KISS ME AWAKE

A NOVEL

KISS ME AWAKE

A NOVEL

by

Julie Momyer

Goody 2 Shoes
Publications

Website: http:/juliemomyer.com
Blog: http://juliemomyerblog.com

Editing by Renee Gray-Wilburn @
www.awaywithwordswriting.wordpress.com

Published by Goody 2 Shoes Publications.

For my family

"As for me, I will see your face in righteousness; I shall be satisfied when I awake in your likeness."

~Psalm 17:15

PROLOGUE

Pomona, California

Spencer Gordon stood alone in center field and decided he was a fool for coming here. He tossed a rock in the air and swung at it with a stick. From behind the tinted lenses of his sunglasses, he surveyed the distance of his line drive. His skills had improved since he was a boy, but considering the magnitude of what he had lost that gain wasn't much of a consolation.

He'd come here looking for a way out, or maybe it was a way back in that had him driving fifty miles inland. He wasn't too sure anymore. He dropped the stick and rubbed gritty palms on his jeans. It was time to go.

Low and warbling, the arid Santa Ana winds howled. It was the sound of a soul in mourning, and he felt it clear through to the marrow of his bones. He ducked his head against the sharp gusts and started across the field for the parking lot.

When he arrived half an hour ago he looked for the row of oleanders, but they were long gone. Bermuda grass cropped short and tinged brown from the perpetual drought, grew in their place.

Spencer leaned an arm on top of his Lexus and stole one last glance over the lot. Everything had changed since he was a kid. This generation played on a ball field landscaped and maintained by the city. Instead of denim jackets or tee shirts, anchored rubber bases divided the ninety-foot chalk line square. It was a far cry from the crude field he and his friends got by with using an eighty-five-cent can of spray paint.

Another angry gust of wind battered his face and ruffled the open collar of his shirt, the potent blast sending a white-throated sparrow reeling like a drunkard in mid-air. He opened the car door and climbed in, shutting out the elements, the noise.

He didn't come all this way to dredge up the past, but the memories tugged, and when he leaned his head back against the headrest and closed his eyes he was eight years old all over again…

>━━

A shrill cry split the air and the hair on the back of Spencer's neck stood on end. Was it an animal? His arm stilled where he had it shoved inside the oleander bush, his mind racing with images of a wolverine, its razor-sharp fangs bared and ready to strike. His heart pounded hard underneath his dirty tee shirt and he jerked his arm out, rubbing at the imaginary teeth marks it left behind.

Behind him he could hear the guys yelling, telling him to hurry up. Spencer wiped the sting of sweat from his eyes and looked over his shoulder. They were still holding their positions. They were waiting on him, waiting on the ball.

He turned back and faced the bush. He didn't want to stick his arm back inside only to have it gobbled up by a wild beast.

Just thinking about it made his heart pound hard again, and this time it felt as though it was in his throat.

What did it matter? They were losing the game anyway. He should tell them he couldn't find it. He *would* tell them that, but he wasn't a quitter.

Spencer stood there for a long moment and then gathering his courage he dropped to his knees and crawled underneath the low hanging branches. Inching a little further in he rolled to his side and looked up into the web of leaves and clusters of pink flowers that smelled like Play-Doh.

There it was, wedged in a grid of branches. He reached up, closed his fingers around the red stitching and crawled back out.

"I got it!" he yelled, waving it in the air. He turned to run back to the field when another loud cry stopped him in his tracks. Spencer jerked his head around, his gaze traveling the row of bushes, searching for the source, but nothing was there.

He sucked the inside of his cheek between his teeth and bit down. It was not a wolverine, he told himself. It was probably just a cat. And now that he thought about it, it sounded more like a baby than an animal.

He tightened his fingers around the ball. He should go now. He got what he came for. But he didn't move. Still ripe with fear, he squatted down and squinted into the shaded gaps between the leaves.

The cry was more of a squalling now. He was afraid. What if it was a baby? He couldn't leave it, but he was holding up the game.

"What are you waiting for Spence, the grass to grow?" He spun around and Noah Wiley reached for the ball. Spencer snatched it back.

Noah scowled. "At least give us the ball back if you're not gonna play."

"I am gonna play."

3

The squall had softened. "Did you hear that?" Spencer asked. He stumbled, moving down the line of bushes, and then stopped.

"It's just a dumb old cat, let's go."

The front of the bush quivered, and that was when Spencer saw it. Spindly and purplish-blue, stick-like arms flailed and the soles of tiny wrinkled feet kicked at the leaves. "It's a baby, Noah!"

"Nuh-uh." Noah dropped to the packed dirt and shoved Spencer out of the way taking a look for himself. "Wow, it is a baby."

"Help me get it out."

Noah held up the branches, and Spencer crawled underneath. The baby let out another loud cry. They were probably scaring it. His hands shook as he slid the tiny bundle out into the open.

"It's a girl," Noah said, a tinge of awe in his voice. His grubby fingers stroked the golden hair matted to the baby's head.

Something inside of Spencer's stomach twisted. Who would do something this awful? Who would leave a baby outside, naked, and all by itself?

The baby's bottom lip quivered and a howl came from the pale miniature face. Spencer pressed his palms against his thighs and hunched over the tiny human being, studying her. The porcelain skin was almost see-through. It looked like a road map with the fine blue lines running underneath.

He looked up at Noah. "Give me your jacket."

"What? No way." Noah pulled it tighter around him.

"For the baby. I wanna wrap her in it."

"She's gonna ruin it."

"Please?" Spencer begged.

"Oh, all right." Noah jerked his arms out of the sleeves and tossed it to him. "Just make sure you wash it when you're done."

Spencer watched her kick her legs and wriggle her arms. His heart skipped and his eyes stung with unshed tears. He rubbed at them, quickly doing away with the evidence before Noah could see.

Crouching down, he spread the jacket out and lifted the baby up. Her head flopped back and he laid her down on the satin lining, afraid he hurt her.

"Go on. Take the ball back," Spencer said. "I'll take the baby to my mom and dad." They would know what to do.

Noah ran off and yelled at the guys to come see what they found. Spencer quickly wrapped the front panels of the jacket over the baby's body and lifted her into his arms. He didn't want them around her. He just wanted to get her somewhere safe.

This was the first time he held a baby. She was so wobbly, and it felt like she was going to fall right out of his arms. What if he broke her? His heart squeezed at the thought.

Spencer pressed her close against his chest and hurried toward home. "Don't worry," he whispered. "I will always take care of you."

1

J aida Martin sat poised on the edge of the rickety barstool and struck a seductive pose. The smile she wore was a mock one, a working girl's cover for the disdain that lurked like an evil twin just below the surface.

She rolled her lips in, working in the fresh layer of ruby lip stain, and shifted on the stool, tugging at the hem of her black leather mini. With every move she made, the shiny red sequins on her halter-top winked under the can lights. She stood out like a flashing neon sign in this get-up.

She hated this part of the job, hated the atmosphere of the dive she was sitting in, thick with a breed of men several rungs lower on the evolutionary ladder than most of humanity. If there had been any other way...

"Frozen margarita." The bartender called her order out then tossed a square-cut napkin in front of her. For the first time tonight she took her eyes off the gold-veined mirrored tiles lining the wall and watched him as he centered the glass on the paper.

He was young. Barely north of twenty was her guess. Maybe just out of college or still in college. He didn't smile, not for her anyway. She might not be very good at pinning down ages, but one thing she was sure of. She made the man nervous.

With a lift of her chin she offered him the pasted-on smile and the last of her cash, a fold creasing the center of Alexander Hamilton's face. "Keep the change," she said.

He slipped it from her fingers and tucked it in his shirt pocket.

"You manage this place?" she asked.

He nodded, swiping a damp rag over the counter. "On the weekends I do."

She leaned in closer eyes narrowed, elbows on the bar. "You're not used to seeing my kind in here are you?"

"Your kind?" he parroted. His brows lifted as if he knew her secret. He shook his dark mop of curls and moved down the counter, abandoning her for a more respectable customer. She spelled trouble and this man knew it.

Jaida poked the straw around in the lime green slush and settled in. From where she sat, the mirror provided a clear view of the entrance, and she went back to watching the door, watching for him.

Three days ago he called the agency and asked for her by name. He identified himself as Ray, but if the moniker he gave matched the name on his birth certificate it would be a first. No one ever revealed their true identity.

But she didn't care about the name. It was what he brought to the table that counted. And Ray had promised her plenty. The question was: Would he deliver?

The door swept open behind her ushering in warm night air mingled with exhaust. *This was it.* Adrenaline surged and her heart beat hard against her ribcage. She scanned the mirror then stopped cold at the gray eyes staring back.

It wasn't him.

She looked over her shoulder and verified what she already knew. There wasn't one white male in here wearing a plain red ball cap and a navy blue Angel's jacket.

He was over thirty minutes late. She couldn't have missed him. She'd watched the door like a hawk. But even if he had slipped past her there was no way he could have missed her.

She reached for her drink and took a large swallow. When she looked up again, the man with the gray eyes was still watching her. Mac was his name. She knew this because it was embroidered on the patch, stitched to his shirt pocket.

Was he a substitute? A stand-in? Eyeing him, she licked the salt from her lower lip and swallowed. Had Ray sent someone else to hand off the information?

Mac's hands hung limp at his sides. They were empty. No folder or briefcase. A slight bulge pressed against the striped fabric of his shirt pocket. It was the right size, the right shape for a flash drive.

Their gazes reconnected and held; hers burning with the question: *Are you him?* But something other than recognition, a look she'd seen too many times tonight, flickered behind the glassy sheen of gray fastened on her. Jaida pressed a hand to her brow and ducked her head, a flush of embarrassment warming her face. This wasn't what she was here for. How could she have misread his intentions?

She pushed her full glass aside and toyed with the strap of her purse. She should leave. She moved to stand when an arm grazed hers and she drew back. It was Mac. What did he want? She tensed, preparing to defend herself, but without a word he left his card beside her drink. And to her relief, he vanished like an apparition into the din and dusky light of the main floor.

She exhaled the breath she'd been holding and settled back on the seat, rethinking her escape. If she were here for the indecent purposes these men supposed, she would be walking away with a big fat bankroll tonight. She smiled at the irony. It was a real smile this time.

Jaida spun on the stool and faced the door of Hank's Tavern. The brown tint on the glass was bubbled and peeling like sunburned skin. When Ray named this location for a meeting place she assumed it was one of his haunts. But this place, these people, they just didn't fit his grandiose sense of self. Not the one he portrayed over the phone.

Maybe he'd selected it randomly, or perhaps strategically. Whatever his reasons, the confidence she had in him was beginning to fade, apprehension trickling through her veins like a slow IV drip.

He'd called all the shots right down to the clothes she wore, satisfying what was a clear need for control. So where was he?

From the far right corner, red and yellow lights flashed and "Should I Stay or Should I Go" blared from the jukebox. Jaida sighed, rested her elbows on the edge of the bar and wondered the same thing.

She mouthed the words to the first line, her foot bobbing in time to the beat then glanced down at the pink dial on her watch. She would give Ray five more minutes.

"Hey, blue eyes." Jaida frowned. It wasn't Ray's voice. The tenor standing beside her had an accent that was honeyed, a southerner who'd gone west.

She didn't look up right away. Didn't want to deal with another one. Maybe he would take the hint and move on.

"Not much of a talker, are you?" he asked.

"Is that what you want? To talk?" She looked up into his craggy suntanned face then down to the layers of gold chains tinkling against his chest. The wide lapels of his powder-blue polyester suit were edge-stitched in navy blue. Was he for real? He looked like a throwback from the seventies, a John Travolta wannabe.

"Maybe I do," he said. He smoothed his hand over a thatch of matted brown chest hair, preening like a cat and grinning down at her as though he was a prize and she'd just won him.

Uh, not interested.

He sipped his drink then planted himself on the stool beside her. She turned and gave him her back. *I just want to get out of here.*

Startled, she shrieked and reared back, slapping at the hand that gripped her thigh. "Hands off!" she warned. What did he think he was doing?

Travolta grinned. "It was only one hand." He held up the guilty hand as proof, making a clicking sound as though she were a horse. "And I always squeeze my apples before I buy. I ain't payin' for no woman 'til I do the same."

"What in the…?" The question vanished on her lips when she spotted the fifty-dollar bill crumpled on the counter. Her anger burned hotter at the sight. *Ray, Ray, Ray. What have you gotten me into?*

Jaida sat up straighter. She was dressed the part. She might as well play it. "Do I look like I'm on clearance?" she snapped.

In one swift move, she snatched up the fifty and tucked it into the V-cut of her top. "I'm no apple, and fifty bucks is a considerable discount for the privilege of touching me."

He threw his head back and downed the rest of his drink, the ice clanking in the empty tumbler when he slammed it down. His gaze dropped. "With legs like that, I guess another ten is in order."

Thick head, dim wit, he still didn't get it. "I. Am. Not. For. Sale." She said it slow enough that even he would understand.

He laughed. "Honey, if you're not for sale then why are you advertising?"

Her mouth tightened. That was it. She was done here. Why should she stick around just to be harassed? Jaida slid from the stool and reached for her purse.

There was one minute left before the five minutes expired, and her waiting around for the clock to tick off the last sixty seconds wasn't going to change the fact that Ray was a no-show.

She brushed past her admirer and out the door, ignoring the curses that followed for taking off with his money.

"It's over, Auggie," she said. "I'm outside." When her announcement didn't bring him around the corner, she tapped the transmitter in her ear. Was it working?

She paced along the curb under the yellow haze of the streetlights, looking up one side of the street and down the other. A horn honked, a man yelled, and tires squealed on freshly paved asphalt, but Auggie was not behind the wheel.

She looked back the way she had come. The neon Corona sign lit up the darkened window. There was no movement at the door. *Yet.* She had about ten seconds to disappear before the guy inside was out here demanding more than a squeeze for that fifty.

She warded off the shudder that came on the heels of that ugly thought then jogged to the corner. For everyone else it was just another Friday night in Anaheim; for her, it was a poorly executed masquerade that she had no intention of repeating.

"Where are you?" She rounded the corner where Auggie was supposed to be waiting, but the curb was empty, not a car in sight. She'd been stood up.

Twice.

Why would he leave her here? Her grip tightened on her purse. If this was his idea of a joke...

An engine revved. "Need a ride?"

Jaida ignored the offer and kept walking.

The metallic gold four-door crept along beside her, the engine knocking under the hood. In her periphery she could see the dim glow from the dome light. It illuminated a crown of dark hair and little else.

"How much?" The driver's voice carried through the open passenger window. She closed her eyes on a breath and walked faster. *Out of the frying pan and into the fire.*

He sped up, just enough to keep tight with her stride and without breaking her own she reached inside her purse and wrapped her fingers around the can of pepper spray. If he tried anything, she would use it.

The car edged closer until the front tire mounted the curb with a scrape and a squeal, the fender bouncing when the car rolled back down onto the street. "What are you doing?" she yelled.

Jaida staggered sideways away from the rogue vehicle, ran a few steps, and ducked inside the first door that hadn't been locked up for the night.

The hydraulic door fell closed behind her with a silent gasp, the scent of Asian cuisine filling her nostrils. She moved to the edge of the plate-glass window where the "Open" sign flickered, and watched the car idling at the curb.

"Can I help you?"

Jaida startled and turned at the woman's voice. She forced a smile and waved a hand over her clothes. "Costume party," she said. "I'm waiting on my ride."

She did need a ride, but not in the back of a police cruiser. And from the look on the woman's face that was where she was going to end up if she didn't get out of here quick.

"We close in fifteen minutes," she said before taking her leave and disappearing into the dining area. When Jaida turned back to the window, the car was gone.

Outside, the scent of fresh drizzle and wet concrete greeted her. She stood under the shelter of the awning and dialed her cell phone, the patter of raindrops pelting the canvas arc. No ring, no answer. Her call was instantly routed to Auggie's voicemail.

You can't trust anyone. She shoved the phone back in her purse then slid her arms around herself and glared at the empty street. How was she supposed to get home now? The bus?

She walked to the bench at the corner, the heels of her stiletto boots wobbling on the uneven cement. She stopped when she realized her mistake. She couldn't take the bus; she didn't have any cash.

What was Auggie thinking leaving her like this? It was unprofessional. It was dangerous.

As though her last thought was premonitory, a hand came from behind and clamped around her waist, yanking her backward. She screamed and tried to pull free, but the hold tightened and lips were pressed against her ear.

"How 'bout a little something for Daddy?"

The sound of his voice brought on a wave of rage. Jaida spun, shoving against the immovable chest. "You big jerk, you scared me to death." She bent at the waist and pressed a hand to her heart. It was galloping behind her ribs like a herd of wild horses.

She glared up at him. "Where were you?"

Auggie laughed, his shaved head gleaming in the light of the street lamp. "I've been right behind you the whole time, chica."

"Right behind me?" Her pulse pounded in her neck, and she was yelling at him now. "Why didn't you show yourself when I came out of the bar?"

He reached for her arm and she pulled it away. They had a plan, and without a second thought he'd digressed from it.

"Chill out. I didn't want to scare our guy off, *detective*. I was giving him space. If he was out there I wanted to see if he would follow you. You do want this don't you?"

She bristled at his deliberate use of the word *detective*. What was he implying? That she wasn't a professional?

Her eyes narrowed as she shot back, "I do want this, but I also want my backup to back me up."

"Look, Jaida, I did my job. I was there for you."

"Fine," she said, "but this is the last time I do this. Next time you can go in drag."

He draped his arm over her shoulder and this time she didn't pull away. "I would love to, babe," he said, "but I wouldn't fool anyone with biceps like these."

"Don't flatter yourself."

He pinched her arm, and she swatted his hand away. "Thug."

Auggie pulled his keys from his pocket. "C'mon, let's go get the car."

2

Jaida stood at the living room window nursing an iced tea, staring into the fog that swallowed up the whole of Newport Beach. In the distance, hazy yellow dots of light along the pier smoldered through the wall of white. It was the only thing visible beyond her patio.

Tonight played out like amateur night. If she had followed protocol and vetted Ray properly would it have turned out any differently? Auggie thought so. And he reminded her of that all the way back to the office. He said they would have known Ray was a fraud if she'd done her job right. But was he truly a fraud?

Their case against William Gale was shriveling up at the edges. She needed Ray to be who he said he was. Without him, everything she had on Gale was worthless.

She'd put in nearly two years of her life on this, and the proof of her labors were stacked and separated in piles on her desk. The photos, the tape, and the documents she had accrued were enough to put an ordinary man away for a long time. But this was no ordinary man.

All she needed was one warrant, and she would have access to everything, including Gale's private records. She was looking for something specific, but would it even be there? Her heart skipped a beat at the thought, the possibility thrilling and frightening her at the same time.

Theoretically, a mere two hours ago she'd been one step closer to having it in her hands, but in the midst of her pending victory fear still taunted. What if she was disappointed? Or worse, what if *she* was the disappointment?

Jaida took another sip of tea. Stiff and cold, her fingers tightened on the glass. With no new leads, it looked like she would never know the answer to those questions.

She traced her finger in a circle over the moisture on the windowpane. *Zero.* That's how many options she had left, and if she didn't come up with a new strategy to keep herself in the game, everything would be lost.

She set her glass on the end table, whisked the blue jacquard drapes across the rod then sank into the softness of the leather couch. The cushions yielded under her weight, cradling her like a baby. Her whole body sighed. It had been one long twelve-hour day, and the only thing she had to show for it was her throbbing feet...and Mac's telephone number. The corner of her mouth lifted on that last thought and her eyes slid closed.

What if they were wrong? What if Ray's call wasn't a hoax? She was grasping at the wind, but what if, in her persistence, she managed to catch it? There had to be some legitimacy because everything he'd told her was spot on.

Was he a psychic? She half laughed at the notion. Now that *would* be a hoax because she didn't buy into the paranormal.

Ray had Gale's private number, and he quoted it as if he dialed it often. In their brief telephone conversation, he'd casually made light of Gale's fondness for unusually young women, and Cognac-infused cigars. But it was his subtle remarks on the Dennison murder that sold her. No one could guess at those details and be accurate. No one was that good.

His standing her up just didn't make any sense. She tugged her boots off, each one hitting the floor with a dull thud. She leaned back and tucked a throw pillow behind her. If Ray was the real deal he would be calling back.

As if on cue the phone rang, but it was the landline. She closed her eyes and ignored it. The machine could get it. Her number was unlisted, and Ray only had access to her through Baseel. Anyone else could wait until tomorrow.

The answering machine came on after the third ring. "Hey Jaida, it's me." Auggie cleared his throat. "As of tonight, we're calling it quits on Gale."

No! She jumped up. He was going to ruin everything.

"We have what we have," he continued. "Let's just turn it over and be done with it."

Jaida yanked the receiver from the base, an electronic screech piercing the air. "You can't do this to me, Auggie."

He sighed that same heavy sigh when he was annoyed with her. "Jaida, we're already breaking under a heavy caseload. We're just spinning our tires on this one."

"Just, don't be so quick on this."

"Quick? Do you know how much time and money we've already put into this investigation?"

"Can't we just take the weekend to get some perspective?" she asked. "Besides, what if Ray calls back?"

When he didn't respond, she said, "We're getting close, I know it." It was a lie, but what else could she say?

"What difference is two days going to make?" he asked.

"Like I said, maybe Ray will call back. He may still intend to work with us. Maybe he was sick, or delayed." Maybe she left the bar too soon. There were a number of circumstances that could have detained him. Including Gale.

"That's an awful lot of maybes, Jaida. How about offering me something concrete?"

She pressed a hand to her forehead, defeat sinking her. "What do you want me to say?" If she had anything concrete she wouldn't be wasting the last hour of her day begging for more time.

"Do you know what I honestly think? There *is* no Ray. This is just another wild goose chase that Gale concocted to throw us off."

The last of her hope withered. That would explain his intimate knowledge of the murder. She ran the concept over in her head before shaking it. "It's not true." It couldn't be true. "This is too important to me," she said, the pitch of her voice rising.

"Why? Why is this case any different than the others?"

She pressed a hand to her mouth, wishing she could take it all back. If she told him why, he would pull her from the case.

"Jaida?"

"It's…it's…he's not any different."

"I know what he did to you, but you can't risk the credibility of the agency for revenge. Besides, you came out clean in the investigation."

"This isn't about revenge." Is that what he thought?

"Then what is it about?"

Nothing the agency would be interested in. Not when she was on this side of it. "What about public safety? We have an obligation to put him away. You know how dangerous he is."

This would have been easier if she'd hired the Baseel Agency to find her mother instead of going to work for them, but they would have kept her planted on the sidelines, and she couldn't abide that.

Auggie went quiet. Was he caving? A soft sigh rattled through the phone. "I'll take the weekend and think about it," he said. Relief flooded her. She'd bought herself two more days.

"Thanks, Auggie."

"Don't thank me yet," he said, then hung up.

She set the receiver back on the base and pressed her palms to her head. Like steady drumbeats, the stress pulsed at her temples. She had forty-eight hours to come up with something that would change his mind.

The couch beckoned. Jaida turned toward it when something caught her eye. *Where had that come from?* There was an envelope dangling from the mail slot in the front door. She snatched it from the grip of the brass flap and turned it over. There was no stamp, no return address. Someone dropped it off.

Inside was a full-sized sheet of copy paper with a single typed line through the center.

The past is called the past for a reason. Leave it there.

No heading, no signature, nothing to identify the sender. But a name wasn't necessary. She already knew. She crumpled up the veiled warning and threw it in the kitchen trash. Did he really think she would be scared off so easily?

The upstairs lights switched off and she spun around, her breath catching in her throat. With knees like jelly, she stood unmoving, her gaze riveted on the two doors at the top of the stairs. It was only the timer, she knew, but a tremor still traveled the length of her spine reminding her who she was dealing with.

Jaida set the alarm and switched on the floor lamp next to the armchair then checked the locks on all the doors and windows, turning on one light after another as she went.

She stood in the middle of the living room and looked over the downstairs. Everything had been secured, and the alarm was set. If he dared venture further than the other side of the front door, she would know it.

Jaida snatched up the empty glass she'd left on the table then wiped up the wet ring it left behind with the heel of her hand. Why had she ever initiated contact with him? She must have been out of her mind. And why didn't he want her probing into her own past?

The worst of it was, she'd let her heart get involved. She tucked the glass in the dishwasher and picked up the mailer from the kitchen counter. His name was printed across the top in bold, bright, red letters outlined in black, and underneath in royal blue were his political credentials: *Former councilman, two-term mayor, district court judge.* And presently he was a gubernatorial candidate for the state of California.

Gale's plastic smile took up half his face on the oversized postcard. His new wife, Patrice, was nestled protectively under his arm, her red hair tumbling over her shoulders in a cloud of curls. Seeing the two of them together brought an unexpected twinge of jealousy, and she hated herself for it.

Councilman, mayor, judge, murderer, it was quite a resume Gale had established...If she could just prove the latter. But his money insulated him, his power protected him, and the high-level connections he kept in his back pocket were his guarantee that he would come out of this squeaky clean.

Jaida tore the card in two, wondering why she'd saved it in the first place. Exhausted, she collapsed on the couch for the second time. She drew her legs up and leaned back. Did Auggie really think she was going after Gale for revenge? Maybe to some degree she was, but not for the reason he thought.

She yawned and tugged the afghan from the back of the couch, gathering the softness and warmth around her like a hug. She worked the edges of the blanket between her fingers, soaking up its comfort.

Years ago she watched her mother work the variegated yarn, shaping the soft cashmere strands of purples, oranges, and reds into chains and butterfly stitches, and bullion stitches, and... Her eyelids slid closed on another yawn, too groggy to remember what else.

"Love," she mumbled to herself. That was it. Her mouth quirked into a faint smile then slipped into a frown. What did she know about love? And why did people always leave? Whether death ripped them from your life or they walked out willingly, no one ever stayed. Not even the woman she called 'mother'.

She scrunched the scalloped edges of the blanket in her fists. The only thing she had left of Eva was this afghan and her Bible. They were her parting gifts, an unsatisfactory consolation prize for when she breathed her last and surrendered the ghost.

She recalled the coolness of Eva's hand gripped in her own, her pulse weak but steady. At the time, it brought a semblance of comfort, but her final words did not: "This Bible holds the truth. Hold onto it, Jaida. I want you to read it."

But Eva was wrong. The Bible didn't hold the truth, William Gale did. And she would do whatever she had to, to pry it out of him.

She rolled to her side and curled into a snug ball. She'd been reared by the finest. Eva Payne *was* her mother. So, why the need to find the name of the woman who gave her life and then left her for dead?

Jaida reached for the remote and turned on the television. Jimmy Stewart's desperation carried through the airwaves as he begged to return to his former life. She could relate to his character, George Bailey, and empathize with his despair, but whatever was missing in her own life hadn't been discovered and wasn't going to be happily concluded like a two-hour drama.

Striking out tonight was evidence of that.

3

The rubber soles of her shoes buffeted the boardwalk. Jaida found her rhythm, her pace in the noiseless cadence. She didn't like to run, but the physical exertion released the pent up stress and helped to ease the nightmares.

The past few months the dreams had worsened, so she doubled up, running after rising and shortly before retiring. She skipped last night but made it through the six hours without an episode of terror and sweat-drenched sheets.

She clamped a hand over the stitch in her side and blew out a sharp breath. Like clockwork, the paperboy was about 100 yards ahead of her. He pedaled his beach cruiser past her house and with a curl of his wrist he propelled the Saturday edition of *The Register* over her wrought-iron fence, swerving just before he rode away.

She lengthened her flagging stride, and pressed into the last stretch of the run, her quads quivering like stretched-out rubber bands. Her thirsty lungs drank in the air as her foot landed over the imaginary line that marked her fourth mile. Done. She was finally done.

Hands pressed to her hips, she expelled a breath and walked off the exertion until her heart rate normalized. Someone called her name and she turned, looking over the row of houses that lined the boardwalk. Who was it? She turned again, this time scanning the beach for a face.

"Up here!" She spun around and shaded her eyes, squinting past the screen in her neighbor's upstairs window. Marilyn Carter's hunched form was little more than a vague shadowy outline behind the nylon mesh.

"Newspaper's on your porch." She lisped the latest neighborhood intelligence report past her dentures. "Thought you might want to know."

Marilyn was a widow, an aging eccentric who lived alone, and a self-appointed window watcher for the neighborhood watch. She missed nothing.

Jaida smiled to herself and released the latch on the gate. "Thanks, Marilyn." Baseel should hire her. Or maybe she should. Marilyn would probably have her standing in the same room with her mother in a matter of hours.

She picked up the paper and tested its weight in her hand. It was heavier and thicker than usual. More bad news to report, she guessed. She slipped the key from the pocket in her running shorts and went inside, tossing the paper on the dining room table.

She had two days to work on Auggie, to sell him on sticking with the Gale case. He was being hasty, irrational even. Walking away now didn't make any sense.

After downing a large glass of water, she pulled the elastic band from her hair and headed upstairs to shower.

Inside the steamy stall, she leaned her head back, dunking it under the stream of hot water. For the first time in weeks, she allowed herself to relax. What if she told Auggie the truth? Told him everything? They were friends. Good friends. He would understand. Wouldn't he?

But then she remembered what he said last night about not risking Baseel's credibility. His loyalty was first to Baseel, which meant that even if he agreed to keep the case open, he would surely pull her off it.

Jaida washed the sweat from her body and then stood under the stream until the water ran tepid. Behind the shower tiles the pipes groaned like a wounded whale. It had been more than a week since she put in a call to the plumber to diagnose the noise, but he still hadn't shown up.

With a shiver, she twisted the water from her hair then wrapped herself in a bath towel and stood before the oval mirror, foggy with moisture. She swiped a hand over the surface and through the rippling beads of water, Jaida studied the outline of her face, her features, the blonde hair that hung in a wet clump between her shoulder blades. Who did she look like—her mother, her grandfather? Who was genetically responsible for her small stature and her square jaw line? Who was she?

She leaned in closer until she was eye to eye with her own reflection. "Who are you?" she asked. The question had haunted her since she was old enough to ask it, and two decades later she was no closer to learning the answer.

She dried her hair then dressed in a pair of denim shorts and a fitted yellow tee shirt. The waistband of her shorts slid down to her hips and she hitched them up. She'd lost a few pounds, but then regular meals hadn't been a priority the past few months.

Jaida hung the wet towel on the rack then rushed down the stairs when the doorbell rang.

She squinted at the distorted image through the peephole and then opened the door. Carina Keller stood on the porch, her eyes concealed by an oversized pair of white-framed sunglasses.

"It's about time," Carina scowled.

Her early morning appearance had Jaida worried. "What's wrong?" she asked. Was someone sick or in an accident?

Carina waved off her concern. "You worry too much. Why would anything be wrong?" She stepped over the threshold, the flowery scent of Pure White Linen filling the foyer.

"It's 6:30 in the morning. If you're out of bed before noon, then something has to be wrong."

Irritation flushed her cheeks. "*Nothing* is wrong."

"Fine." Jaida held up her hands in surrender, wishing she'd left her standing on the porch. "Have a seat," she said, collecting the discarded fishnet stockings from last night. She wadded them into a ball and set them on the stairs.

If this is what she was like early in the morning, she pitied the man who married her.

"What *is this*?" Carina asked.

She looked up. The leather mini from her botched escapade was dangling from the tip of Carina's finger.

"It's my new uniform." Jaida picked up the newspaper she'd left on the table and snapped off the rubber band.

"Made a career change, did you?" Carina let the skirt slide to the floor.

"Temp job," she said, then shook open the paper. The inserts fluttered to the floor and she picked them up.

"Oh, I almost forgot." Carina did a graceful pirouette then posed to show off her bronzed legs. "Do you like it?"

Jaida lowered the paper and looked her over. The dark shade of her skin stood out against her white shorts and mint green blouse. "It actually looks like you've been outside," she said.

The color was natural enough, but with Carina's aversion to the outdoors, it had to be from a tanning salon or a bottle.

"Well, you know me. I'd rather do South Coast Plaza than the beach."

"No shame in that," she said, although she didn't share Carina's fondness for chilly air-conditioned stores and fawning sales assistants.

The strong scent of newsprint and ink brought her attention back to the paper she held in her hands. Jaida folded it up and set it back on the table. She'd flip through it after Carina left. Right now what she needed was a dose of caffeine to ward off the subtle throbbing that was building in her temples.

"Do you want some coffee?" she asked then headed for the kitchen.

"I'll take a double shot," Carina muttered past a yawn. She dropped her handbag on the floor, a Gucci knock-off. For a prosecutor she made good money but not enough to buy the real thing.

Jaida poured the steaming hazelnut into two mugs. When she turned to hand one to Carina, she found her sifting through the stack of unopened mail on the counter.

"What is this?" Carina waved the envelope from Edison in the air, the pink paper in the cellophane window announcing to the world that she hadn't paid her bill. There ought to be a privacy law against that.

"They're shutting off your electricity, and you haven't even opened the bill?"

Jaida set the cups down. She yanked the envelope from Carina's fingers and tucked it under the stack. "It's just a warning. They aren't going to shut it off."

"That's a shut-off notice if I ever saw one."

"Yes, but they aren't going to shut it off *yet*. I have time."

"You see? This is exactly why you need Kevin."

"Don't bring Kevin into this, Carina." Kevin was a bad idea from the start.

"I'm talking strictly business here. Nothing personal. He's a genius at handling money. Just swallow that pride of yours and let him help you."

"I can pay my own bills, thank you very much. I just haven't had the time." Besides he would mistake it for something more.

Carina scolded her with a look and then surrendering the argument, she shrugged. "Suit yourself."

That was what she intended to do. Jaida scrounged the nearly bare refrigerator for a carton of milk and found one between the Styrofoam take-out boxes. She swished around the small trace left inside and added the remains to Carina's coffee.

Her friend raised the mug and eyed the intricate floral swirls etched in the jade ceramic. "I think my assistant has one just like this," she said. She set the mug down and hot coffee sloshed over the rim and onto her fingers.

"What do you want, Carina?"

Carina looked up, paused, and then shrugged with her face. "Maybe a doughnut to dunk in my coffee? If you have any." She shook the dribbling coffee from her fingers. "And, I could use a napkin."

Jaida wrung out the dishrag and handed it to her. "No. I mean, why are you here?" Showing off her tan, small talk about coffee cups, digging through her mail. Carina never did anything just because. There was always a reason.

She looked up at that, her mouth twisted in a frown. "Do I need to have a reason to stop by?"

"Yes, you do. Apparently no one is dying, but something must be up for you to be sitting in my kitchen at the crack of dawn on a Saturday."

She watched Carina wipe the stickiness from her fingers. "Speaking of dying," she said, "did you hear Mark Vickery passed away?"

Jaida calmly shook her head, giving nothing away, but inside chaos reigned, charging her heart and leaving it pounding in her ears. "No, I didn't know."

"I heard about it at work, but there's a decent article in the obits."

Her gaze drifted to the table where she'd left the newspaper. That was about as far as she'd gotten with the weekly copies. Opened, but unread. No wonder she didn't know.

Carina sipped her coffee. "You knew him didn't you?"

Jaida nodded. Not personally, but she knew of him, and his passing could change everything. Mark Vickery was the attorney who handled her adoption.

She'd called him once to request Eva's files, but he'd refused, claiming that attorney-client privilege didn't end when a client passed. But what about when both client *and* attorney passed?

"The funeral is Monday," Carina said.

Jaida looked at her then. Would she know? "What happens to the client's files when an attorney dies?" Did they become public record? Could she request them? Or did they destroy them? What if she was too late? The thought of all those secrets being run through the shredder left her shaken. *Was* she too late?

Carina lifted her shoulder. "I don't know. But that is a good question. What are you doing today?"

Houdini couldn't have changed the subject faster. Carina was a master at putting her concerns above everyone else's. Jaida answered with a disappointed shrug then crushed the empty milk carton and tossed it into the trash.

The phone was closer than two feet from where she stood. She looked at it, her fingers itching to pick it up, to dial Vickery's office.

"A shrug? All I get is a shrug for an answer? Does that mean you don't have plans?"

Jaida looked at her. "What?" What was she rambling on about?

"I just asked what you were doing today."

"Nothing. I'm not doing anything." She took a drink from her mug, her mouth twisting at the bitter taste. She forgot sugar.

"Sorry. I shouldn't have said anything. I didn't know Vickery's death would upset you. Were you two close?"

"What? No, I wasn't close to him. And what makes you think I'm upset?" She scooped some sugar into her coffee and stirred.

"Oh, I don't know, maybe it was that stricken, deer-in-the-headlights look you got when I mentioned it. And since when do you take that much sugar in your coffee?"

Was she keeping tabs on everything she did? Jaida glanced down at the mug braced between her palms wondering how many spoonfuls she'd put in. She wasn't about to ask.

She looked up then and waved off Carina's observations. "It was just unexpected, that's all."

"So you're free then?" Carina pressed.

"To do what?"

"Lance borrowed his uncle's catamaran. We're going to Catalina. Auggie was supposed to tell you last night, but I guess he forgot."

"Is that why you're here?" Why didn't she just say so in the first place? "I don't know…" Jaida made a face at the dirty dishes stacked in the sink.

Carina followed her gaze and said, "I'll do the dishes while you throw some things in a bag."

She glanced at the telephone again. With Carina here she wouldn't be able to talk openly anyway, and it was the weekend. No one would likely be in until Monday.

She nodded. "I'll go." If she stayed, she would drive herself crazy counting down the hours until she could make that call.

"You'll want some extra clothes. We're staying overnight."

Overnight? Jaida turned at the bottom of the stairs. "I thought it was just for the day."

"Is that a problem? You said you didn't have any plans."

She shook her head. "No, it's not a problem." But already she found herself wanting to make an excuse and back out. If she could just remember the name of Vickery's assistant, she could look her up and call her at home. It started with the letter B. Was it Barbara? But Barbara what? She couldn't recall, and it nagged at her.

At Carina's urging, she climbed the stairs, dragged out her overnight bag, and reluctantly packed.

4

It was going to be a scorcher. The sun's rays pulsed against Jaida's face as she shuffled along beside Carina, the heat of the marina's blacktop burning through the thin soles of her sandals.

This was supposed to be fun, a good time, but she couldn't seem to rally her mood. She adjusted the duffle strap on her shoulder and looked up at the gulls circling overhead. Their cry was a cacophony of second sopranos, the notes dangerously off-key.

Water lapped against the vessels secured in their slips, the fiberglass hulls knocking restively against the wooden planks. That same restlessness infected her. She was edgy and impatient, the records in Vickery's office dominating her thoughts.

She glanced over her shoulder, searching for Carina's car. The silver Volvo was locked up at the south edge of the lot. It wasn't too late to beg off. She could insist that Carina take her back, but it wouldn't be without a fight. They were already getting a late start, and catering to her would set them back even more.

Besides, she could find out just as much from the island as she could from home. She brought along her laptop. This afternoon, she would visit Vickery's website, do a search for his assistant, and track down her phone number.

The Black Diamond was tethered at the far end of the dock. Clad in a white tee shirt and a pair of gray plaid swim trunks, Lance stood on the lower deck staring off into the distance. But whatever had him riveted no longer held his attention. His gaze lowered, landing on her.

"Hey there, beautiful." He reached for her, helping her aboard then slipped the overnight bag from her shoulder.

"Did she put up a fight?" he asked, offering Carina his hand.

"She was easy," Carina said. "With the way she's been buried in her work, I thought I would have to tie her up and drag her here."

Jaida frowned. "*She* is standing right here."

"And we're so happy that you are," Lance said with an Irish brogue. She paused and squinted in the direction he'd been looking when they arrived. What had been so enthralling?

She didn't know much about Lance. None of them did. He'd been at Baseel for less than four weeks. What she did know was all surface. He had a dangerous appeal, a boyish charm that drew even the most resistant of women, which meant she needed to be on guard.

He wrapped an arm around her. "We may have brought the boss along, but just so you know this is a work-free weekend," he said, stroking the faint shadow of a mustache that lined his upper lip.

"Hey, you made it." Auggie came up behind Lance, shifting the baseball cap that shaded his face. "I should have told you last night, but…" He shrugged and gave her a look that said, what? That last night was her fault? That reaming her took so long, he'd forgotten to tell her about this last-minute outing?

"Put that inside, will you?" Lance tossed her duffle to Auggie. It hit his midsection, and he winced.

"What do you have in here?"

"Your ego."

He shook his head. "Nah, too heavy. Feels more like my brains." She made a face at his retreating back as he and Carina disappeared inside the salon.

Jaida followed Lance up to the cockpit. He eased the catamaran out into the open water, and she sank back on the bench behind him. Instead of sitting in the seat at the helm, he gripped the wheel and stood with his feet braced for balance. A black smudge marred the tan leather of what looked like a new pair of boat shoes.

He reached over his shoulder and scratched at an unseen irritant between his shoulder blades. "You're watching me, aren't you?" he asked. So caught off-guard by his remark, she didn't think to look away when he turned his head and proved himself right.

It wasn't what he thought, but it bothered her that he caught her staring. "You're so conceited."

A subtle dimple carved the lower part of his right cheek when he smiled. He was tipping the mask, revealing his intentions. But they were unwelcome.

"Don't hold your breath," she mumbled. Curling inside of herself, Jaida withdrew and looked away. Her life was already too complicated.

"What was that?" he asked.

She shook her head. "Nothing." But his chuckle told her he knew exactly what she had said.

Auggie came up the stairs and poked his head around the corner. "Either of you want anything to drink?"

"Pepsi," Lance said.

"No thanks." Jaida dropped the sunglasses over her eyes and leaned back. She just wanted to shut out her problems and enjoy the ride.

"Five miles behind us. Twenty more to go." She groaned when Lance announced their progress. He was ruining her moment.

"Are you going to do that all the way there? The ride over is the best part." Jaida kicked her sandals off and drew her feet up onto the cushioned bench seat.

He laughed. "Testy today, are we?"

"Sorry," she said. She supposed her tone had been a little rude.

"I would have thought you were a woman of refined tastes. You strike me as the champagne and caviar type."

"That would be Carina." She looked up at him then. "But what does that have to do with my enjoying the ride?"

"If you were the pampered type I would see *this*," he tapped the wheel, "solely as a means to transport you to your natural habitat."

Again, that would be Carina. "My natural habitat, being...?" Where was he going with this? Should she be offended?

"Never mind. I was just thinking out loud."

Both of them turned and looked as Carina ascended the steps. *What was this?* Her skin glistened with a generous layer of tanning oil, and the two-piece bathing suit she wore left little to the imagination.

Carina swept past and spread a bright orange beach towel out on the deck, then planted herself in the middle of it.

Had they entered the twilight zone? Jaida couldn't tear her eyes away. "What are you doing?"

"Just getting a little sun," Carina snipped. "You don't need to make a federal case out of it."

It was all for show, it had to be, but who was the audience she was playing to? Auggie? She'd been discreet about her attraction to him, but Jaida saw it. Besides, why else would the avowed sun hater be sailing to Catalina?

"Hey, Senorita Martin." Jaida turned. *Speak of the devil.* Auggie tossed Lance a bottle of Pepsi then waved at her to follow him down the steps.

What did he want? If he thought he was going to harp on her about last night he had another thing coming. She had the weekend off.

Down below Auggie reached for the salon door then hesitated. He drew his hand back. Angling his head, he eyed her from over his shoulder.

"What's wrong? Is it locked?" In answer he slid the glass door over the tracks and ushered her inside. *Guess not.*

The chilled air against her warm skin made her shiver. It was like a miniature apartment down here. She had never been on a catamaran this lavish.

"I could live on something like this, travel around from port to port."

It had an open floor plan. Two love seats, the color of burgundy wine were centered in the room. A narrow oak table stocked with magazines and decks of cards still in their sleeves sat between the two sofas. Beyond the living area was the kitchen. It was small; a galley, but appeared as functional as her own.

Two closed doors. One must be the bathroom, the other... There was movement, and her gaze darted to the right, to a corner where dusky shadows and the narrow space conspired to hide the vague form of a man.

A splash of light from the window revealed a stony face. Kevin? What was he doing here? Is this why Auggie was behaving so strangely?

How dare he do this to her? She spun around and speared him with a glare. He offered a half-hearted shrug, had the decency to look embarrassed, and then muttered some excuse before fleeing the scene. *Coward.*

Jaida stood facing the door he'd hastened out of, wanting desperately to follow. But they were in the middle of the ocean. Kevin would catch up to her sooner or later.

When she turned around he had emerged from the shadows. He was watching her with that same shyness, that painfully awkward timidity.

"Hey," he said. His shoulders were slouched, and he had his hands stuffed in the pockets of his khaki shorts. He was a man of few words and most of them borrowed from movie scripts.

She saw her duffle bag on the floor near the breakfast bar and picked it up. "How are you?" Her greeting was flat, almost perfunctory. But she had no real desire to know the answer, just to escape this awkward situation.

He spread his hands. "Sorry about this. Carina said you wanted to give it another shot, but I can see you had no idea I was even here."

Of course, this poorly planned rendezvous had Carina written all over it. And as Lance said, they were five miles out. There was nothing she could do about it now.

Kevin looked so mournful, like a human Eeyore. She almost felt sorry for him, but no amount of pity would change her mind.

"Friends is good, Kevin," she said. She never wanted anything more than that.

He nodded again, strands of chestnut-colored hair hanging in his eyes. He was letting his hair grow long, and the ends already grazed his unshaven chin.

"I'm still willing to help you out with your finances. Setting up some investments, building a portfolio. Anything you need."

"Thanks for offering, but I've got that covered."

A brief flash of disappointment crossed his face, and then he smiled. "Money's only something you need in case you don't die tomorrow, right?"

She recognized the quote, but couldn't recall the movie he'd pulled it from. He was an odd man.

Bag in hand, Jaida walked away and closed herself inside the bathroom.

Lance contemplated the empty stairwell to his right and the fact that Auggie had come back up alone. He was now occupying the seat Jaida had vacated and his mood appeared to have soured. Just what transpired down below?

He cracked a grin. "What happened to my view?" he asked.

"She'll be along." Auggie was tight-lipped, as usual. The man was easy to read, but hard to crack.

Lance surveyed the surroundings. He glanced at Carina, who was absorbed in a novel, then turned his gaze back to the water where rows of cresting swells the size of speed bumps rumpled the glassy sea.

Auggie said, "The review board approved your 30 day increase yesterday. They'll send you a formal notice on Monday."

The news gave him the opening he needed. "And not a moment too soon. I don't know how I'm supposed to survive on what they pay. How does Jaida manage so well? I barely made rent."

"I have a good broker."

Lance jerked around and blew out a sharp breath. Man, she was stealth. Where had she come from? He eyed the melon-colored swimsuit she changed into and held up an appeasing hand. "Didn't mean to pry."

He drained the last of his Pepsi then crushed the plastic bottle in his palm. "I was just curious. Maybe you can offer me some tips later on."

"Maybe," she said then sank down beside Carina on a towel.

"So, what's the name of this broker?" Auggie asked. "I know what you get paid, and he must be a magician. You couldn't possibly have anything left to invest at the end of the month."

The corners of her mouth curled up, and Lance smiled to himself. She had a secret. And he was just the man to dig it up.

Auggie snorted and adjusted his hat. "Broker my eye."

"What are you reading, Carina? Is it any good?" Jaida asked. Lance watched her tilt the book clutched in Carina's hands to get a glimpse of the title.

Carina said, "Nothing you'd like. It would keep you up at night."

"I don't know how you can read those gruesome horror stories. They creep me out."

He noticed the unnatural pitch to Jaida's voice. Something had her riled. Was it his probing about money, or the *cargo* they were hauling downstairs?

Allowing Kevin to join them was a regret he would have to live with. At Carina's request, he'd agreed to include her friend, but that was before he knew her purpose for inviting him. Kevin was just one more obstacle, and right now what he needed was a clear field.

Besides, there was something off about him, but he couldn't get a clear read on what it was. And he wasn't too sure he wanted to climb inside that brain and wade around unless he had to.

Footsteps sounded on the stairs, and in his first appearance since boarding the Black Diamond, Kevin joined them on the upper level. He was less than cordial. Much less.

He stood alone, looking ill at ease in his own skin when Lance called him over. "Want to take the wheel for a while?"

He scratched his head, looked down at his sandaled feet then said, "Sure, why not."

They switched places, and Lance gave him a brief rundown on the basic operation of the vessel then stepped aside. "Thanks, man." He could use the break and the opportunity to mingle.

He pulled his tee shirt over his head and tossed it on the seat next to Auggie, fully aware of the attention it elicited from Jaida. He smiled to himself, glad that he didn't have to work too hard to attract it.

"I didn't know you had a tattoo," she said. "Wicked-looking dragon."

Auggie snickered. "Who is that supposed to be? Puff?"

"If you weren't such a woman, I'd punch you."

"Go ahead. You hit like a girl anyway."

Lance chuckled at Auggie's gibe. Waving it off, he insinuated himself into the narrow spot left beside Jaida then dropped to his stomach.

She angled her head, their eyes connecting, hers full of questions, the wheels turning. She was analyzing, trying to make sense of his motives. Not something she ought to do.

"The dragon needs a little sun," he said. He watched the corner of her mouth tip up and then spread into a brilliant smile. He knew then this was going to turn out better than he'd planned.

5

She'd been trained to fake it, to let people see only what she wanted them to see, but today her façade had slipped. Today it was personal.

Jaida slid her bag from her shoulder and left it on the floor in the hall. She followed Carina inside her hotel room, gently closing the door behind her. Carina turned when the latch clicked, a look of surprise on her face.

"Did you need something?" she asked.

"How about an explanation, retribution, a little remorse. Maybe all three?" Jaida's fists clenched. "How *dare* you do that to me?"

Carina sighed and dropped her head back, "Oh, please, can't we act like an adult, Jaida? You're overreacting."

"Don't patronize me. And for the record, I'm not looking for a relationship."

"Well pardon me for thinking you might want to be more than a fling to some man, but now that I think about it, it's the other way around isn't it? You're the one who gets what you want then bails out of the relationship."

Carina sank the venom deep and Jaida drew back. Is that how she saw her? She opened her mouth, a retort on her tongue then changed her mind and reached for the door, but she wasn't quick enough to dodge Carina's parting shot.

"You have no appreciation for a good man. Kevin isn't like those losers I've seen you with. He's an auditor for the county—a fiscal genius—and he's gone out of his way to help you manage your money. You, the woman who's too busy to pay her bills."

Jaida stood there and took the verbal bashing then quietly let herself out. Shaken, she drew in a breath and reached for the strap of her bag. Confusion washed over her anew. What just happened in there?

She was the one who'd been wronged, but Carina turned it around and went at her again taking pot shots. Numb, she walked the carpeted corridor, scanning the doors for room 212.

Original landscapes of the island set in matching frames were displayed on the saffron walls. Her weekend might be ruined, but at least Lance booked a five-star hotel.

He reserved three rooms. How he'd even found one room during tourist season was beyond her. This time of year the island's hotels were booked solid weeks in advance. One room was a fluke, but three rooms qualified as a supernatural miracle. He must have connections.

"Jaida, hold up." Auggie called to her from behind, but instead of turning she glanced at the number on the door to her right and kept walking.

"I'm sorry." His voice carried down the hall followed by the soft thudding sound of rapid footsteps coming closer. They were right behind her, then beside her. He'd made his apology, what did he want from her?

"I shouldn't have meddled." His arm brushed against hers and he reached for her hand, squeezing her fingers.

"No, you shouldn't have," she said.

"But in my defense I was only thinking of you."

She stopped then and looked up at him. "Of *me*? Really? How so?" This she had to hear.

"Cut it out."

"Cut what out? I'm only asking for some clarification since the answer isn't obvious to me."

"You're a handful to look after. All right? It wouldn't hurt you to find a nice guy and settle down."

A lump swelled in her throat and tears pricked her eyes, but she quickly blinked them away. "What makes you think you're responsible for me?" she asked. "And who do you think you are, trying to pawn me off like that? What am I? Some kind of community project?"

"I didn't mean any..."

She waved her hand, cutting him off. "Just go away."

"It was Carina's idea."

"Did you really just say that? That is so first grade, Auggie. Can't you take a little responsibility?"

"I just said I was sorry. Isn't that taking responsibility?"

Any hope she had of redeeming the weekend was shot. A pre-paid room at a five-star hotel no longer seemed like a fair trade.

He gripped a strand of her hair and gave it a playful tug. "Are we good?"

Unbelievable. "No, we're not." she said, watching the hope that lit his dark eyes fade. "Not yet."

Jaida walked away, lugging her bag down the hall, and leaving him to think about what he had done.

The hotel's internet service was down, and her hope of tracking the name of Vickery's assistant was once again pushed to Monday. Jaida picked up her camera from the desktop and sat on the bed with it. She pressed the "On" button, and the blackened LCD screen lit up.

They did some hiking earlier then spent the afternoon diving at Ship Rock. Even with the temperature at 90 degrees, the chill of the ocean was still buried under her skin. She slipped her feet under the rose-colored bedspread to warm them and settled into the mattress, clicking through the pictures.

She'd snapped a few candid shots of Auggie and Lance, but it was the blue-banded gobies, anemones, sea fans, and purple hydrocoral that took up most of the space on the camera's memory.

It was just the three of them. After Carina's blistering censure, the woman made a beeline for the nearest spa, and she hadn't seen Kevin since they stepped off the shore boat.

She turned off the camera and dropped it on the bed. Maybe Kevin had gone back to the mainland. Not likely, but she could always hope.

Why was Carina suddenly so interested in her personal life? And what was so special about Kevin that she chose him to foist on her?

Jaida slid the screen door open and stepped out onto the terrace. She leaned against the iron rail that wrapped the perimeter and wedged her foot between the bars, turning her face into the breeze. All around the grounds palm leaves rustled, and somewhere down below, meat was grilling. The smoky scent left her mouth watering.

The view from up here was perfect for people watching. Men, women, couples, and families; she observed them all from her lofty perch. It was the way she imagined God, sitting back on His colossal throne in the heavens, scrutinizing their every deed. What did He see when He looked down at her?

She sent a fleeting glance into the blue sky. "What do you think of me, God?" There was a thread of mockery in her inquiry, and on its heels she shivered with fear. Would the answer be sent in a bolt of lightning? She certainly deserved it.

On the other side of the street, a curly haired child in a yellow dress laughed and ran after her older sister. A graying man dressed in golf gear zipped by in a golf cart, his bag of clubs on the seat behind him. All of them were entertaining to watch, but it was the man and woman in the right corner of the quad area below that stole her breath and won her undivided attention.

They stood close, intimately close. The man lifted a gentle hand and stroked the woman's cheek. The way he looked into her face—into her soul—left Jaida's heart aching with a familiar longing. His fingers traced her cheekbone to her hairline, tucking the auburn hair behind her ear. Sunlight played on the gold band of his fourth finger, left hand. Married.

He leaned even closer and whispered in her ear. She giggled and gave a playful push against his chest. Their laughter carried up to her easily enough, but the whispered endearments, the lighthearted banter were lost to her.

Jaida pushed away from the rail. She'd seen enough. He was married, but who was to say that the woman was his wife? He could be wed to another and that painted the scene playing out before her in an entirely different light.

He was no better than she was. She went inside and shut the sliding glass door behind her. She would not pine for what wasn't meant to be.

6

The karaoke bar was indistinct; a small white stucco structure with a blue and white striped awning that shaded the entrance. Lance held the heavy wooden door open letting the live karaoke music out and Jaida in.

Auggie had already abandoned them for a dark-haired beauty in the corner, but the rest of their crew straggled in behind her with all the enthusiasm of death-row inmates being led to their execution.

Carina immediately excused herself and headed for the ladies room. She had been pleasant enough over dinner, but neither one of them broached the subject of her earlier outburst. It couldn't be done without an argument. Besides, what was there to say?

Lighted strings of colored bulbs decorated the beamed ceiling, but the rest of the décor was a nautical motif. Lance grabbed her hand and wove a path through the crush of customers. Music, laughter, and conversation filled her ears. They slid into the only booth available, and a server took their drink order.

Up front, a shapely brunette stood on the portable stage and clung to the microphone, belting out a rock tune with a country twang.

Kevin slid into the seat across from them. He shook the hair from his eyes and leaned back against the green vinyl seat. "Whatever happened with those charges against you?" he asked.

Why was he bringing that up? It was so off the cuff and it happened over six months ago. "They weren't charges." Not legally anyway. "William Gale made an accusation and it was investigated." That was it. She'd been cleared.

Lance nodded his head. "Yeah, I remember hearing about that. What was it? Eight million dollars he said you took?"

"Eight and a half."

He whistled through his teeth. "What I could do with eight and a half mil. Some men have all the luck."

Kevin glowered at Lance then settled a sympathetic gaze on Jaida. "I was afraid you'd get fired. I'm glad nothing came of it."

Jaida appreciated his kindness and nodded a silent thank-you. It had been a difficult time for her.

"So why is it you were afraid Jaida would get fired?" Back from her detour, Carina slipped in the booth beside Kevin. He took the purse she handed him and tucked it in the corner.

"Gale's money," Jaida said abruptly. Could they just move on to another subject? Why did they want to rehash the details?

"Oh, that." Carina rolled her gray eyes. "You know I never understood why he blamed you. If the bank account number had been sent through Baseel like he said, what made him think you were the one who took it?"

All three of them turned their eyes on her, and she shifted under their hawk-like stares. Was this what it was like to be on the witness stand, cornered like prey by a prosecutor?

This felt less like a discussion and more like an inquiry. Gale was the one they should be asking. How was she to know his mind? Jaida glanced down at the saltshaker in her hands. When had she picked that up?

She pushed the dispenser aside and told them the story she'd been telling herself. "It was his way of getting me off the case"— And his plan to keep her from learning the name of her mother.

The intro to a ballad played while the next rising karaoke star took to the stage. Jaida craned her neck to see the performance. If she feigned interest in the amateur act, would it put an end to their prying?

The waitress brought their drinks and pulled a handful of straws from her apron, leaving them on the table. Lance passed Jaida her Sprite.

"I ordered you a Coke," Kevin said, handing Carina the glass. Carina bit the end of the paper from her straw like a seasoned smoker biting the tip of a cigar then blew the casing at Jaida. It shot across the table and fell into her lap.

Carina stuck her straw in the glass and whispered something to Kevin. "We'll be back," she said. The two of them rose and disappeared into the crowd.

Jaida frowned at Lance. "Guess it's just us."

He yawned then scrubbed his face with his hands. "All right by me. This feels good after that grueling hike," he said. "Especially after carrying that one hundred-and-twenty-pound weight on my back."

"One hundred and eighteen pounds," she corrected. "And it was chivalrous of you to carry me the rest of the way." She had blisters on her blisters, and they had been scraped raw by the heels of her tennis shoes.

"Chivalrous?" He snorted, mocking her use of the archaic word. His free arm slid behind her coming to rest on the back of the seat. "I'm no boy scout." His hooded green eyes captured hers telling her things she didn't want to hear. Hadn't she made herself clear on the ride over?

Jaida pulled away from him, but she was cornered in the booth. She tried to mask the flush of embarrassment with a half smile. She wasn't new to this game, to men's advances, just at pushing them away. She looked around the seating area searching for something, anything to transfer her attention to.

"It's packed tonight," she said, catching a whiff of someone's coconut shrimp. It smelled wonderful, but after dining on roast lamb and herbed red potatoes she had nowhere to put it.

"Guess so." Lance raised the bottle his fingers were wrapped around and took a swig of his Blue Moon.

She watched his gaze drop to her hand where it rested on the seat. Almost hesitant, he opened and closed his fingers then without an ounce of caution moved his hand from the thigh of his jeans to cover the back of her hand, his fingers expressing a form of confidence when they slid between hers like pieces of a puzzle.

He didn't waste any time. But she had sworn off men and was now trying for some semblance of virtue. Hadn't she done enough damage? Before she knew what was happening, Lance leaned in and kissed her. She should pull away, scold him for crossing her boundaries, but she didn't.

Nose to nose, she watched his eyes crinkle softly at the edges, the attractive result of the casual smile he wore. "Cold lips," he said.

She smiled back. "The warm heart makes up for it." Warm heart? That was laughable. Her thoughts went to Spencer, and her smile faded. What would he say to that? If he were sitting here right now he would surely argue that it was a frigid block of ice occupying the left side of her chest.

Jaida leaned her head back against the seat, appraising Lance. Pale green eyes, ash blond hair with a short practical cut that would have been standard for a military man. The sun had marked him with a faint streak of red down the length of his nose and a wide swathe across his forehead. He was strong, confident, good looking, and for her, dangerous.

She looked down at her lap. "So, outside of the few places we've been together in our brief friendship, where do you like to go? What do you like to do?"

He chuckled. "You have me pegged all wrong. I'm a homebody. I only venture out of doors when you're around."

Jaida shook her head. "That was the sorriest line I've ever heard. You can do better than that." Have done better than that, no doubt.

He laughed without a hint of shame then leaned closer until she could feel his lips brush against her ear. "I find you very attractive."

She resisted the wooing, the softening of her will, and pulled back. "Not too creative, but definitely better."

"I just can't please you." Lance grinned and drained his bottle.

Jaida tipped her head, her eyes narrowing as she zeroed in on Auggie standing across the room. "Would you look at that?" she said, pointing at the girl clutching Auggie's shirt.

"Yeah, Auggie lays on the Latino charm like a farmer spreads manure."

Jaida snorted when she laughed. "A deeply profound analogy. And I would bet you his Cuban accent is twice as thick. Women love an accent."

"Do they now?" Lance studied her a long moment then raised her face with a light touch of his fingers, his lids thick and lowered, he looked into her eyes. "Avete un bel viso e un bel corpo."

The rhythm of the foreign words sounded so beautiful. "What did you say?"

He shrugged. "I don't know, but it sounded good, didn't it?"

She shoved him. "What do you mean you don't know?"

"Just because I'm Italian doesn't mean I speak the language. Besides, I thought the only thing that mattered was the accent." He grinned and cocked his head. "How was it by the way?"

"Muy bueno," she said.

He shook his head. "This multilingual thing isn't working for me. I declare English the official language of Catalina."

"Not until you tell me what you said."

"Okay, okay." He held up a hand. "Just give me a minute here. I'm sure I butchered it, but if I got it right, it was something along the lines of, you have a lovely face, and a lovely body."

Heat burned her cheeks and she looked away. "Auggie isn't the only one spreading a load of manure," she said.

"You don't think I mean it?"

Oh, she knew he meant it. She would have to be blind not to notice the way he looked at her, but it was all about the physical. He saw her as a good time and nothing more. Jaida shrank in her seat. For the first time in her life, she felt cheap.

But wasn't this what she wanted? Non-committal, one-dimensional relationships that never grew roots or put her heart at risk? It had never been about love, so why did she feel cheated when those were the offers she attracted?

"We're ba-a-a-ck." Carina sang out, her voice and her presence grating on Jaida. She set a basket of deep fried mushrooms on the table. "Eat up."

Jaida arched a brow at the golden batter-fried fungus, "Are they poisonous?"

"If they are, we'll die together." Carina snatched one up out of the basket and popped it in her mouth.

Lance nudged Jaida with his shoulder. "Want to take a walk?"

"Sure."

He looked from Carina to Kevin. "Hope you don't mind if we take off."

Silent, they stared blankly across the table at the two of them. Apparently they did mind.

Kevin ran his hands through his hair, shoving it back from the rounded line of his forehead. Why did he look so upset?

"Get over it, Kev. Jaida just isn't the kind of girl you take home to Mama."

Jaida bristled at the remark. So, she was still being punished. She felt her mouth twitch at Carina's deliberate meanness. *Sticks and stones*, the cruel words should roll off of her carefully constructed armor. Instead they slipped through the unseen chinks and sank deep.

She felt the warmth of Lance's palm come to rest on her back. "That's enough, Carina," he said then stood, pulling her to her feet.

Carina didn't know when to hold her tongue, but she was right. She wasn't the kind of woman men brought home to their mothers. Why would they? Even her own mother had left her behind.

7

Lance never waited for daylight to make his exit, but this morning the sun rose before he did, and he had no desire to leave.

It was the first time he'd stuck around to watch a woman sleep. He stroked the soft blonde hair fanning the white pillowcase, his gaze trailing the blanket-draped figure beside him. What started out as business had turned personal, and it was a clear conflict of interest.

He'd been hired for his professional services because he was the best in the field and those who were bankrolling him would expect nothing less than the results he'd guaranteed.

He shifted to his side atop the rumpled sheet and blanket and rested his cheek on his palm. Lungs filling and emptying, he watched the rhythmic rise and fall of Jaida's chest, each descent punctuated with a faint breath passing through a part in her lips.

He had never met anyone like her. She was an enigma, a dichotomy of harlot and virgin, imp and angel. It seemed an impossible, even a perverse juxtaposition, but he was trained to know the psyche, the heart and mind of an adversary, and he would stake his reputation that at the core of her was the antithesis of how she lived, and even she didn't know it.

Lance rubbed a strand of silky hair between his fingers and considered his dilemma. Paradox or not, she'd managed to slip under his skin and it wasn't conducive to good business.

Affections warred against duty, but affections could be tamed. He already knew it was duty that would win out. He named his price, the deal was set, and he would give his people what they wanted.

Lance released her hair and rolled onto his back. *Sorry Jaida.*

Jaida pressed her cheek against Mommy's softness and listened to the thumping drumbeat in her ear. The rocker creaked, the battered wooden runners carving a groove in the polished hardwood floor, carrying them back and forth.

She resisted the heaviness of her eyelids, the languid tug of her limbs. Sleep wooed, but didn't claim her. She knew if she allowed it to win she would wake up in her bed alone.

Jaida opened her eyes wider and stared into the shining tawny gaze smiling down at her.

"I want down," she said.

"No. Sit with Mommy for a while."

Mommy rubbed her hand in soft circles on her back. Her shoulders slipped lower slouching at the gentle caress, her body curling into a ball in the crook of Mommy's arm. She was drifting, floating on a cloud of dreams that were taking her deeper. Jaida jerked, her eyes popping open with a start.

She tried to slide free from the clasp of soft arms, the curve of the warm lap, but those same arms clamped around her and slid her back into place, holding her tight.

Jaida yawned. She was not going to sleep. "Where is Spencer?"

"He isn't coming today."

"Can I see him?"

Mommy stroked her hair. "Later," she said.

Jaida sighed and laid her head back down. Mommy hummed then told stories of how Mommy and Spencer's mommy and daddy used to play at the ocean.

"Sunday, after church, we'll go there to play."

"When you played at the ocean, how come I wasn't with you?" Blinking the sleepiness away, Jaida lifted her head again, waiting for an answer.

"You weren't born yet."

"But where was I? Was I with you?"

Mommy shook her head. "No. God didn't make you yet."

Jaida rubbed her fists into her eyes, tears stinging the rims and spilling down her cheeks. She wailed and pressed her face into Mommy's softness again her shoulders and back shuddering with every audible cry.

Mommy stroked the back of her head. "What's the matter? Why are you crying?"

"Because I was all alone, and I didn't wanna be alone."

Jaida's lips responded to the warmth, the gentle pressure. Her eyes opened to the dark blond head leaning over her. Spencer? No. Not Spencer. It was Lance.

He drew back, his face hovering over hers. Her heart raced in her chest. Was it him or her dream that caused the erratic beat behind her ribs?

His cupped hand slid from her shoulder, down her arm and he took her hand in his, his fingertips toying with her own. "You were sleeping pretty solid, but then you started whimpering. When your breathing accelerated…" He shrugged. "I thought you might need a diversion from whatever held you captive in that beautiful head of yours."

Confused, she blinked. It sounded so clinical and detached, his words making no sense at first, but then she realized he was explaining why she woke to find him kissing her.

She furrowed her brow. Whatever made her think it was Spencer? Her heart paused then resumed with a pounding when she remembered what Spencer's kiss was like: tender and sweet and born of love. Her heart swelled then shrank.

Swallowing, she lifted her face and gave Lance a feeble smile. "It was better than waking up to an alarm."

His eyes warmed, telling her it was the right answer. He turned her hand over and stroked her palm. "Do you want to talk about it?"

The dream? No. It was the last thing she wanted to talk about. She shook her head.

He offered a patient smile then stared into space as if weighing out each word before he spoke again. "I once read that dreams are one of the most powerful insights into the human psyche."

Lance watched her, then silently encouraged…no, more like urged her to respond, to tell him what tormented her, but his psychology wasn't going to work, even if his reference was true…especially if it was true. Her psyche was the last place she wanted anyone poking around.

Jaida's nerves were still on edge. A brief shudder sent her body quivering and then took flight, leaving her utterly still. She said nothing, just turned to her side and snuggled against Lance's chest, timing her breathing. *In two counts out four.*

The weight of his arm draped over her and she closed her eyes, frantically searching for a place of peace and safety, but the corner she was trapped in was terrifying, the aloneness a great yawning giant.

She squeezed her eyes tighter; shutting herself inside the world she feared most.

Lance must have sensed her agitation. His arm tightened around her, drawing her closer. He kissed the top of her head. "Sleep," he said. "We don't have anywhere we have to be."

Her breathing leveled into a light cadence, and Jaida slipped into a sound sleep. Lance rolled off the bed and pulled the covers around her shoulders. He stood over her, watching, considering the anxiety that gripped her in the throes of sleep.

Was it just a meaningless collection of thoughts that plagued her, or was it something deeper, something that would point him in the right direction?

With light steps, Lance crossed the room and collected the rest of his clothes that were laid out across the desk chair. He was only guaranteed one more day alone with her on the island, and he intended to use it to his advantage.

The doorknob rattled followed by a sharp thud that shook the wooden door in its frame. He tugged his shirt over his head and opened it.

"I thought I'd find you here." Auggie's fist was still suspended, ready to crash against the door one more time. He let it drop to his side, his searing gaze burning holes through Lance. He pushed his way inside, the back of the door slamming against the wall.

Did he always play the irate father and bust in on her like this? "Am I missing something? Did I need your permission, *Dad*? I didn't think you had any interest in her."

That earned him a dark look. "I do have an interest, just not the kind you're suggesting. I look out for her."

"Keeping her safe from the likes of me?" Last night it was his shoulder Jaida cried on, so to speak. He found Auggie's suggestion that she settle down amusing. Less amusing was the fact that he wasn't considered suitable company for the fair Jaida.

Auggie shoved a stiff finger against his chest. "Just watch yourself, man."

The camaraderie between them was gone. Lance could take it or leave it since it wasn't formed to last in the first place, but it would be a wise decision to hold onto it a little while longer.

He nodded. "Will do."

After Auggie left, Lance stood at the foot of the bed mulling over the woman in it. He was surprised she'd slept through their skirmish.

She was something special. He wouldn't mind delving deeper, establishing an honest relationship without ulterior motives clouding it. But that was unrealistic. Once she discovered why he was involved in her life, she would have his head on a platter.

8

The line was busy. Jaida dropped the phone in the cradle and yawned. She'd been dialing Vickery's office for an hour and a half and still could not get through.

Either the machine was full of condolences to Vickery's staff or someone left the phone off the hook. She stood, laced her fingers, and stretched her arms over her head then took a few steps across the black-and-white tile to work the numbness from her backside. The waiting was making her crazy.

She had an early morning meeting scheduled with the head of Baseel or she would already be on the freeway headed to Ventura. It would be tasteless to crash a funeral, but at the moment, need trumped etiquette.

She hit 'speaker' then 'redial' and got the same result. If by the end of the day she couldn't reach a live person, or a recording to leave a message, she would drive out there first thing tomorrow morning.

Vickery's assistant was Barbara Ellenburg. She had located the woman's name and was in the process of pulling up her cell number.

Her only concern was that Ms. Ellenburg would stand by her boss's views on attorney-client privilege. What if she refused to let her see the records? There was no reason they should be withheld. She was the only one they affected. Besides, who was left to object or even care what was in them?

She had always wondered if Eva knew the name of her birth mother. If she had she never let on, and Jaida could never bring herself to ask. What mother, adoptive or biological, would want to share her child's heart with another woman?

She glanced at the clock. It was nearly eleven, and it was Monday. Her weekend grace period had officially ended. Soon, Auggie would make his appearance and inform her that the investigation on Gale was closed. Once again, she would be on her own.

She sat back down at the desk and reached for the styrofoam cup. Sipping at the lukewarm coffee, she looked over the open folder. The pages of the year-old summary stared up at her. It was the last report in the file. How many times had she read through it already? Twenty? Thirty?

Jaida rolled the desk chair forward, the seat squealing in protest, and read the investigators remarks. She considered every angle the prosecutor could approach this from. Anything turned over had to be strong enough to stick. She had to be missing something that would seal this up for her, something small but significant, and that's what she was searching for. Again.

Gale deserved more years behind bars than he had left to live. The video footage she'd viewed was macabre. A murder preserved on film, it mimicked a violent scene straight out of CSI. Only this was real.

The video alone should be enough to guarantee that charges would be filed, and a conviction would follow. But the quality was so poor it could be argued that it wasn't Gale—that he was the victim of a look-alike's heinous actions, another man with a similar face and build. And she had nothing in her arsenal to shoot that theory down with.

Even after video forensics spent hours cleaning it up, the image alone didn't prove beyond a reasonable doubt that it was William Gale wielding the knife.

Jaida picked up the second page and looked it over, reading the first line once, twice, and then a third time before she gave up and tossed it back into the pile of loose papers. She couldn't do this. Not today.

She dug her fingertips into her temples and rubbed, but the tension clawed tighter. This was not part of her job. She was to present the facts and the evidence then pass the baton onto the police in a collaborative effort. It was the State that would choose to prosecute...or not.

And therein lies the rub. It was the 'or not' that had her stressing out and scrambling for surety in a system that was so unpredictable.

Her own motives in this were hardly altruistic, but if she got what she wanted there would be a double win. She would learn the name of her mother, and for the victim, Marcus Dennison, justice would be served.

Jaida shrugged out of her sweater and let it slide between her and the back of the chair. With the thermostat set at an arctic chill, the white cashmere had become an office staple. Even in the middle of summer.

She eyed the long-stemmed red rose draped over the top of her inbox. Lance left it for her. She lifted it and pressed it to her nose, the sweet fragrance a stench in her nostrils, a reminder of one more mistake.

Her face burned hot with shame at what she'd done. But what was one more indiscretion? Why should it matter? She pressed her eyes closed. Maybe it shouldn't, but the ache behind her ribs told her it did.

She rubbed one of the velvety petals between her thumb and forefinger. The shade of the rose was an uncommon deep purplish-red. Carmine red. Not true red. Not true love. No surprise there. If it weren't for the art classes she took a hundred summers ago, red would just be red to her. But what did the color represent?

She set the rose down and typed "colors of roses and their meaning" into the internet's search engine, and in the blink of an eye there were twelve million, seven hundred thousand results at her fingertips.

She scrolled down, randomly selected a link, and with a click of the mouse, the page opened to a spread of professionally photographed roses. She scanned the bullet list below it. Red meant true love—she knew that one. Her gaze drifted down the page, past the pinks and yellows. There it was. Carmine red—deceitful desire.

What kind of meaning was that? And whose deceitful desire did it refer to, the giver or the receiver? Jaida closed the page.

She was reading too much into a simple gesture. The idea of Lance choosing a flower based on the color was ridiculous. To most men a rose was just a rose.

The phone rang. She lifted the receiver to her ear. "Detective Martin."

Silence.

She glanced at the caller ID. *Unknown caller.* Jaida opened her mouth again, but it was another voice that spoke.

"I told you to come alone."

Her fingers tightened on the receiver. "Who is this?"

"You don't know?"

"I do now," she said. It was Ray. His voice didn't sound natural, but it had been altered in some manner since the first call. Not electronically. It was just unusual.

"Did you recognize me at the bar?" he asked.

Was this a trick question? "You weren't at the bar."

"No, I wasn't. I gave you very simple rules, Detective Martin. Did you think you could break those rules and get away with it?"

"I don't understand. I did exactly as you asked."

"I told you to come alone."

"I don't know what you're talking about," she said. It wasn't a lie. Not really. Technically she had come alone. She didn't know where Auggie was until he grabbed her on the street.

"I won't tolerate being played. If you want my cooperation, you'll stick to my rules."

"How about tonight?" she asked. "Same bar, same get-up if you like."

His anger was palpable. "I will say where and I will say when *if* I choose to meet you at all."

Pompous, self-important, little… She bit back the angry words and worked an agreeable smile into her voice. "As you wish, Ray. Feel free to call me if you decide you're still interested in talking."

The phone clicked. He hung up first. It was a waiting game now. Jaida set the receiver on the hook and pressed her eyes closed. *Please, please, call back.*

She had the leverage she needed now, the excuse for keeping the case open. Ray's call had given her that much if nothing else. Her office door banged open, and she swung around.

"Delivery." Auggie entered carrying two white paper sacks. "Something wrong? You look troubled," he said then shoved the door shut with his foot.

"I had a phone call."

"Was it our man?" He found a small square of exposed wood in the sea of her paperwork and set the bags down on the desk.

"It was," she said, hesitant to say much more. His hand disappeared in one of the sacks then reappeared with a paper carton. He handed it to her.

Jaida opened the flap and a small burst of steam released the scent of General Tsao's chicken. It was her favorite.

Auggie opened another one and handed it to her. "Mmmm, pork lo mein. You are my hero." This was just what she needed after living on coffee all morning.

He grinned and licked an orange sauce from his thumb. "I take it the conversation didn't go well." He drew another container from the bag and set it in front of him. Drinks followed.

"He knew you were there," she said. He looked up at that. Let him mull that over for a while. That way when she stepped outside his authority and handled this herself, he would understand, because the next time their informant made her an offer to meet she would be going alone.

"Impossible. Did he specifically identify me?"

"No, but he knew I had backup." She twisted the plastic fork in the middle of the noodles and tucked the bite in her mouth.

"When does he want to meet?"

She chewed then quickly swallowed. "We haven't gotten around to that yet. I think right now he's about proving he's the one with all the power."

"Next time we'll just have to be more careful. No meeting up with me afterward unless it's an emergency. Maybe it was just a hunch on his part until he saw us together on the street."

"Maybe," she said, but she wasn't convinced. She sank into the chair and waved her fork over the food. "Thanks for the Chinese."

"No problem." Auggie slouched down in the armchair across from her and propped his feet up on the desk.

"Just to be clear, this means you're keeping the case open now, right?"

He nodded then jerked his chin at the open file lying next to the shabby Nikes he wore. "I see you're hard at work on it. Are you making any headway?"

"Trying." But not succeeding, though she wasn't inclined to reveal that little nugget of information. Auggie might be her friend, but he was also her superior.

"Let me guess. Lance has you sidetracked."

In a way, yes he did. She grinned and pointed her fork at him. "You are just too good of a detective."

He eyed her over the tops of his feet. "Just a friendly suggestion, but I don't think you should see him anymore."

"Why?" She hadn't expected that, not after he tried to pawn her off on Kevin.

"I don't know." He shrugged. "Intuition. Something tells me he's a bad idea."

"Yeah, and you thought Kevin was a good idea."

His feet dropped to the floor, and he held up his hands in surrender. "All right, I admitted I was wrong there, but the guy is so pathetic when it comes to women, you in particular. It's like he's some awkward adolescent tripping all over himself. You can't help but have a little compassion."

"You make him sound like such an attractive prospect." Jaida laughed. "Besides, I thought you liked Lance."

"I'm just telling you what I think. Let's leave it at that."

'Let's leave it at that,' implied there was more, but she wouldn't ask. Not today. Not with everything else she had to deal with.

"Fair enough." She bit into the shrimp-stuffed egg roll Auggie unwrapped for her.

His fork invaded her territory and speared a piece of her chicken. She leaned forward and guarded the remains of her food with her arms. "Eat your own."

"You can have some of mine." He shoved his carton at her, and she looked inside the empty cavern. Empty, save for a skimpy mouthful of white rice, tinted red from the sweet-and-sour sauce.

"Thanks." She made a face at him then frowned, a somber mood overtaking her. "Why do you think Ray wants to help? I mean, what exactly does he get out of this? He's putting himself on the line, and the man he's about to expose repays favors like that with a bullet to the head."

He shrugged. "A grievance, a vendetta…he didn't get what he was promised. Could be anything. Guys like this have revenge in their blood. Once we're through with him, if he's still breathing, he'll probably be begging for a new identity and a boat ride to some uncharted island."

Auggie popped the rest of an egg roll in his mouth and cleared away the trash then tossed her a pre-wrapped fortune cookie. "Fresh out of the oven."

She tore into the plastic wrap. Without breaking the crisp golden cookie, she slid the edge of the fortune out with the tips of her fingernails and held the faint red print up to the light. "Charm is deceitful, and beauty is passing, but a woman who fears the Lord, she shall be praised."

"Where did you get this? From a Chinese restaurant or an evangelist?"

"Both. The owner is a Christian man." He chucked her chin. "If nothing else, they're wise words. Now, get Lance off your brain and get back to work."

Nettled by the self-professed heathen defining Scripture as "wise words," she pinched the fortune from her cookie into a tiny ball and flicked it into the wastebasket. Was he crossing over?

Wise words, truth, or mere babble, they had a mild impact. But she learned to shut them out before, and she would do it again.

9

Jaida sat back and watched the fax machine kick out page after page of her adoption history, and now the final sheet inched its way to the top of the tray.

When she reached Barbara Ellenburg and explained the purpose of her call, the woman was more than accommodating. The only thing she required of Jaida was proof of her identity. But the question of legality swirled in the back of her mind. Was the move lawful without going through the courts? She kept the concern to herself, afraid this gift she'd been handed would be snatched away from her.

The hum of the machine went quiet, and she collected the stack of papers from the tray. She carried them to the kitchen table then settled into the padded chair, every beat of her heart pronounced.

There were eight pages including the cover page. Pen and highlighter in hand, she uncapped them both and looked over the first document. It was the Court Report of Adoption.

She skimmed over the legalese and focused on the portions that mattered. No birth name was given. Her date of birth had been listed, but was it the actual date she was born, or just an educated guess?

Based on the story she'd been told, the date recorded had to be within a day of her birth. Other than her gender, most of the fields in Part One of the form were either listed as unknown or left blank: place of birth, birth parents' names, attending physician. Had there even been one?

Jaida slipped the page from the top of the pile and set it face down on the table then started on the next document. It was a legal form that terminated parental rights. According to this, voluntary consent had been given. But how could that be? Unless... Her gaze raced down the page. If consent had been given, then her birth mother's name would have been documented at the time of the adoption. Legally it had to be.

She picked up the next page and read the header: Affidavit for Termination. This should be it. She made quick work of skimming over the document then homed in on the name typed in the box. She slammed the paper down on the table. "How could they do this?" she yelled at the ceiling. Jane Doe. They had her listed as Jane Doe.

No name, but they did manage to include "Jane's" birth date. She was seventeen years old, a minor when she gave birth.

She read the instructional paragraph above the empty fields. As a minor, the parents' names and address were required, but the indicated spaces were left blank. Convenient. But for whom?

What kind of sham adoption was this? How could a judge approve this? Nothing made any sense. And why would her mother come back after dumping her in the park? Why step forward at all?

The rest of the fax was her medical history compiled shortly after she'd been found, and some photocopies of handwritten notes. She highlighted the name of the hospital and the physician who examined her, wondering if the hospital and the medical group involved had more detailed records than this.

The jotted notes were Mark Vickery's work product. It surprised her that Ms. Ellenburg included them. Jaida read through the scrawled drafts. Doubling back over the second paragraph, her breath caught. She *had* read that right. Laurel Gordon, Spencer's mother, was present throughout the adoption process.

Eva was thirty-five and single when she adopted her. A longtime friend of Laurel's, she was visiting at the Gordon home the day Spencer found her. Still, she had no idea how involved Laurel had been.

How much did she know? She pushed up from the chair, slipped her shoes on, and reached for her car keys. She would just have to find out.

>⟶⟶

Fueled by sentiment, Jaida sat in the idling car and flipped through the CD case. What she was searching for was her Achilles heel, her kryptonite, but right now she was desperate for the poison.

She slid the disc out of the case and fed "That's Amore" into the slot, giving herself permission to reminisce. She put the car in reverse and backed out, squinting as she passed from the darkness of the garage into the harsh sunlight, her fingers scrabbling for the sunglasses in the console.

Across the alley, Marilyn Carter wrestled a heavy-duty trash bag into the plastic bin, the point of her red scarf flapping over her short gray hair. She slapped the lid on the can then turned and waved Jaida down, signaling for her to stop. Jaida hit the brakes and lowered the window.

Marilyn leaned close. "Do you have someone staying with you?" She rolled a mint over her tongue and tucked it inside her cheek. "A man in his mid to late forties? Looks like he wears a rug?"

Jaida frowned and shook her head. "No. Why?"

"Then you better make sure your house is locked up tight. I saw a man snooping around your back door yesterday. He even jiggled the handle. I would have called the cops, but I wasn't sure if he was a friend or maybe you had a relative who was locked out."

"I'm expecting a plumber," she said. But they were supposed to call first.

Marilyn stepped away from the car and moved in the direction of her house. "Maybe that's all he was about, but you better watch yourself. Especially since you live alone."

"Will do." Jaida rolled up the window, the outside heat already encroaching on the cooled interior. Whoever Marilyn saw may have been harmless—a peddler or the plumber—but her warning resonated, and she would take heed.

She turned up the volume on the stereo and pulled onto the street. The warble that was unique to Dean Martin's vocal cords came out sharp and clear. If Dean was still alive, would he have minded that she borrowed his last name? Spencer had. It wasn't her choice in replacements that bothered him, but rather her choice to change it at all.

"My One and Only Love" was already half played out. She tried to recall the lyrics about the April breeze, but they escaped her until the line repeated and she crooned them in a duet with Dean.

Spencer had made it her song, their song. Her lower lip trembled and she bit down hard, trading the emotional pain for the physical.

Her participation in the vocals had long since ended, and she gave Dean the privilege of serenading her with one more verse before she turned off the music, turning off the past.

Jaida parked in the lot of the nursing care facility then craned her neck for a quick look in the rearview mirror. She dabbed at the corner of her eyes, then sat back in the seat long enough to chase away the sorrow her nostalgia had conjured up.

She didn't want Laurel to see her like this. She took a few calming breaths and practiced smiling as if it mattered. Happy or sad, her mood would go unnoticed. And if today turned out to be one of Laurel's bad days, she wouldn't notice her at all.

With a manila envelope tucked under her arm, Jaida walked past the main desk. On the other side of the chest-high blue laminate counter, a nurse and two aides conversed. The tall one in print scrubs waved at her as she passed.

Jaida nodded back, her mouth only lifting slightly with a smile then headed toward Laurel's room. She exhaled a nervous breath then drew in another, inhaling the fresh pine scent. The maintenance crew kept this place near to immaculate. And the staff was exceptional. They treated the residents like family.

This facility was a cut above the home her Grandpa Payne spent his final days in, but then social security didn't cover much. Spencer had researched the corporation that owned this place and interviewed the director thoroughly before he signed on the dotted line. He always provided the best for those he loved.

Jaida turned the corner at the connecting hallway and clutched the envelope tighter to her chest. She would show this to Laurel. She had to ask. She'd been there. Why had she never said anything? If the memory was still stored in her mind, if this was a good day and she could process the question, and if she could just form the name on her lips...

She laughed at herself. *Look at me. I'm a fool, a desperate one.* Did she honestly expect to be pointed in the right direction by a woman who could barely communicate? A woman whose lucidity wavered from one minute to the next? But with her case against Gale falling apart, what alternative did she have?

"Well, look who's here, Roger. It's Miss Martin." Jaida turned. Mary, one of the full-time aides was gaining on her with a wheelchair.

"Where are you off to?" Jaida asked.

"Roger just finished rehab for the day," she said. Mary's passenger beamed up at Jaida, his wide smile yellowed with age and nicotine.

"He is such a flirt." Mary laughed then wheeled the chair around the corner.

Jaida stepped inside the open door to her left. Bright with sunlight and buttercup colored walls, Laurel's room held warmth. She was seated quietly in the center of the bed with her back to the door. She didn't move, didn't turn from the window. The hummingbirds hovering over the feeder had her spellbound.

"Good morning." The words came out raspy, and Jaida cleared the thickness from her throat.

Laurel shifted and then pivoted her head on a delicate neck. She raised her chin to get a better view of Jaida, but her glassy gaze went straight through her as if she wasn't even there.

It would be one of *those* days. The visits were getting harder. It was a cruel twist of nature to watch someone you cared for deteriorate until there was nothing familiar but the shell.

She was told this was to be expected. According to the medical world, any improvement at this point was impossible. So why did she always come expecting more?

On the upside, Laurel's quarters were cheery. There was a twin bed, a whitewashed nightstand and matching dresser with a beveled mirror mounted on top. Like the room, the attached bathroom was private.

Jaida sank down on the bed beside Laurel and opened the crumpled envelope she brought. She slid her hand inside and for reasons she couldn't explain, bypassed the newsprint, her purpose for coming today, and pulled out a frame with tiny orange stones encircling the perimeter.

It was a color print of the two of them standing arm in arm in Laurel's yard. Brilliant yellow flowers blooming on the sweet acacia tree dominated the background. She held it out for Laurel to see. "I framed this for you. It's a picture of the two of us."

It was one of the last pictures of Laurel before she'd been disabled by the stroke. Jaida watched her face, looked into her eyes. Was any of it familiar?

Laurel's jaw worked up and down, her larynx straining but turning out only a grunt. Her eyes flicked up at Jaida then dropped again to the frame.

Again her jaw worked. "J-J-aida."

She said her name. The words were pinched and garbled, but she knew who she was.

Jaida lifted Laurel's hand and pressed it to her cheek joy swelling inside of her. "Yes, it's me. It's Jaida."

Laurel jerked her hand away and tucked it close to her side. Like a pricked balloon her joy deflated. It was a reaction, not a rejection, she told herself.

The bed creaked when Jaida stood. She set the picture on the dresser, tilting it enough so Laurel could see it. The photographs arranged on the wall were different than when she was here last. Spencer must have changed them up when they painted.

The grin on his face in one of the pictures sparked something inside of her. She touched the tip of her finger to his lips. A smile touched her own then quickly slipped away when she considered the state of his humor the last time she saw him. But could she blame him?

The door swung open behind her, and she turned. For one insane moment, she expected to see him standing in the doorway instead of the chunky blonde aide.

"Sorry to interrupt but it's time for lunch."

"Thanks. I'll bring her down," Jaida said. She picked up Laurel's sweater folded at the foot of the bed and draped it over her shoulders.

"All righty." The aide ducked out and closed the door.

Jaida glanced up once more at the picture of Spencer thinking how odd it was that she'd never run into him here.

She helped Laurel into the wheelchair then picked up the envelope she brought with her. For now, the newspaper clippings would have to wait.

10

Hidden by the slant of afternoon shadows, Lance sat back in the wrought iron chair on Jaida's front patio and looked up at the two-story Mediterranean. It was prime property. The front and sides were loaded with arched windows offering high dollar views. A shack on the beach would sell for a few million, and this was no shack.

On her salary, Jaida couldn't afford this house even with the top-notch broker she laid claim to. He smiled to himself recalling the line she'd fed him about her investments. She was quick and sharp. He appreciated that in a woman. Soon he would see just how quick and how sharp.

The rumor making its rounds at the agency was that she inherited the house, but she could have ingeniously circulated that tale herself. He hadn't yet confirmed it as fact and even if it proved true, it didn't shed light on where the brand-new BMW came from or how she maintained her high-end wardrobe, or where the funds came from that she'd used to build her stock portfolio.

But public records had exposed one of her secrets. On a personal level the revelation was a bombshell, but it didn't bring him any closer to his objective.

Did Gale know? He'd briefed Lance on the basics, but when it came to Jaida's personal life he got the impression that he wasn't forthcoming. The more information he had on her, the easier this would be.

There was a rustling sound, and Lanced looked up, a smile catching his mouth. *And here she is.* The gate clanked shut, and he stood. "Hey there, beautiful."

She let out a startled cry. "You scared me to death! What are you doing here?"

"I was in the neighborhood. Thought I'd stop by."

"Lucky for you I wasn't armed."

He looked her up and down, taking in the yellow bikini. "Don't know where you'd carry a weapon in that."

Judging from the look on her face, his comment didn't go over too well. She dragged the beach towel from her shoulders and worked it over the ends of her wet hair.

"How's the water?" he asked.

"It's decent. Did you come for a swim?"

"Maybe. Are you inviting me?"

"It's a free ocean."

His company wasn't expected and it showed. He guessed she didn't like being caught off-guard and wasn't big on surprises. Ironic, since he was going to be her biggest surprise yet.

"Come on inside," she said. He followed, but before she reached the door he took her by the hand and pulled her into his arms. Her body tensed at his touch. He was losing his in with her. Not good. He needed her to cooperate, and he would rather persuade than demand.

She pulled away from him. "I'm getting you all wet." She dabbed her towel at the water spot she left on his navy blue button-up shirt.

He took it from her, caught hold of her wrist and turning it over he pressed his lips to the delicate skin. "It's fine. It'll dry."

She shrugged, a silent 'whatever' implied. What was up? They had connected. Why was she pulling away from him? She opened the front door and at the crook of her finger he followed her inside.

And what an inside it was. He looked down at his loafers. The soles of his shoes were tracking dust on the gray-veined, Italian, marble floor...expensive, Italian marble floor. Did she have a maid too, to sweep it up?

Vaulted ceilings, custom wrought-iron handrails along the stairs, he took it all in, marveling at the opulence. She disappeared into a hallway at the back of the first floor. Bedroom?

He edged his way toward that same hall. "Is this a bad time?" he called out then bit down on his tongue the second the words were out of his mouth. Stupid question. What if she said yes?

Jaida emerged from a doorway off that same hall absent her towel. Must be the laundry room. "Do you want anything to drink?"

"Coke or Pepsi's good." Lance observed the sculpture displayed on a pedestal at the bottom of the stairs. He lifted the porcelain piece and checked the mark on the bottom, the white patina catching the light. He was no art aficionado, but he knew enough to determine the piece was not a cheap reproduction. Everything was top shelf. He carefully set it back down. No yard-sale junkie lived here.

He did another quick scan of the living area and mentally calculated the cost of the furnishings. It was just an estimate, not exact figures, still he winced at the sum. He didn't think it was possible, but maybe she could blow eight and a half million that quick.

His chest tightened in what was the nearest thing to work-related stress he'd experienced to date. Gale expected his money, at least the majority of it. If Jaida owned this house outright it was likely all gone, every penny.

He startled at her sudden presence then composed himself. She handed him a full glass with the ice still crackling. "So, this is your place?" he asked then took a drink of the soda.

Jaida looked it over as though seeing it for the first time then nodded, an odd look in her eyes. "Do you like it?"

"I heard you had a nice house, but I wasn't expecting anything quite this…posh. Are you moonlighting or what?"

"Or what," she said with a wink. It was another one of her vague non-answers. It was deliberate, this ambiguity. Just as it was the last time he'd probed.

He gave her a half grin. *Don't you worry little Miss Jaida, I have ways of getting what I want.*

She picked up a stack of magazines from an end table and unloaded them into a cabinet. "Carina asked me to host a little get together here for her friends tonight. You're welcome to stay."

She was fast tracking him to another subject but he played along. "I thought you two weren't on speaking terms?"

"We weren't, but Carina apologized. That's just how she is."

Lance sat on the couch, propped a throw pillow behind his head, and patted the seat beside him. "There's plenty of room."

He frowned when she shook her head and moved away. "I need to rinse off and change. I don't want to be caught looking like this."

"Looks all right to me," he called after her, but she was already halfway up the stairs.

Lance chugged down half the Pepsi then set the glass on the table. Carina knew how to work Jaida. He had her pegged as a user the first time he laid eyes on her, and she had proved him right.

His own motives could be misconstrued as such, his actions placing him in the same category as Carina, but for him it was different. It was business. You did the job you were hired to do.

The sound of running water reached his ears. It was his signal to move. Lance stood and took himself on an unguided tour of the mock Italian villa.

Gale was convinced Jaida had his money, but he wasn't. Not until today. From what he'd seen, it wasn't looking too favorable for her. The offshore account opened in Gale's alias was emptied, the full sum electronically transferred to another offshore account with a bogus name and no valid contact information. The second account was emptied as soon as it went from the clearing account to the recipient's. And Jaida was sitting pretty, rolling in the dough.

He moved down the hall, heard the low hum of the dryer and found the laundry room right where he thought it would be. And across from that was…what? He pressed his palm on the half-open door, swinging it open. *Bingo.*

He switched on the light and sat down at the desk. *Sweet.* Constructed of solid mahogany, it was a work of art. The woman had impeccable taste. He opened the top drawer and sifted through the contents but found nothing of import. He went on to the next one.

The tape was equal priority. Gale wanted his money, but he also needed assurance that he wouldn't be linked to his advisor's death. A scandal would ruin his shot at the governorship. Lance had personally deleted the video footage on the agency's computer and destroyed the disc it had been burned to, but he had yet to track down the original.

Marcus Dennison, Gale's advisor, was the subject of that tape. Before he died, he'd forwarded all account numbers and passwords to Gale's offshore accounts to the Baseel Agency, and more specifically, to Jaida Martin.

Dennison had been on a mission to expose Gale and take him down for money laundering. The man lay six feet under, but if Lance didn't get the job done, Dennison could still destroy Gale from the grave, taking his fifteen percent commission right along with it.

Quietly, he rolled the second drawer closed and reached for the third. His breath hitched at the neatly organized cache before him. Bank statements, checkbook registers. He switched on the desk lamp then flipped through Jaida's financial records noting the fat balances at the end and the beginning of every month. If this was Gale's money keeping Jaida so comfortable, he would be happy to know that she hadn't spent all of it, but unless she had the rest stashed somewhere else she had devoured one hefty chunk.

He unfolded the deed to the house and held it under the light. What was this? Two names. Joint ownership. He made a quick perusal of the room and shook his head. Imagine that. This place was on the upscale end of the market, and it was paid in full. Maybe she did inherit it.

Lance looked back down at the deed. *Spencer Gordon.* It wasn't the first time he'd seen that name printed next to Jaida's. It was time he found out more about this man. He wrote down the account numbers, the bank name, and other pertinent information before tucking the items back inside the drawer.

One task in progress, he shoved the paper in his pocket and stood. The tape had to be here. He had picked her office clean at work and found nothing except notes on Gale along with her hostile opinions of him. But that was all they were—opinions. Not much damage she could do with those.

Jaida took her cases personally; at least this one she did. Was it possible the two of them had been romantically involved at one time? Is that what Gale was keeping from him?

Jealousy rippled through him. For a man on the downside of fifty, Gale took reasonable care of himself, but he was still too old for her. Lance gave his head a shake and chuckled to himself. He was getting way too involved. What was it to him if she was looking for a daddy? And a sugar daddy at that?

He turned off the lamp and put the chair back where he found it, his attention gravitating to the unit along the wall behind him. The shelves were custom built, teeming with books and paper-filled folders. This would be an all-day job. He threw a quick glance toward the door, guessing at how much time he had left before Jaida came looking for him, then turned back to the shelves. Where to start?

Lance picked a random spot and ran his hands over the tops and sides of the books then slid them inside the folders one at a time. "Come to Papa." He had landed one sweet deal when he was offered this gig. The woman, the money...

He tucked his hand behind a messy stack of folders. His heart charged when his fingers grazed the plastic edge of what felt like an 8mm tape. He smiled to himself and silently cheered his victory when he pulled it out and read the name, William Gale, scrawled along the side in blue ink. He raised it to his lips and kissed it. Tonight was his night.

"What are you doing?" Lance stiffened at the voice behind him.

Keep your cool, your back is to her, she can't see anything. He eased his open fingers a fraction to the right and latched onto a figurine of a small child then dropped the tape into his front pocket with his other hand.

He turned then and flashed her an artless grin. "Just touring your home since the owner didn't offer." He feigned an interest in the stone piece he held in his hand before setting it back on the shelf.

"Nice," he said, rubbing the inside of his wrist.

"Would you like to see the upstairs?" she asked. "Or have you already been up there?" Her eyes narrowed in suspicion.

"No, I haven't been up there, and I would love to see it. Great Italian flavor, by the way, you must have been thinking of me when you decorated." He caught her by the shoulders before she turned and brushed her lips with a kiss.

Lance followed her up the stairs. Her white cotton capri's skimmed her hips, a fine line of tanned skin peeking out between the waistband and the pink shirt she wore. The label stitched on the back told him they were as pricey as everything else he had seen today. Maybe it was a good thing this was a temporary relationship. He couldn't afford to keep her.

"This is the guest room." She swept a hand into an open doorway and he poked his head inside. It was sparse, but nicely furnished with a hint of the old world complementing the décor.

The next room was her bedroom, and where she had skimped on the other she had gone all out on this one. Not masculine, but not feminine either. Classy, that was how he would describe it.

Furnished with a combination of black wrought iron and dark wood, it was tastefully decorated. Lance eyed the shiny blue-gray comforter and the thick pile of pillows smothering the top. He slid his arms around Jaida and decided he wasn't going to wait for an invitation.

11

Shame singed the back of Jaida's neck. What had she gone and done? It wasn't one mistake, a random fall from grace, but a freefall that left her hurtling through space and wondering how long before she would hit bottom.

Lance stayed. She wished he would leave. It was her earlier offer that kept him there, but that was before. Before she'd gone and...

"I never thought of Carina as an intellectual," he whispered in her general direction then stretched his arm over the back of her chair, leaning in for her response.

It was to Carina's advantage that she came off as an airhead. "That's why she wins so many cases. The defense doesn't take her seriously." But she was as shrewd as they come.

They were sitting in on Carina's reading group, the sectional in her living room occupied by six stuffed shirts. It was next to torture, she thought, listening to these pseudo-intellectuals ramble on as though they alone knew the answers to the universe, but Lance seemed caught up in it. Did he take their intellectual arrogance seriously?

She nibbled at the whole grain cracker smeared with the liver patè Carina brought. Not a favorite. She washed it down with the rest of her tea.

Lance picked up her empty glass and stood. "I'll get you a refill."

Not without me. Jaida quickly leapt to her feet and followed on his heels, escaping to the haven of her kitchen. "Are they ever going to leave?" she asked. Was *he* ever going to leave?

Lance seemed to find her dilemma humorous and laughed to prove it. She watched as he made himself at home opening her refrigerator and filling her glass as though he belonged there.

"You should have told Carina to hold her snobfest somewhere else." He opened the freezer and fetched two ice cubes, dropping them into her glass. "You need to learn to say no."

"It was her turn to host the group. She was having her apartment sprayed." And why was she explaining herself to him? He was the one she needed to learn to say no to.

He handed her the glass. "And how is this your problem? Like I said, you need to learn to say no. You're a pushover, and she knows it."

Resentment reared up. Is that why he showed up today? Because he knew she was a pushover? She had deliberately avoided him since Catalina, and she didn't want him here now.

He must have sensed the downturn in her mood. He took a step back and looked at her. "You're angry," he said. "Why?"

She sent a fleeting look up the stairs, her eyes narrowing at the open door to her bedroom. Understanding lit his eyes.

"Look, when I said you were a pushover, it had nothing to do with that. Carina works you and you let her." He shrugged. "Maybe it's the result of not knowing what you want. You think you do. That's why you're so tenacious. You run deeper than you know, and not knowing yourself makes it easy for you to fall prey to deceptive desires."

Really? Her mouth slid open and she quickly closed it. Did he psychologically analyze people on a regular basis, or was it just her? How arrogant. He thought he had her all figured out.

Wait...what did he say about deceptive desires? His remark was too close to the meaning of the rose he left for her. *Deceitful desire...deceptive desires.* She paired the two phrases in her mind and wondered if that really was the message he intended to send with that rose.

The anger cinching her lungs withered. She had no right to it. He was right. She needed to learn to say no. She reached deep and managed a small smile, but underneath something indefinable was crumbling and she wasn't sure she knew how to function without it.

One by one, Carina's friends filtered into the dining room, filling their platters with honey-lime sake shrimp, smoked salmon cocktail crepes, and Vietnamese lamb riblets. This wasn't a chip-and-dip crowd, although there was a bowl of smoked paprika potato chips isolated at the end of the table. Untouched, of course.

"Well, Sleeping Beauty, it's about time you woke up and joined the party." Carina rested a hand on her shoulder then looked at Lance and flashed a smile that was half sweet, half acid.

Jaida frowned. "I wasn't..."

"Too late. Don't deny it. I saw you nodding off during the most riveting discourse." Carina slid the toothpick poised in her fingers between her teeth, the pimento-stuffed olive vanishing behind her lips.

Jaida almost laughed. "Riveting? I suppose that's a matter of opinion."

Carina looked at Lance. "Why don't you go fetch Jaida a plate, Sir Galahad?"

His mouth tightened and puckered as though he'd tasted something bitter. As soon as he excused himself to do her bidding, Carina cornered her. "I don't trust that man. He's up to no good. Probably after the money."

"What…"

"You heard him the other night. He already has that cash spent."

"But I told you, all of you, I don't have it."

"As if you would admit your guilt to a prosecutor. I could put you away."

The object of their discussion was back with a plate of food. Carina gave her a knowing look, reminding her of the warning before she wandered back to her friends.

"Thanks." She took the plate and studied him. He had analyzed her; maybe it was time she did a little psychoanalysis on him.

Both Auggie and Carina were warning her off. Although Auggie never made his reasons known, Carina didn't beat around the bush.

Jaida bit into one of the salmon crepes. What if she was right? What if he was after the money? In just how many ways could she be used?

She looked up to see Lance shrugging into a lightweight jacket. "Are you leaving?"

He laughed softly and kissed her on the cheek. "Weren't you listening?"

Apparently not.

"I have an early appointment. I'd love to stay, but…" He frowned and spread his hands. "I'll call you later."

Please don't. She held the sentiment in, concealed it with a smile, said good-bye, and closed the door behind him, thinking again about the rose and what he'd said.

She didn't want to admit it, even to herself, but he was right about her. The question was: what was it that she truly wanted?

12

Spencer swiveled in his chair and looked out the large-paned tinted window that took up more than three-fourths of the back wall of his office. Fifty-two floors below, vehicles waged war over parking spots on a Los Angeles street too small to accommodate a population bursting its seams.

The clock dictated their lives. There were appointments to make, deadlines to meet. The madness spilled from the streets to the sidewalks, the concrete disappearing under the leather soles of a singularly focused workforce. It was a new morning, and from the top of his building he watched the daily rat race playing out from the best seat in the house.

His building marked the hub of the city and boasted an art deco architectural design, clad in terra cotta tiles that was planned and executed by L.A.'s finest. It was no façade. The inner workings of this business lived up to the success the exterior design suggested, but the achievement was a triviality seeing as he'd built it for one purpose. And she was gone.

Spencer squeezed his fist, his thumb clicking the ballpoint pen wrapped inside, open and closed, open and closed. An hour into his day and he was ready to call it quits and head home. He huffed a sharp laugh at the thought. Head home to what? What did he have waiting for him there?

He rocked back in his chair feeling every ounce of tomorrow's date weighing down on him like an anchor, his legs thick with lead. This sullenness was par for the course. He could label it as seasonal something or other and clock it annually.

Spencer swung around in the chair and settling in behind his desk, he flipped the page on the calendar. It was the second one he'd purchased since Jaida walked out. *Well, cheers to her.* He lifted the chilled glass of water from the sandstone coaster and drank it down. At least one of them was satisfied with the outcome.

Seven hundred and sixty-two days after her inglorious exit he was coming to terms with what's what. A half-week ago he'd relived a moment, left the nostalgia at the park, then drove home and emptied the shed where he'd stored her belongings. For too long the steel structure housed a hope that he refused to let die. But hardening the shell of his bruised soul he did the unthinkable and pulled the plug, carting off the remainder of her possessions to the Salvation Army.

They were just things—things that bound him to another time, another life. He wanted a future, not the past all dressed up and looking pretty. He'd like to say that he felt nothing; that removing the last traces of her existence from his life didn't affect him, but who would he be kidding?

He'd reached for the phone at least a dozen times to call and ask if there was anything she wanted back before he gave it all away. But it had been more than a year since he sorted through it and hauled it out back, and just as long since they had spoken. That was answer enough.

The intercom buzzed and Spencer's finger grazed the button. "Yes?"

"Mr. Rose is here."

Spencer closed his eyes on a sigh. *Eugene Rose.* This meeting had been planned for weeks, and he'd forgotten. If he didn't pull himself together he was going to lose his shot at a major deal.

"Give me one minute and then send him in."

He released the button, crossed the slate-woven carpet, and used the mirror to straighten his tie. *Focus Spencer.* He would get past this. A few days out and this dull mood would begin to fade. He ran his fingers through his hair and said a quick prayer.

His time up, the door swept open and Spencer held out his hand…

Spencer stretched his legs out in the back of the company Lincoln Town Car and twisted the cap from the water bottle. Taking a long draw, he grimaced as it wound its way down his throat. Mineral water. He'd grabbed his assistant's bottle by mistake. He liked his water straight, no frills. And he could do without the irritating carbonation.

He recapped it, set it in the cup holder then hoisted his briefcase on the seat beside him. Popping the lid, he took out the folder that was tucked in the back slot and flipped through the bound pages.

His meeting with Eugene Rose more than exceeded his expectations. The new program Rose developed rocked him. His design for security systems possessed capabilities that made what they were peddling now seem archaic and inept, and considering that what they produced and delivered was cutting edge, it was a remarkable feat Mr. Rose had accomplished.

Spencer thumbed through the thick black folder, perusing the details of the plans and statistics that made this idea worth developing, worth pinning his name to.

For him, the need to protect was instinctual, and that instinct was the stimulus that led him to form Seraph, a security solutions business that in four short years had climbed well past the hundred million-dollar mark in annual revenues.

Eugene Rose's plans would dramatically enhance what Spencer already created. It was impressive technology, ideal in that it covered every aspect of security and protection at the private and corporate level. When governments understood how it would enhance national security, he was confident that Seraph would pick up those accounts without trying.

He made a few notes in the margins then slid the information and the pen back into the briefcase.

"Landon, drop me off at the corner." He snapped the briefcase shut, set the code, and then tucked it under the back of the driver's seat.

"Sure thing, Mr. G."

The car rolled alongside the curb, stopping at the double-mirrored doors. Spencer reached for his gym bag and then the door handle. "Be back in two hours."

"Will do."

At the reception counter, Gina flashed him a newly veneered smile. She wore her dark hair pulled back in a long ponytail at the nape of her neck.

"Good afternoon, Mr. Gordon. Racquetball today?" Her manicured nails hovered over the computer keys, anticipating his response.

He grinned. "Am I that predictable?"

She shrugged. "You know what you like."

She had him there. "Yes, ma'am, I do."

"Ma'am?" She gave him a look that seared. "That makes me feel like an old lady." She shuddered for effect, and he smiled, amused at her aversion to the natural course of life.

"Sorry, Gina." She couldn't be more than forty-five, and the subtle cosmetic procedures she'd had done since he'd been a member at this club did a decent job of erasing about eight of those years.

He leaned on the counter and watched her type in his name. She rattled off a number and he headed for the elevators. In a silent glide, the doors rolled open and his gaze followed the blonde that stepped out. He continued to watch as she crossed the lobby and exited the building.

"Like what you see? I can introduce you."

Spencer gave the fitness trainer a sidelong glance then held his hand out to stop the door from closing. "No thanks, Dave." Spencer chuckled at the irony. He supposed his reaction could be mistaken for interest.

Dave nudged him in the ribs, a goofy smile spanning his narrow jaw. "You sure?"

"Yeah, I'm sure. She just reminds me of someone I once knew." There were some similarities. Enough to catch his eye and for a split second make him wonder, but it wasn't Jaida. It never was.

Gina paged Dave, and the trainer headed for the lobby. Spencer stepped inside the elevator. An hour on the court should get his juices flowing and pull him out of this disabling funk.

The locker room was empty. He hung his gray suit on the hanger provided then changed into shorts and a tee shirt. He reached for a fresh can of Penn balls that were tucked in his bag and locked the rest of his belongings inside the locker.

He stood outside of court four where Gina had assigned him and studied the player through the glass, impressed when the man drove the rubber ball into the wall and without any effort, picked up the rebound.

It didn't take her long to find him a partner. It wasn't anyone he recognized. He must be new to the club or a member who had changed schedules.

He hung back a moment longer and watched, sizing up his game. Spencer was no lightweight, but given the man's overly developed musculature, and his power-centered wield of the racquet, if the game could be won by brute strength, Spencer would be no competition for him. But fortunately skill was a necessary component, and he was semi-accomplished in that department.

He waited for the ball in play to fizzle out then opened the door and stepped inside. "How's it going?"

His assigned partner turned and gave him a sweeping once over, a stick of gum working his jaw up and down. "Lance Palermo," he said, offering his name and his gloved hand at the same time.

Spencer tucked the racquet under his arm and gripped the man's hand. "Spencer Gordon."

"Well, Spencer Gordon, let's get to it."

Palermo bounced a ball on the tight weave of his racquet strings. Sensing the man's impatience, Spencer took his position and prepared to engage.

13

She was in so much trouble. Jaida's hands shook as she dug through the box of papers. Just papers. No tape. She shifted from her backside to her knees where she sat in the middle of the floor, her home office littered with emptied files, drawers, and boxes. Auggie was going to kill her.

"Don't take evidence home. Make a copy." His instructions rang in her head like warning bells that came too late. How many times had he told her that? Too many times to count, that's how many.

She picked up a stack of loose papers and stuffed them back inside the empty box then pivoted toward the desk, pulling out a lone shoebox shoved under the bottom drawer. She lifted the lid. There was nothing inside but old photographs.

This tape was the backbone of their case. The backup file stored in the agency computer had been deleted along with a few other files. But those files were of little importance. She had the original; had to take it because the copy that was burned to a disc had been missing for a couple of weeks. Now all three copies were gone.

Puzzled, she glanced at the bookshelf to her right. She left the video on that shelf right there, second down from the top. She was sure of it.

Where was that tape? She dropped her head back and closed her eyes. Was she so thickskulled that she had to learn everything the hard way? Gale just might walk after all, and it was her fault.

"Leave me alone!" She yelled at the ringing cell phone then pushed herself up, her legs tingling with life where the blood had stanched. She darted for the kitchen counter where she'd left it, catching it on the last ring.

"Hello," she said. Breathing, heavy and strained rattled through the airwaves. Was this a prank call?

"Hello?" she tried again, anger clipping her tone. No one answered. Her finger slid to the off button. She hesitated and second-guessing herself, brought the phone back to her ear.

The connection crackled then cleared. "Detective Martin?"

Ray. She never thought she'd feel this way, but the sound of his voice elated her. The timing couldn't have been better. He was the only man who could get her out of this predicament. Not her first choice in heroic relief, but at this point, she would take what was offered.

"Are you ready to talk?" She blurted it out, baring her need, her desperation. Maybe it was for the best. She was tired of the games, the hoops she had to jump through. If it wasn't his aim to deliver what he promised then she would rather know now.

"You sound eager, detective."

"Yes, well, um, you do know and can appreciate that we're in need of your assistance." She stumbled over the words.

He laughed. "What's with this 'we' bit? Tell it like it is. *You* need my assistance. You need *me*." His voice went low and flat. "Now, let me hear you say that."

Jaida caught her tongue between her teeth and held it before she said the wrong thing and ruined any chance she might have with this informant. Her grip tightened on the phone. *Just do it. Just tell him what he wants to hear.*

Like sand, it was all slipping through her fingers. The months, the hours, the late nights; all of it a waste. She held her eyes closed long enough to draw in another breath and do what he asked. "I need you," she said, the admission even more painful because it was true.

"Very good," he taunted, his condescension raising her ire. He might flaunt his win, but as long as he came through for her, she would endure whatever he dished out.

He cleared his throat. "I just needed to..." The connection broke up leaving her with nothing but dead air.

"Don't cut me off now! Hello. Hello. What about a meet?" She groaned and slammed the phone down on the counter. He was gone.

He just needed to what? Hear her say that she needed him? She was dealing with an unhinged man. An unhinged man who was holding all the cards and somehow he knew it. But how did he know?

He called her cell phone. How did he get her number? She didn't give it out to just anyone and never to an informant. She was so relieved that he had called she hadn't even considered...

The phone vibrated against the counter. He was calling back. Jaida answered, and this time she buried the enthusiasm under a formal tone. "Yes?"

"Where are you? I've been waiting for you." It was Auggie, not Ray. She wouldn't have picked up if she'd known.

"I'm on my way," she said. She slipped her purse over her shoulder and grabbed the car keys. She had to tell him about the tape sometime. It may as well be now.

"Good. We need to push this meeting with Ray. Get him to talk and turn over the documents. I have a bad vibe that we're losing this thing."

It was more than a vibe, but now wasn't the time to confirm his fears. Not over the phone.

"If he won't cooperate, Jaida, we're done. I've extended this long enough."

"I just got off the phone with him," she said.

"And…?"

"I lost the connection." She opened the car door and paused before climbing inside. "He called my cell phone. You didn't happen to give him my num—"

He cut her off. "Are you crazy? No way would I be that careless. I guard that with my life. Just like I guard you."

He'd done a better job with her than she'd done with the evidence. "Thanks, Auggie. See you in a few."

When she arrived at the agency, he was gone. She hung up with him not twenty-five minutes ago. Why didn't he wait for her?

She switched on her office light. Fluorescent tubes flickered behind the plastic ceiling sheets. A yellow sticky note was stuck to the center of her phone. She peeled it off.

Urgent call. Had to leave. I'll catch you later.

Auggie.

She sank into the chair behind her desk. She'd missed him. It wasn't as though she had a death wish, but she was prepared, her nerve built up along with her resistance to the verbal flogging that was surely coming, and perhaps her termination.

Maybe his absence was fate saving her hide. Maybe the tape would turn up and he would never have to know. She shook her head, a weak smile playing at her lips. That was just a little too Pollyanna.

Her desktop looked like a warzone. In a way she supposed it was. Good fighting evil, facts the weapons of warfare. She sifted through the debris of paperwork along with the evidentiary photos then collected the information she didn't have at home and shoved it into an empty folder. Unwilling to make the same mistake twice, she flipped through the files and scanned the computer records to verify that what she was about to take home were duplicates.

She would finish what she'd started. Unless her luck changed, she would have to find something more incriminating in these documents, even if she had to fabricate it. She smiled at the tempting thought.

Files in hand, she locked her office door and hurried through the hall. Rounding the corner at a fast clip she ran smack into something hard enough to stop her in her tracks and knock her backward.

The folder of papers clutched in her hand slid sideways, its contents spilling, fluttering to the earth one page, one picture at a time. Jaida teetered on her heels. Losing the battle for balance, her arms flew back, tensed and straight, prepared to hit the tile, but large hands grabbed her, sparing her backside from making a painful connection with the floor.

"Slow down. What's the hurry?" She looked up at the amused chuckle and saw that Lance was the wall she'd run into. He pulled her upright.

Jaida wriggled one hand loose and adjusted the shoe that had slipped from her heel. "Where did you come from?"

"Me? You were the one flying around that corner like a bat out of hell."

He bent down and rounded up the scattered documents then shuffled the skewed pile until they were all uniformly stacked. The folder was lying open wide and face down. He picked it up and slid everything inside then handed it to her with a slight bow.

"Thanks," she said. At least he had contained the fallout.

"Nice save." Grace from the coffee shop passed by carrying a cardboard holder filled with steaming coffees. Her broad grin lifted the corners of her eyes. "Is that how you do it, Jaida? Get all the men, I mean?"

Not quite feeling it, Jaida smiled back. "Only the ones who are hard to catch."

Grace winked. "I think you already have this one eating out of the palm of your hand." She gave Lance an appreciative look. "Wish I could say the same."

When Grace moved on, he said, "You do, you know. Have me eating out of the palm of your hand."

Not wanting to go there, she let his remark slide without commenting and crossed the hall to retrieve a stray sheet he'd missed. She glimpsed the date at the top of the memo. Her brow tightening, she looked up at Lance.

"What's the date today?" she asked.

"The 16th."

Innocuous, it was only a date. So why did she feel like this, flashes of hot then cold and a churning in her stomach? Maybe she was getting sick.

She turned, her feet struggling to keep up with her desire to escape. Lance caught up to her and grabbed her elbow. "So, what's the big hurry? I thought you just got here."

"I can do what I need to from home. And I want to stop and get a quick bite to eat."

She hadn't thought it through, just reacted. She hadn't been back there in years, but she wanted to go there now.

"Sounds great. I'm loaded." He draped his arm over her shoulders. "I'll take you wherever you want to go."

14

Seclusion was good. Lance took a bite of his burger and gazed up at the steel-framed arch overhead. It was painted green. Two-toned roses of fuchsia and white grew in a tangled vine over the top.

The bench he shared with Jaida was a hard marble slab, their grease-stained sack of food the only thing between them. That and a few lies. He licked a drip of mayonnaise from his finger and frowned. He would have splurged on her. He was thinking along the lines of the infamous Mr. Stox, not fast food, but he'd given her the choice.

Where the cuisine was a bust, the atmosphere of the botanical gardens they picnicked in made up for it. It wasn't what he had in mind, but it worked.

He stretched his legs out and crossed his ankles, watching her dainty fingers twirl a greasy French fry in a blob of ketchup she'd wrung from the small foil packet. She brought it to her mouth and bit off the saturated end.

"Good food?" he asked. Considering what he had just packed in his belly, that was an oxymoron.

Jaida nodded and swallowed, then dabbed her mouth with the small paper napkin she had spread on her lap. "Today it is."

He laughed, but tucked those words away for further dissection. "Why today? Special chef on duty? I'm thinking it would taste pretty much the same every day."

She lifted her shoulder slightly and then let it fall, her face almost pained with a wistful expression. "I don't know. I guess I was just looking for something different."

Not different, just something to fill the void. She didn't say it with words, but he could see the hollow pit that was consuming her. He watched her closely, watched the fan of dark lashes close over those scandalous blue eyes in a long drawn-out blink. So, the money she rolled in didn't feed the need. In that respect, they were nothing alike.

Lance took her fingers in his, thinking again how their lives could have merged, been bound together by something real if their relationship had developed under different circumstances.

Her carefully lined lids flicked up, and her eyes met his, telling him quite bluntly that he was part of her confusion. *I won't be for long, baby.* She tugged her hand away and reached for another fry.

He'd considered the best way to approach her. Good cop? Bad cop? Both described his role in this, but after he considered her temperament and how she might react, good cop won out. Bad cop would be waiting in the wings to swoop in and take over should the need arise.

She swept the hair from her eyes with her fingers, etched silver bracelets clanking at her wrist. Her gaze roamed over the well-dressed grounds from one object to another until she saw him staring at her. Startled, her focus became solid and clear, and he was the center of it.

His lip tipped up at the corner. "Forget I was here?"

"I told you I wouldn't be good company." She tilted her head to the side, her hair tumbling over her shoulder in soft waves. He reached out and ran his fingers through it.

She drew back, her face failing to conceal her discomfort and...what? Guilt? She raised her half-eaten cheeseburger to her mouth and bit into it.

Jaida Martin couldn't be a thief, he mused. It just didn't fit her profile. But then that was hard to pin down. Forensic science hadn't met up with this woman yet.

She was an anomaly, or perhaps a chameleon, her colors changing to suit the need. The well-oiled transition from one mode into another was perfected so that it was almost indiscernible. Even her preference for inferior food had him working his brain to comprehend the digression from her high-end taste in clothing, furnishings, and vehicles. But wasn't that the modus operandi of a good con?

Lance poked his straw into his cup, breaking up the clumped ice and searching out another draw of Pepsi. Plastic on plastic, the straw squeaked against the lid.

"I have a confession to make," he said.

The overture won her attention and she looked at him. "Do I want to hear it?"

He ran his tongue over his top lip then smiled at her. "That all depends."

"On what?"

"Whether you're guilty or innocent." He heard the soft intake of breath. She was scared; the elevated pulse was visible, pounding against her throat.

"Guilty of what?" she asked.

"Making off with Gale's money." He locked gazes with her. "I'm with internal affairs. The department Baseel collaborates with instructed me to investigate the unauthorized wire transfer of William Gale's offshore accounts."

Her body stiffened at the revelation, and she drew back. He'd betrayed her, and she wasn't handling it well. He had no choice but to show his hand. Doing this without her cooperation wasn't yielding results. The money was still missing.

Her tone was sharp. "Read the report for yourself. I had nothing to do with emptying his accounts."

He set a reassuring hand on her arm and she pulled away. "I'm not accusing you. I was hired to get to the bottom of this. Personally, I believe you, but I need to do my job and prove that what you say is true. Your word is good enough for me, but it isn't enough for my superiors."

Her eyes turned hard. "William Gale has ruined my life. He deserves nothing."

Her emotional state, the disdain in her voice, was telling. He was beginning to believe his own theory that she'd been intimately involved with Gale. Gale liked his women young and beautiful. And she was both.

"How do you explain your assets? Baseel doesn't pay that well."

"I shouldn't have to explain anything. I'm not on trial. You'll just have to take my word that my assets weren't purchased with Gale's money."

Spencer Gordon? His earnings made Gale's eight and a half million look like pocket change. Is that where it came from? He could ask, but he didn't want to bring Gordon up just yet. He couldn't risk her closing up on him and ending the dialogue.

The wind blew a wrapper on the ground. Lance picked it up, crumpled it, and stuffed it in the empty sack.

"Let me ask this another way. If you don't have the money, do you know where it is?"

She dropped her head and shook it. "I have no idea."

She looked battle worn. Why was she so weary if she was innocent? Answering a few questions wasn't that hard. Other than her brief suspension, she had endured only a little suffering over the accusation.

"Who else had access to the email address that Dennison sent the information to?"

She gave him a sidelong glance, straightened, and with a defiant lift of her chin, she said, "Every single one of my superiors. And if they printed, forwarded, or shared the account numbers with anyone, you can include those names."

For a split second he thought she would tell him to go to Hades. But she remained calm, the picture of professionalism. She smoothed her gray skirt with the palms of her hands and stood. Was she leaving? He had driven, but that wouldn't stop her.

He threw out some bait, just enough to keep her here a little longer. "Did you know that William Gale is filing a civil suit against Baseel and against you?"

Her mouth gaped. "For what?"

"For stealing his money." He shrugged with his face. "Like it or not, the money belongs to him."

"Maybe it does belong to him legally, but ethically..."

"Ethically nothing. And you can bet your last dollar he'll win this."

"And," he continued, "with the agency named in the lawsuit you're the designated scapegoat since Gale accused you personally."

The news left her visibly shaken, but she rallied, her spine stiffening. "I'll bring Gale down if it's the last thing I do."

"An eye for an eye, eh?"

"Something like that."

"I'm with you on that, believe it or not. I'm here only as a messenger. If you can help me, I can help you." He spoke softly, hoping to smooth the feathers he'd ruffled and ease his way back into her trust.

"Sure." The hint of sarcasm he heard in her tone told him he had a ways to go. Another couple appeared by the water fountain and Lance stood.

"How is the case against him looking?"

"It's coming along." Her smile was a thin veneer, unable to mask what was written all over her face. She folded her arms and glanced away. "I have an informant that says he has information."

"Is it enough for a conviction?"

She met his eyes then. "I think so." But she didn't. Not really. Gale was a free man. His confiscation of the tape had seen to that.

He cracked a smile. "Good for you."

She nodded and looked toward the exit, signaling her desire to leave. He collected their trash. "If I had my hands on that kind of cash, I'm not so sure I wouldn't take it and run myself."

She just stood there. Waiting. What did he need to do to get a confession out of her? Don a collar and robe?

"I'm ready to go," she said, as if he didn't already know that.

He drove her to where her car was parked and climbed out with her. Testing the waters, he reached for her hand and pulled her into a hug. He was prepared for a slap or an angry rant, but neither came.

"I'm sorry. I didn't want to hurt you like that, but I had no choice. You of all people should understand. I'm sure you've had to portray yourself as someone you're not many times over."

He heard her sigh and she drew back. He took the keys from her hand and unlocked her car door. She slid inside, and he placed them in her palm with a soft peck on her cheek. "Drive safe."

Lance shut the door. He would let her stew over the news of a lawsuit. Maybe that would be enough of a threat to get her talking.

He watched her drive away and moved for his car when a hand gripped his arm. Lance spun at the contact ready to strike.

"Do you have anything for me?" His cheek twitched when he saw that it was Gale's man. What was he doing following him?

He flung the hand off. "I told you I would contact you when I had something." Lance spread his hands. "Have I contacted you? No. That means I don't have anything yet."

His eyes thinned. "Mr. Gale and I feel that you're taking too much time in securing his cash. He isn't paying you to romance your target."

Lance laughed at the squatty man's attempt to place himself in the same rank as Gale, stretching what some would call a neck just so he could look him in the eye. He was a grunt, a bottom feeder; his knowledge limited to bad toupees and cheap suits.

"Don't tell me how to operate. I got you the tape. No prison, no death sentence, and Gale's political reputation is still intact. I think he should be grateful."

"Don't take too long, or I may have to move in on your little sweetheart and get answers from her myself."

"Stay away from her. I work alone."

15

Cradled in the crook of his arm, Spencer carried the damask roses to the car. It was the sole reason he was here. They were cut fresh this morning at his request and draped in green tissue. The day deserved some recognition.

He reached for the car door then paused to watch the familiar figure emerging from one of the paths. She remembered. And the gardens where they'd recited their vows meant so much to her that she brought another man along to pay tribute to the occasion.

What was Palermo's game? He walked beside Jaida, his arm curled about her waist as though he had a right. Spencer's teeth clenched. His brief appearance at the club was no coincidence. But what was he after? His blessing?

Her stride was stiff, her chin held high at a sharp angle. She was miffed about something. Palermo stopped her and turned her toward him, cupping her face in his hands. A jealous heat singed the back of Spencer's neck. What did he think he was doing? He took a step forward intending to break it up, but then stopped. What good would it do?

He watched them leave then slid behind the wheel, the inside of his Lexus already pulsing with heat. Black interiors were a big mistake...in cars...and women. He turned the key in the ignition and rolled the windows down until the air conditioning could overtake the high temperature.

Since she'd left him, Jaida's collection of men had been plentiful to say the least. But for God, he would have ended it a long time ago. That's what he told himself anyway. Maybe involving God just made it easier to stay the course. Vows meant something to him, and he held himself to every one he'd ever made her.

Sweet misery, that's what she was, and he was the pushover that kept coming back for more. If he had any sense of self-preservation, he would turn around, go home, and do whatever it took to forget she ever existed. But how did you quit loving someone?

Spencer gunned the engine. He wasn't turning back. Running away was her way not his. She had an easy time of it, putting him behind her and moving on. He hadn't been as fortunate, and it was about time she faced the damage she'd left in her wake.

He headed west toward Newport and turned down the narrow street that ran along the north side of Jaida's house. He parked at the curb and dialed her house number, disconnecting when he got the machine. Spencer rolled the windows down and turned the car off. Wind chimes tinkled in the breeze. A few minutes later, a bald Latino and a slender brunette entered Jaida's front gate. He leaned forward for a better view. A blur of blue steel whizzed by in his periphery. She was back.

Spencer picked up the bouquet from the passenger seat and climbed out. *Lord, have your way, even if it isn't what I want.*

The front patio was swept clean. Aqua and gray flowerpots lined the perimeter of the porch, two on the right and two on the left. Inside, the soil was dry and pulling away from the sides of the pots, the stems and leaves dried, and the fading buds wilted.

Spencer rang the bell. He shifted his neck and worked one of the buttons free on his stonewashed oxford shirt. The day was too warm for it.

When no one answered, he rang the bell a second time and the door swung open. It was the Latino.

"I'd like to speak with Jaida," Spencer said.

The man standing in the doorway eyed the roses. "Is this a delivery?"

"No, this is personal." He glanced down at his jeans. Did he look like a delivery boy?

"Give me your name, and I'll see if she's in."

Whoever he was, she sure had this one trained. "I'd rather not," he said. He wouldn't give her the opportunity to refuse.

Sandaled feet spread, and wearing a green tee shirt with a Ford logo on it, the man stood there looking torn between guarding the fort and playing host.

In an unexpected gesture, he held out his hand, catching Spencer by surprise. "I'm Auggie Garcia. Step inside, and I'll see if she's taking visitors."

Spencer waited in the foyer he half owned and watched Garcia take the stairs two at a time.

He didn't have to wait long. Jaida stood at the top of the staircase in a pale pink tea-length sundress. She had changed clothes.

He knew the moment she saw him. Heard her gasp, saw her eyes light with pleasure then watched dread leach the color from her cheeks, leaving her a sickly shade of white.

Auggie Garcia picked up on her distress. He gripped her elbow to keep her from going down the stairs. "Is this man trouble for you? Do you want me to show him out?"

Spencer met her gaze and held her with his eyes, waiting for his sentencing. After making it past the warden, would she have him thrown out?

"Why are you here, Spencer?" Her brow tensed, leaving lines of worry creasing the middle. She sounded breathless, almost hopeful and afraid at the same time. But what was it that she hoped for and what did she fear?

He straightened, glanced down at his feet then back up at her. "I'm here for our anniversary."

16

Less than two minutes inside and Spencer had been branded bad news. And from the extended silence he was floundering in, it appeared Jaida wasn't about to say anything to change that perception.

"You said you were here for your anniversary. Anniversary of what?" Garcia asked.

Spencer didn't answer. He looked past him and settled his gaze on Jaida. "Can I speak with you privately?"

The woman who came with Garcia emerged from the downstairs hall. She followed his gaze up the stairs and noting the tension, made quick strides toward him. "Who are you, and what are you doing here?"

"I'm Spencer. Spencer Gordon," he said, his eyes never leaving Jaida. "And Jaida is my wife."

The silence at his announcement was chilling. Garcia started down the stairs at a fast clip stopping just short of Spencer's personal space. Jaida followed, but went no further than the foot of the stairs.

"I've known this girl a long time, and she is not married," Garcia said.

"She is my wife, ask her." Spencer looked beyond the bulky shoulder and saw Jaida with her hands balled into tight little fists, her body poised to strike, but she didn't make a move. Did she hate him now for outing her?

"Look, I didn't come here to cause problems for you." Uncomfortable with this whole scene, he shifted and glanced at the door. He should leave, but before he could make his move, the woman insinuated herself between him and the front door.

"Don't you mean ex-wife?" she asked.

Her eyes narrowed at the cross he wore around his neck. "You religious people don't believe that divorce ends a marriage, but trust me it does. Besides, the law takes precedence over your beliefs."

Spencer said, "I know quite well what I mean. She's my wife, present tense; in the eyes of God *and* the law."

Garcia looked stricken. "Is this true, chica? Are you really this man's wife?"

She nodded, her eyes bright with tears.

The other woman threw her hands up in the air and laughed. "Oh, this is rich. What else don't we know about you, Jaida?"

Garcia shot her a silencing glare. "Be quiet, Carina."

Spencer pulled a card from his shirt pocket and tossed it along with the flowers on the couch.

"I'm sorry, man." Garcia apologized. "Carina and I will get out of your hair and give you two some space."

He wasn't sure he'd be staying, but he welcomed the unexpected support. "Thank you, Mr. Garcia."

"Just Auggie," he said. "Do you have a card on you?"

Spencer pulled out his wallet and handed him one.

Auggie glanced at it before pocketing it then nudged the woman he called 'Carina.' "Let's go."

"You don't speak for me. I'll go when I'm good and ready."

Auggie ignored her protests then turned and said, "We'll have to get together sometime." He forced the arguing woman out ahead of him and closed the door.

They were alone.

He could hear himself swallow, hear Jaida breathe. Every sound was amplified in the brittle silence. Spencer turned, rocked back on his heels and studied her. She moved to sit on the arm of the couch, and he searched her face for a cue, for some direction as to what to say next.

"Jaida. Look at me." Her chin shifted slightly, but she kept her gaze fixed on the hands folded in her lap.

"Please," he said, his voice firm, unwilling to beg. Not this time. Not again.

When she didn't look up, he closed the space between them, hesitated, then reached out and traced his fingers down her bare arm. She flinched at his touch. He heeded the message and backed away from her. Unless she invited it, he would keep his hands to himself.

What am I doing here? He massaged his tightening brow, swallowed against the thickness in his throat. He couldn't sever the ties himself. Wouldn't, not yet anyway, but he was drowning while he waited for change to come. He'd wanted to back her into a corner, force her into a decision. Either come back and be his wife or call an attorney and legally end whatever it was they had going on.

"What more could I have done, Jaida? What is it you needed that I failed to give you? Haven't I loved you well enough? Provided for you well enough?"

This was a conversation they should have had two years ago, but just like now she closed herself off, folding her arms over her chest, effectively shutting him out. His anger welled at her silence. "Don't I at least deserve an answer?"

She was trembling, her eyes still downcast. "Just leave, Spencer. I have nothing to offer you."

He moved to stand in front of her. "I saw you today with Lance Palermo." She raised her head, surprise on her face, and for one brief moment he held her undivided attention.

"Did you know that he paid me a visit?"

Guess not. Not with the flash of anger he saw cross her face. She wanted to say something, he could see it, but she fought against her own will and looked away again.

He ached at the chilling chasm that filled the space between them. Her body cast off a slight shiver, and her palms clamped tighter on her arms. She felt it too. The oneness, the intimacy they once knew was dead.

Was this why he was supposed to come? To see firsthand that it was over, that it was time for him to let go? There was so much he wanted to say, but she wasn't ready to hear any of it. Maybe she never would be.

"Your friend, Auggie, it sounds like he looks out for you." *Something I should be doing.*

She said nothing. She wasn't going to engage him. He'd worn out what little welcome there was. Spencer gripped her fingers that had fallen limp and brushed a light kiss across her warm forehead. "Happy anniversary, Jaida."

He pressed a business card in her palm and squeezed her hand. "In case you ever need me."

17

Even if it isn't what I want. It was with deep regret that Spencer recalled his prayerful concession. Not that it would have changed the outcome.

He slammed the car door. The sound ricocheted off the bare white walls and concrete floor of the garage. Failure. Regret. Defeat. He owned them all.

He picked up the hammer and screwdriver he'd left lay on the workbench and hung them on the pegboard above it. He'd been prepared for a fight with her. He knew how to handle that. But how could he win against indifference?

He went inside the house, the door banging closed behind him. The curtains were drawn, the rooms dark. He hadn't opened them in days. He needed to snap out of this.

Jaida had his card. Not that she couldn't find him without it, but with him personally handing it to her there would be no mind battles, no reason to doubt when her call never came.

But God's call *had* come, and Spencer reluctantly answered. It was the last thing he wanted to do. He dropped to his knees in the center of the living room floor and lifted his hands in a weak attempt at surrender; rebellion still lingering, weighing down on his arms like lead.

The sacrifice came grudgingly. It was a feeble offering of praise that floated from his lips, the flow building little by little until it became genuine and the faith behind it grew.

Jaida was created for him alone. A point no one could argue with him and win, but he was done, past the point of weary. He was tired of loving a woman who didn't love him back. A woman who despised and rejected all that he was.

He wanted to terminate the relationship, end the crushing attachment. For his own sake he needed to quit loving her. *Help me to quit loving her, God.*

"Husbands, love your wives, just as Christ also loved the church and gave Himself for her, that He might sanctify her..."

Hadn't he already been doing that? Spencer dropped his head and wept. The question was: Would his love be enough?

The sound of the door clicking shut behind Spencer was the sound of finality. It was finished. She should be relieved. Strange that she wasn't.

Jaida scooped up the roses and stood, squeezing her fingers around the business card in her hand. Her legs went weak, and she reached for the back of the couch to steady herself.

Why did he show up like that, out of the blue, with no warning for her to prepare or to guard her heart? And why did she push him away when she wanted to hold onto him, shut him out when she wanted to let him in?

But she already knew why. She just didn't know why it couldn't be different. Why *she* couldn't be different.

His hair, the color of golden wheat was cut shorter than the last time she'd seen him. Not close-cropped, but a stylish short. His complexion was paler than normal, the hint of shadow under his eyes darkening the sage green of his irises to a dull gray.

He probably spent his days locked away in that high-rise growing the empire that paid for this house, the car…everything she owned. She was plagued by the shame. But why? She hadn't asked for any of it. He was the one who had insisted.

She gazed down at the bouquet in her arms then pressed her face into the perfectly formed rosebuds, breathing in the scent. Long-stemmed and absent thorns, these roses were red. True red.

Spencer was everything Lance was not. Offered what Lance did not. He was faithful, longsuffering, patient, kind; he was perfect. He was perfect, and she was flawed.

Jaida set the bouquet on the kitchen counter, unfolded the card, and worked her thumb over the crease that ran down the middle. Did he know she wouldn't call? Couldn't call?

She was still trying to wrap her mind around what happened. She managed to keep her life private, and in a matter of seconds, Spencer had ruined it. And the worst of it was, he'd already won Auggie over. A two-minute conversation and they were instantly buddies.

She picked up the flip-flops she'd left by the front door and set them on the third step, then straightened the afghan so that it was centered on the back of the couch.

Spencer had been the reason for everything she'd done today, from the food she ordered at the ramshackle stand where they'd had their first date, to the secluded botanical gardens where they were married. And to see him standing there in the flesh—so real, so vulnerable—it was the best and the worst moment of her life.

She couldn't bear to look at him; couldn't meet his gaze. She'd been master over her shame. She had tamed it, prevented it from rising to the surface, but not today; the reins she'd kept in a firm grasp had slipped from her fingers, and she was suddenly helpless, falling prey to its reproach.

He remembered their anniversary of all things. Remembered her with roses and a card. *The card!* How could she have forgotten? She rushed to the couch where he had discarded it. It was wedged between the cushion and the arm. She picked it up and tore it open.

Love never fails.

Her eyes stung and she sniffed. *Why?* Why did he have to show up? Why did he have to remind her? Jaida swung her hand and flung the porcelain figurine from the table sending it flying across the room. The molded piece spiraled into the air, arced then came crashing down on the tile, severing the head from the body and shattering the remains. The lopped-off head spun across the floor and rolled under a chair.

Jaida crumpled to the floor, her hands pressed to her face, the hot tears trickling through her fingers. Spencer wanted her to run to him, to throw her arms around his neck and love him. But she couldn't do it. She was broken, defective. She didn't know how to let someone love her or how to love back, and she wouldn't martyr her heart for a cause that would lay her bare and leave her defenseless.

She wiped her eyes with her fingers and slowly lifted her face. The light from the lowering sun glinted on the mirrored chest and she startled, drawing back from the distorted image, the hollow eyes that stared straight through to her soul.

Stripped bare of every pretense, she was seeing herself from the inside out. She flattened her palm over it, willing the image away, but the ugliness that masked her face and the mocking eyes were still staring back between the slats of her fingers.

What have I become?

It was distant—the faint, almost raspy mewling, but the quiet sound was like a jolting crash of cymbals in her head, jarring her from this supernatural spell.

She dropped her hand from the cool, mirrored surface. There was nothing there to see now except the oily imprint of her palm and fingers. Had she imagined it?

She stood and looked around her for some explanation, but there was nothing, just the whining meow. She tracked the sound to the foyer and opened the front door. Uninvited, a white ball of fur made the leap over the doorstep and into the house as if it belonged there.

"Where did you come from?" Jaida scooped the scraggly kitten up in her arms and nestled it close to her chest. Did it belong to Marilyn? She stepped outside and looked up at the house next to hers. It didn't appear anyone was home to ask.

She carried it to the end of the stone walk, stopping short of the gate to look up and down the boardwalk. There was no one about other than a few straggling beachgoers carrying their ice chests and beach towels to their vehicles.

She lifted the kitten up and looked into its pitiful gray-flecked eyes. "Who do you belong to?" A pink tongue poked out as if to taunt her.

Jaida dug her fingers into the fur and felt for some identification, but the scraggy neck underneath was bare. No collar, no tag. Must be a stray. She carried it inside and set it on the kitchen floor with a bowl of milk then rummaged through the cupboards for something that would satisfy its palate and fill its belly.

A can of Swanson chicken was shoved in the back corner. That should do the trick. She ran the tin can under the opener and loosened the packed chunks with the tines of a fork then set it down beside the milk.

Sitting cross-legged on the floor beside the kitten, she stroked the fur that clung to its bony spine, thinking back to the things Spencer had said. Where did he see her and Lance together? Was it at the botanical gardens? If so, then he'd witnessed more than he'd mentioned. Her face heated with a fresh wave of shame.

Lance may have been with her this afternoon, but emotionally she arrived and left alone, and in between, she'd taken the liberty of remembering Spencer taking a knee in the middle of that dusty ball diamond. She bit into her quivering lip, resisting the emotion the memory stirred. Her big mistake had been saying yes.

The kitten brushed against her thigh bringing her thoughts back to the present. Sluggish, it carried its full belly into the living room and leapt into a chair. Jaida pushed up from the floor. She pulled the lid from the magnet still dangling on the opener then dropped it into the trash along with the empty can.

What reason would Lance have to meet with Spencer? Was it part of the investigation through internal affairs? And how did he know about Spencer in the first place? She hadn't told anyone about him, about her life.

She rinsed her hands under the faucet, glancing at the clock on the microwave. She couldn't think about this right now. It was a distraction she didn't have time for. Both Lance and Spencer had thrown her day off while her work sat on the desk untouched. And she still hadn't talked to Auggie about the tape.

Jaida dried her hands and slipped inside her office. She switched on the lamp and pulled the desk chair up behind her. The first folder she opened contained two photographs and she held them up. In rich digital colors, William Gale and his former political aide, Marcus Dennison, stared up at her, their eyes bright with life. She tilted the picture under the light and took a long look at their faces wondering if Dennison was cut from the same cloth as Gale.

"Don't judge a book by its cover, and don't judge a man's character by his photo," she mumbled to herself. Dennison sold Gale out. Why? Was it a moral decision or a political one? Or something else entirely?

She dropped her head back and blew out a heavy breath. Did any of those things matter? Dennison's motives could be speculated on and debated until the cows came home, but those questions didn't get her any closer to her mother.

Dennison handed them everything they needed to charge Gale with money laundering and end his political career, but now there was no trace of the money and the accounts were closed. What could she do with that?

Jaida rested her chin in the cup of her palm and stared into the image of Gale's long, lean face. It was disturbing—his soulless blue gaze too much like what she'd seen in her own eyes just a little while ago.

The similarity was undeniable. She couldn't stop the shudder that gripped her body and left her shaking. *God help me.* Was that a prayer? And if it was a prayer, would God answer and save her from herself? Save her from becoming like the man she despised?

Her visual shift to the second photo was quick and deliberate, but that image was just as unsettling as the first, and she looked away. The slain corpse of Marcus Dennison was sprawled on his bedroom floor. She'd seen the graphic display of his death many times over, but there were some things you never grew immune to.

Her eyes watered, and she blinked to clear her vision, giving herself some time before she looked at it again—at the face hidden underneath the layers of caked and dried blood. It had been a brutal death at the hands of a malevolent being.

It was in that moment that everything changed. This was no longer just about her, about finding who she was. William Gale took this man's life, took him away from his family. And somehow she was going to prove it.

18

Auggie raged, his dark eyes stormy. "You what?" he yelled, jerking to his feet. The desk chair rolled out from under him and slammed into the file cabinet behind.

Jaida flinched, her stoic demeanor wavering under the pressure. He was just getting warmed up, but she was prepared to take whatever he dished out. She'd earned the fullness of his wrath and then some.

From the hallway, curious eyes watched the fireworks through the office window like Auggie's reprimand was a sideshow. With one well-placed kick, his foot sent his overflowing trashcan in motion, its airborne contents scattering across the floor like confetti at a parade.

But this was no celebration. He crossed to the window and gave the cord on the blinds a yank. Cheap white vinyl tumbled down over the sheet of glass, shutting the spectators out.

Eyes wide, Jaida pressed a hand to her mouth. She guessed he wasn't as good at pretending that they didn't have an audience as she was. But her co-workers didn't have to watch to know what was happening. Not when they could hear it all the way down the hall.

Auggie slammed his fist into his open palm and Jaida reared back as though he'd hit her. He was back behind his desk. A thick, corded, blue vein bulged at his temple beneath a layer of purpling skin. She squeezed her eyes shut, bracing herself for the next round.

"I trusted you with this. How could you have been so careless?"

She looked at him, saw the strain in his face and eyes and opened her mouth to offer a defense, but what defense could she give? She'd messed up.

He gripped his hand across the back of his head, his face a mixture of fading rage and empty defeat. "How many times have I told you not to take anything out of here unless it's a copy?"

She shook her head. "I'm sorry. I know an apology means nothing considering what my actions have cost us, but…"

"Are you sure? Are you absolutely sure that you didn't just misplace it?" He looked at her with the same desperation she felt burning inside. But she was sure. She wouldn't be standing here if she wasn't.

Jaida turned her face away and shook her head. "It's gone, Auggie."

"Have you checked your office at home, here at work, your car, your purse?" Without taking a breath, he rattled off all the possible places the tape might be. Places that she had already considered and already searched.

"I've torn apart everything in my house, my car, and my office. It's gone."

He stared at the calendar dangling from a thumbtack. He was probably wishing that it read "April 1" and this was all some kind of tasteless prank.

Auggie clamped his hands over his head then slid them down to the back of his neck and paced the floor, shoving the litter from his wastebasket aside with his foot. Would he fire her now?

She flopped into a chair and threw her hands up. "None of this makes any sense. The same day I brought the tape home, I put it on a shelf in my office and I never touched it. I planned to review it one more time and fill in any gaps in my notes, but when I went to get it, it was gone."

Auggie stopped his pacing and waved a hand, silencing her. "Wait a minute, wait a minute." He came around the desk then shoved a stack of papers back and sat on the edge right in front of her.

Resting his palms against his thighs he leaned so close that she could see what was left of the Rolaids tablet on the center of his tongue. Great. She was probably giving him ulcers.

"Now let's just slow down and backtrack a few steps here," he said. "When was the last time you saw the tape?"

Jaida frowned. When *had* she seen it last? She remembered taking it out of her handbag and sliding it onto the shelf along with her files. She went out that evening and that was seven, maybe eight days ago. She'd been busy and hadn't touched it since.

"The last time I remember seeing it was about a week ago. That was the day I brought it home."

"Who could have taken it? Who would have known what it was, known where it was, and had the opportunity, Jaida? Think." He tapped the side of his head with his forefinger, the tension between the two of them mounting once again.

Jaida raised a hand in the air and let it fall limply into her lap. "No one. I don't even allow anyone in my office. I would never be..." Her mind flashed to Lance's back, his hunched head, standing in front of that same shelf in her office. She chewed the inside of her cheek. *It couldn't be. Could it?*

She remembered Carina's warning, but that was about the money. "Lance." His name was out of her mouth before she could stop it.

The air grew deathly still, and Auggie's eyes narrowed to angry slits. "What about Lance?"

"No." Lance was not a plausible choice. She pressed her hands to her lips and thought back to that day, then gave her head a shake. "No, he would have no reason to take it...he..."

"Let me decide that." His voice was low and monotone, his expression so dark, so dangerous, it made her heart stall in her chest.

"Now." He clasped his hands together and leaned back on the desk. "What about Lance?"

"It's nothing really. I came back from a swim and he was waiting for me outside my door. I invited him in. I took a quick shower, and when I was through, I found him in my office. He said he was showing himself around." She spread her hands. "He came out empty-handed, Auggie."

His feet hit the floor, and he was pacing again. "What about his pockets? Did you check those?"

She rolled her eyes. "Oh, sure, I always ask to frisk my guests."

"Our one crucial piece of evidence and that worthless scum waltzes off with it." Auggie swore and sent his fist crashing into the wall. The framed, autographed baseball program bounced off the head of the nail that it hung from, and with a deft sweep of his hand, he caught it by the edge and set it back in place.

Jaida shoved herself up from the chair. "What makes you so sure he's the one who took it?" Wasn't he internal affairs? Why would he steal the evidence?

"Because my gut tells me he took it."

"Since when is that enough to go on? And even if it was it still doesn't explain his motive. You've seen his file, his awards. He does his job. Besides, what possible reason could he have for undermining this case?"

His eyes flashed. "Yeah. He does his job all right. But I happen to know the man a little better than you think."

Jaida frowned at his cryptic comment. What was that supposed to mean?

"Look, he was asking about you earlier. I want you to pay him a visit and see what it is he wants. Do what you can to feel this out. Play it like he was any other punk you're trying to get information out of."

Should she tell him Lance was with internal affairs? He'd asked for her silence on that. Was he lying to her? Was she that gullible? He showed her his ID, but was it a fake?

"This is crazy, Auggie."

He stared her down, challenging her, daring her to argue. "Okay. All right." She would do it, but he was wrong.

Jaida moved toward the door then hesitated. What about Lance's meeting with Spencer? Should she bring that up? Deciding against it, she reached for the doorknob.

Auggie stopped her with a hand to her arm. "Promise me you'll do as I say."

"I promise."

"Good girl." He chucked her chin, and she jerked her face away.

"I hate it when you do that."

Auggie grinned. "I know."

Jaida turned the knob. Lance's office was locked and the lights were off. He must have left for the day. She would come back tomorrow. It was just as well. She had something important to do.

19

Spencer handed Taryn Nichols, an aide at the nursing home, the white paper sack he brought with him.

"I think you know what to do with these," he said.

"Delicious. It's like an orchard in a bag. I could smell these peaches the second you walked through the door."

He could impress her further by telling her he'd picked them himself from the tree in his backyard, but he only said, "Just have the cook pit them and cut them up for her like last time."

She set the peaches down on the desk and wrote the instructions on a sticky note then stuck it to the bag. "Your mom sure loves these."

"Yes, she does," he said, noticing the gray blouse she wore and the way it flattered her figure. Her auburn hair was pinned up in a twist. Tiny tendrils rebelled, sprouting from the smooth coif at the nape of her neck. "You look nice today."

"Thank you." She looked down at her hands, the pink of her cheeks deepening at his concentrated attention. He cleared his throat and looked away when he realized his gaze lingered longer than was appropriate.

"Your mom is in the dayroom," Taryn finally said. It was a polite way of glossing over his lapse. "Jai…I mean, your wife, was in earlier, but I think she left."

He nodded and headed for the east corridor. *You blew it, Spencer.* He just made sure all future visits would be uncomfortable for both of them. The attraction was there. They both knew it, but he never encouraged it, and neither would he act on it.

His defenses were low after being taken down a notch by Jaida. It was more than a piece of paper that bound him to her, but he was human, and he was lonely.

He rounded the corner and stopped when he saw her. She was still here. He ducked his head and did a one-eighty, the edge of the wall concealing his presence. He didn't want to see her, didn't want to get into it with her. Not here. He half laughed at his excuse for avoiding her. Who was he trying to kid? It was her rejection he hoped to dodge.

Maybe he should leave, let her have her time, and come back later. He glanced at his watch. He had an appointment scheduled later this afternoon. He would take care of that first if he could get Paul Norton to bump up the time.

Spencer turned to leave, but something held his feet to the floor, kept him from rushing away. He lowered his head and shoved his hands in his pockets. What was the hurry anyway?

His ears perked at the familiar laughter; laughter that floated with the weight of a feather, soft and feminine. It had been such a long time since he'd heard it.

He leaned his shoulder against the wall and watched his family—what was left of it anyway—fragmented and with pieces that no longer fit. When Dad passed away, his mother became the only existing link between the two of them. When that was gone...

He watched Jaida cup Laurel's hand in hers. Her face was luminous, almost angelic, her eyes soft and full of love that was too genuine to doubt. How could this be the same woman from yesterday? She must save her congenial side for the people she liked.

She smoothed the twisted yellow collar on his mother's blouse then rearranged the blanket spread across her lap. Jaida talked the whole time and his mother listened. But what did she talk about?

He watched her turn in her chair and look down the length of the hall. What was she looking for? Spencer took another step back, but not before he glimpsed the frown forming at her mouth and between her brows. Was she expecting someone? Lance Palermo, perhaps?

He had managed to keep the sorrow at arms length, but suddenly the weight of his loss was suffocating, crushing the breath from his lungs. He leaned back against the wall and closed his eyes. She loved him once. Or had he mistaken need for love? His throat tightened. Love or need, whatever it was, she'd severed their connection and the artery had been bleeding out ever since.

A sharp wail split the air. His heart jolted, and he pushed up from the wall. A few quick strides and instead of heading out the way he came, he wedged himself between the two women. "It's okay, Mom." He stroked her arm, soothing and comforting while he quietly prayed. The crying began to ease.

With a nurse at her side, Taryn rushed toward them, but Spencer held up his hand. "Everything's under control. She's fine now." He pulled away from her enough to see her ashen face. "Aren't you, Mom?"

Her eyes still glistened from the outburst, but a trace of a smile crept to her thinning lips, and she patted his cheek with a chilled palm. He sank back on his haunches with a sigh glad he'd been there, and relieved that it was over.

Taryn seemed uneasy almost reluctant to leave. "Let us know if you need anything," she said. "We'll be right down the hall."

He nodded. "I'll do that." He eased Laurel back in the chair, adjusting the lap quilt that had slipped to the floor.

Spencer glanced up at Jaida. She stood beside him frozen in place, her complexion stark white, holding a square of neatly cut newsprint that trembled in her hand. He rose and reached for it. He slipped the yellowed paper from her fingers, recognizing it before he even read the headline.

"So, you still want to find her?" he asked. This must have been what set his mother off. He looked up from the paper when she didn't answer.

A flicker of remorse crossed her face, and she lowered her eyes. She nodded, telling him what he already knew. She looked like a scolded child the way her teeth worried the plump flesh of her lower lip. He handed the clipping back, disappointment a lead ball in his stomach.

In her mind, he must seem the ogre when he was only trying to protect her. He didn't begrudge her knowing her birth mother, but she was looking for that connection, that relationship to do the impossible. Why he concerned himself with it, he didn't know. She was a grown woman. It was time he let go and let her find out for herself that her worth and her future wasn't buried with her family's past.

Spencer sighed. "For what it's worth, looking back won't give you what you're searching for. Haven't you figured that out yet? It isn't about the past. It's about right now."

She pressed a tight knot of white knuckles to her mouth, and he reached for her. "Are you all right?" It was habit that drove his arm forward to offer comfort, but he pulled back before he made contact, forcefully shoving his hand into the pocket of his slacks. He could communicate without touching her.

Jaida shook her head 'no' then nodded. Not okay, he decided.

She lowered her fist from her mouth. "Why did she do that? She seemed fine and then…" She swallowed hard, staring at the floor. "What have I done?"

Do you want a list?

Spencer reached over and yanked a Kleenex from the lone box on the end table. He blotted at his mom's damp cheeks and eyes. "It just happens," he said. "Emotional lability." That's what the doctors labeled it.

"She's not going to get better, is she?"

He looked up at her then. "The doctors say she won't."

"But you don't believe them?" The hope that lit her eyes bewildered him. How was it that she could have no faith in him when it came to their marriage, but in this matter, one affirmative word from him and all would be made well?

"There's always the possibility of error," he said. The doctors were men, fallible beings, and if medicine or a surgeon's scalpel couldn't reverse the damage from the accident, God could. If it was His will.

Jaida stepped back, her body visibly trembling. Was she leaving? What did he say to run her off this time?

Spencer crushed the used tissue into a tight ball. "I can go occupy myself while you visit. I didn't know you were still here or I wouldn't have come."

Her eyes met his with a flicker of pain, a flash of anger. *The coup de grace.* His innocent comment dealt a deathblow to the unseen remnant of her affection for him. A remnant he didn't know existed.

She stiffened, a wounded soul guarding the injury. "No, I'll leave." Cool and distant, she gathered her things.

Spencer caught her by the arm. "No. She needs you here." This was exactly what he was afraid would happen.

He loosened his grip prepared for her to jerk her arm away and tell him off, but her anger dissolved, giving way to vulnerability. He hadn't seen her so helpless since he carried her home bundled in Noah Wylie's jacket. Was he witnessing the presence of a chink, a crack in the wall that Jaida built?

She blinked and the defensive barrier was back in place. His hope bottomed out, and he released her. "Let's take her back to her room."

He unlocked the wheelchair and guided it toward the main hall, the rubber-bound wheels propelling the chair over the buffed floor. It was a concrete foundation dressed up with hard tile squares and several layers of wax, but it felt more like eggshells underfoot, and if he was careless and stepped the wrong way...

It surprised him that she stayed and that she followed him now at his request. He had no desire to drive her away, but her reactions were so unpredictable that he didn't know how to respond to her or what to expect.

She walked briskly to keep up. When he noticed the discrepancy in their natural strides, he slowed down. He glanced at her then looked ahead. Always in control she'd shut her emotions down. But that rawness he glimpsed earlier didn't just disappear at will. Somewhere behind the controlled exterior it lived, and if she didn't own it, one of these days it was going to own her.

Jaida pushed the door wide enough for him to enter with the wheelchair. "Would you pull the covers back on the bed?" he asked.

She didn't speak, but did as he asked, folding the bedspread and the matching top sheet down. Spencer removed his mother's shoes then settled her under the covers, tucking the loose edge of the sheet under the mattress.

He pulled the drapes and turned off the overhead light. Jaida skirted him, moving to the opposite side of the bed. Was it just his imagination, or was she positioning herself closer to the door?

With a gentle touch, she swept back a strand of hair that hung in his mother's eyes then looked up at him. "Just answer me this. How is it that, before today, we've never run into each other here?"

It was a loaded question, one he'd rather not answer. Spencer found a fresh pitcher of ice water and a clean plastic cup on the bedside table. He'd only done what she'd asked of him, stepped aside to give her the autonomy she desired.

He owed her the truth, but it wasn't going to endear her to him. There was no kind way to say he intentionally avoided her. He filled the cup and offered it to her. When she refused it with a shake of her head, he drank it down. She wasn't going to be put off.

He set the empty cup in the sink. "I have the employees let me know when you're here along with the general schedule of your visits to make sure our paths never cross."

Her jaw visibly hardened. It was another wound he'd inflicted. He was bombing out big time.

"What about today?" she asked.

He rubbed his jaw. "I was late, an unexpected fluke, someone dropped the ball." He shrugged. "Maybe all three." Or God ordained it, making his immutable plans mutable.

"I see." She picked up the purse she left on the table and made a beeline for the door. In one long stride, Spencer moved in front of her, blocking her path with his body.

"What do you see, Jaida?"

She raised a strong chin. "I see how it is."

"I don't think you do, or it wouldn't bother you. The way we're living right now, this was your plan not mine. I'm just staying out of your way, playing things out the way you wanted."

"If you were trying so hard to stay out of my way, why did you show up at my house the other day?"

He locked eyes with her. He owed her no explanation, and he didn't offer one. He took a risk and put himself out there because God told him to. Because for the life of him, he couldn't quit on her, and because, for some insane reason he still loved her.

Putting an end to their silent standoff, a nurse arrived at the room with a chart in her hand. Spencer stepped aside to let her in, and Jaida took the opportunity to slip out.

"Good-bye, Spencer."

20

Jaida rested her shoulder against the steel doorjamb, a cup of hot coffee in each hand. Lance had yet to see her standing there. He sat hunched over his desk. The phone was pressed to his ear, his mouth drawn into a rigid line, his other arm a shield spanning the width of his chest.

He leaned forward, and in the time it took for her to exhale, his expression went from annoyed, to irate, to furious. He shouted into the receiver. "I can't work with you breathing down my neck." The string of colorful words that followed belonged to a side of him she'd never seen before. But how well did she actually know him?

Jaida straightened. She leaned her head back and took a peek down the hall. Auggie's door was closed. She promised she would do this, but it didn't look like a good time to probe.

Besides the negative atmosphere in here, she was still operating below par from running into Spencer. She wouldn't be at the top of her game. Not that she had much game to begin with.

She turned to leave, but before she managed a full pivot, one of the cups slipped through her fingers and fell to the floor. The lid and hot paper cup parted ways. She jumped back at the spreading puddle and looked up, eyes wide. Lance was staring back, panic paralyzing his features when he saw her standing there.

No good-bye, he offered no closure to the other party before he hung up. Just exactly who was on the other end of that line, and what did he think she heard?

He pushed back from his chair and rounded the desk, then quickly turned back and picked up the phone again. "Yeah, can you get some paper towels in here?" He looked down at the spill and the oversized cup lying on its side. "Better make it a mop."

He hung up then and looked at her. Jaida shrugged and smiled. "I brought you some coffee."

"I see that. Did you want me to lap it up like a dog?"

She stared at him, struggling for words, unsure how to take him. Was he joking? Or was he angry?

He flashed his trademark smile then, the tension from her shoulders melting. "It's all good. Job security for the custodian," he said.

She skirted the mess on the floor and handed him the other cup. It was hers that she'd so gracefully dumped.

"Come on in." He pulled out a chair beside his desk and she hesitated. Did she really want to do this right now? May as well. Couldn't very well turn tail and run without raising suspicions.

He raised the cup. "Want to share?"

She shook her head. "I'll survive. But I'm not so sure about you. You having a bad day?"

He sighed and sank into the desk chair. "Guess you heard?" He looked at her then as though gauging her reaction. Was he trying to determine how much she'd overheard?

"I saw more than heard," she said. "Problems with work?" How did she ease into this and walk away with information Auggie could use?

He leaned back and eyed her, his gaze suddenly shifting to the door. She turned. Jerry Schultz, full-time custodian, filled the doorway. His blue shirtsleeves were rolled up over his beefy arms. He went to work swabbing the spill with a wet mop.

"Sorry about that," she said.

He shoved his black-rimmed glasses up on his nose, grumbled something about unions, and then waved her off. "Now, don't go falling down. It's wet," he warned as if she didn't know.

She turned back to Lance, apologizing again.

He sipped his coffee. "No big deal."

She crossed her legs and smoothed a hand over her pant leg, the black fabric a magnet for cat hair. "Still no luck locating the money?" She took a stab. Is that what had him lathered up?

The corner of his mouth hitched. "What would you do if I kissed you right now?"

He set his cup down and moved from the chair to his desk. Perched on the edge, he was inches from her face. Her heart pounded. What was he doing?

She drew back, and he leaned closer. "Go on, tell me what you would do."

She moistened her lips, her heart in her throat. "File a sexual harassment claim."

He looked surprised. "Would you really?"

"Maybe."

"And maybe not." He laughed. "You're way out of your league, Jaida. I'm better at this than you are."

What was he saying? "Better at what?"

"Pumping people for information. Just a tip, sweetheart, your mark can't be onto you, or it won't work."

She felt her face flame and she stood. "Not all of us have ulterior motives."

"Not all of us." Lance rose, his height topping hers by several inches. "But you do. Don't you?"

"I only came by to drop off some coffee. You're the one who invited me in. Remember?"

"You've been avoiding me. Running scared. What changed? Why would you seek me out now?"

She tightened her jaw to keep her mouth from gaping. How did he know? She wasn't cut out for this. Subterfuge, deception, lies. Inept at faking it, she couldn't keep track of it all. This wasn't a career for her, it was a means to an end, and she was failing at that as well.

Before she could respond, he said, "I like your hair like that." Was it sarcasm? Self-conscious at her lack of skill with hair, she tucked a stray into the sloppy chignon.

He smiled. "Etiquette requires that you thank me for the compliment."

She glared, wanting to smack that grin off his face. "What about the insult? You insulted me first. What does etiquette dictate for that? An apology?"

"I'll tell you what. I'll apologize, and you can thank me. Then we both will have done Miss Manners proud."

She rolled her eyes and turned to leave, but Lance stopped her, his hands gripping her forearms. "I'm sorry. Honest. I've had a rough morning. I didn't mean to take it out on you."

Sorry? Maybe. Perceptive? Definitely.

She waved a hand and pulled away from him. "It's fine. Really, it's fine." She just wanted to get away from him.

"You're angry with me because I didn't come to your rescue earlier aren't you?"

"What are you talking about?"

"Auggie sounded pretty miffed."

She hadn't seen him hovering in the hall with the rest of the staff when Auggie went off on her. But then after the blinds had been pulled, and the door shut, who knew what staff members hung around hoping to get an earful of gossip?

"What exactly did you do to get on his bad side? Shoot his dog or something?"

No, shooting his dog would have been forgivable. Of the two evils, letting Gale walk was a greater indiscretion. Lance perked up, his attention fully concentrated on her now. She had gone and done it. He was right. He *was* better at this than she was.

Did he know she was being chewed out over the tape? "It was just a disagreement," she said. "Nothing that can't be fixed."

"Are you sure? I mean, I could go to bat for you, take a guilty plea on your behalf, even."

She eyed him. "You'd do that?"

"Sure, why not? But I would need to know what it was I was pleading guilty to."

Something told her he already knew. *Did you take that tape?* She searched his face, his eyes, for any indication, but she only saw what he wanted her to see.

It was a dance between them, each one trying to take the lead, but she kept stumbling over his feet, looking like a clumsy fool. Just when she thought she had the advantage, he would sweep her over the dance floor with practiced grace, taking her in a direction she didn't want to go.

"I don't think your employers would be happy with their internal affairs liaison admitting to…"

He grinned. "To what?"

She'd only intended to bait him, not give herself away. "Never mind. I have to go." Had to leave before he had it all figured out. His uncanny ability to read people could prove entertaining on a Las Vegas stage, but in real life it was a threat.

"What's the hurry?"

"I have Auggie's dog to bury. Remember?" She took a step and forgetting Jerry's warning, her feet went out from under her. Once again, Lance caught her before she hit the floor, his hands cupping her elbows.

"Now, don't go falling down," he mocked. "Floor's wet."

She shrugged out of his hold and straightened her shirt, shutting out his laughter that followed her all the way down the hall.

21

Jaida leaned back in the chair and from the seclusion of her patio she took in the glory of another sunset. She was alone. Alone was safe, it wasn't so bad, not the death sentence she once imagined it to be.

I'm alone, Spencer, and I'm fine without you. She finished off the last bite of her corndog and licked the trace of mustard that clung to the corner of her mouth. It was a lie. She wasn't fine. Or it wouldn't hurt so much to learn he'd been avoiding her. She crumpled the wax paper square around the empty stick and tossed it on the table. The truth was, she missed him.

He was right though, about all of it. She'd made her choice. It was her wounded pride that took offense and stormed out, yet she blamed him. She rested the soles of her bare feet against the edge of the empty chair in front of her and pulled the pinkish-red cardigan tight around her, the lightweight cotton warding off the evening chill.

A wise girl doesn't love. And a wise girl leaves before she's left. It lessens the sting of rejection when she isn't loved back. The breeze tousled her hair, and she swept it away from her face. She sank down deeper into the chair and yawned. Spencer would have left, eventually. Everyone leaves.

Jaida wove her chilled fingers together. She rested her hands on her stomach and stared off into the horizon. A showoff flaunting its splendor, nature performed for her, singing its own praises. The lit-up sky could put the most elaborate fireworks display to shame.

The sun kissed the pale sky adieu, and it blushed pink with pleasure. For the finale, the fiery golden orb sank, melting into the sea and leaving behind a shimmering puddle of 24-karat liquid brilliance.

Jaida applauded.

The phone rang. She got up and went inside to answer it. *Private Caller.* It was probably a telemarketer or someone collecting for charity. Letting it go, she headed for the stairs then turned around at the next ring. What if it was Ray?

The possibility sent her rushing to the phone. *Stay calm and even-keeled. Show no emotion.* She swallowed then lifted the receiver. "Hello."

"Hello, Jaida."

Her stomach twisted into a knotted ball, the sound of his voice stirring untapped wells of anger. Why was *he* calling?

"Jaida?"

Just hang up. "I'm here," she said, immediately wishing she'd regarded her own warning. "What can I do for you, Mr. Gale?"

"Mr. Gale?" he asked sounding almost affronted. "Why so formal?"

His chuckle grated like nails on a chalkboard. "What would you prefer I call you?" William, Bill, Billy?

"'Dad' would be appropriate, don't you think?"

She'd stepped right into that one with both feet. The thought of this man's blood running through her veins sickened her.

His money wasn't the only thing Marcus Dennison left her. Days before his death he came to the agency, found her at her desk and without warning, dumped the terrible news on her. William Gale was her father.

She had never seen the man before that day. She didn't know who he was, or if she could trust him. He stood in her office looking like a spooked rabbit, his eyes jumping around in his head while he spilled it all—names, dates, and details about Gale's offshore accounts. He knew then that he didn't have long.

His blue suit jacket was rumpled. It looked as though he'd slept in it, his wiry gray hair askew. She gave him her email at his request, and he pulled his phone from his jacket pocket, transferring the information as she stood watching.

The recollection roused her own fear, and her face flamed in anger at the injustice of it all. "What do you want from me, Mr. Gale?"

He laughed. "You're just like me, you know. Chip off the old block. You want it straight, no beating around the bush."

"I am *nothing* like you." She denied the comparison, but deep down she feared the very same thing, saw the signs that said it was true.

She pressed her eyes closed. *God, don't let me be like this man.*

He was silent for a beat. She could hear the creak of his chair swiveling on its base, the hum of his steady breath. And then he spoke. "I want to make a deal."

A deal? "What kind of deal?" she asked. Was it a bribe to get her off his back? What could he want from her, and what was he offering in return? Adrenaline rushed. Could he actually be suggesting...?

"My money in exchange for your mother's name."

He was.

Why did he need it? He had billionaire donors carrying him. Was he losing their support? In the real world, eight and a half million dollars was a large sum, but in a political race with players of this magnitude it was ice-cream money.

"And how would we do this?" she asked. "How would I know that the name you give me is legitimate?"

"That's where trust comes in."

Her laugh was forced. "Trust you?" Did he think she was naïve?

"You trusted me once when you asked for her name. Didn't you assume then that I would be honest enough to give you the correct one? This is no different."

"It doesn't matter because I don't have your money. I never did." Her voice shook, and she cursed him under her breath, resenting the power he held over her.

"Dennison sent you the codes," he said. "And the passwords. I've read the emails."

"And he's dead. To kill a man in cold blood like that..."

His voice was ice. "Be careful what you say. Young women who live alone should mind their manners."

"Or their fathers will have them killed?" She was trembling now, her voice strained to a high pitch. "Is that what you mean to say?"

She could sense his fury, feel his hatred. *No Father's Day present for you next spring.*

"It's a shame you didn't acquire your mother's docile nature."

Her heart tripped at his calculated words. It was his intent to entice. He knew her desire and toyed with it like a master manipulator. She wanted to know everything about her mother; what she looked like, where she grew up, who she was. But out of a million dpi, his depiction of her character was the equivalent of one dot. It wasn't much to build a picture on.

"I assume you were the one who ended your association with her then?" No meek being would dare walk away from this man. Not without a direct order to do so.

"I loved her." There was a lull in his anger. His voice took on a sorrow and a tenderness she didn't recognize, and would have sworn on a Bible didn't exist.

"Why are you telling me this?"

He sighed. "I don't know."

The cool tile sent a chill through her bare feet and up her spine. Or was it this rare moment of honesty between them?

"What's her name?" she asked. "I have a family somewhere. I'd like to know who they are."

"She's dead."

It was a sucker punch that left her winded. Nothing could have prepared her for that. Why hadn't he told her before? The sting of her eyes, the ache in her chest threw her off-kilter. "Was it, was it recent? H-h-how long?"

"A long time ago." No specifics, no details for her to fill in the blanks and make sense of it all. Was he lying to her?

"How did it happen?" she asked.

"You ask entirely too many questions. Don't you know ignorance is bliss? The less you know, the better off you'll be."

"What about my grandparents? Aunts, uncles, cousins?" *But I'd like to start with my mother's name.*

His tone hardened. "I made you an offer. The ball is in your court." The detached politician she was familiar with had wrestled the sentimental man to the ground.

"I can't give you what I don't have. You're suing Baseel for it...and me. I'm sure you'll collect somehow." He had enough judges in his pocket to make that a certainty.

"There is no lawsuit. Who told you that?"

She wouldn't be sharing that information with him. Besides, didn't he just tell her that ignorance was bliss? The less *he* knew, the better.

"It doesn't matter," she said. No longer willing to play his game, she hung up the phone, suddenly plagued by Spencer's remark.

"Looking back won't give you what you're searching for. It isn't about the past. It's about right now." Again he was right. But still she longed for an identity that was legitimate, one that was woven into her cells and stamped into her DNA.

Weary, she dropped down on the stool at the counter, tension pulling at the muscles behind her eyes until they ached from the strain. Her mother was dead. He could have told her sooner, though it wouldn't have changed anything.

The phone trilled, startling her. It was Auggie. She started to transfer the call to her voice mail account then thought better of it. It might be important.

"Where have you been?" he asked. "I've been trying to reach you all day." The five missed calls blinking on her phone were probably his.

"Hello to you, too," she said.

"I sent you to do a job, and you disappeared on me. What's going on with you?"

She pressed a palm to her forehead. *Lance.* She never got back to Auggie about Lance. "I'm sorry. It hasn't been a good day for me, and I forgot to call you. But there is nothing to tell. I didn't get anywhere. Lance caught on to what I was doing and called me on it."

"Didn't I teach you how to play the game, chica?"

"You did." But she'd never mastered the skills required to play and win. "It wouldn't have mattered anyway. He's with internal affairs." She covered her mouth. She hadn't meant to let that slip.

"Is that what he told you?"

"You sound like you don't believe him."

"I didn't say that." His throat was raspy and he cleared it. "Did he ask about the money?"

"I think he believes I have it," she said.

"Well, if he's really internal affairs, he'll be looking into the rest of us too."

"I guess. But how long are they going to drag this out?"

"Until they find it," he said. "Have you tossed names around? Considered who might have it?"

"I've tried, but I can't believe anyone at Baseel who had access would have taken it." Would have let her be investigated for their crime and not spoken up—or would have at least returned it.

She said, "What if Dennison cleaned out the accounts after he sent us the information? He knew he was going to die, and the amount Gale had amassed was more than enough to take care of Dennison's family for the rest of their lives. His giving us access might have been an act of genius—setting us up to take the blame while no one even considers that his wife might have it."

"Wow. I'm impressed." She could hear the smile in his voice. "I never considered that," he said.

Theory or fact, it should be looked into, but she didn't have the nerve to broach such a sensitive subject when their grief was still fresh. It didn't seem right.

"Yeah, well, when it's your hide they want to put in jail you start thinking outside the box."

She turned at the sound of snagging claws digging into the fabric of her damask accent chair. The kitten was going to ruin it. She darted across the room and snatched up the cat, cuddling its furry head under her chin.

"I'm sorry about the tape," she said.

"Yeah, well, without Ray it was probably worthless anyway." His admission surprised her.

"By the way," Auggie said, "Kevin left you a note at the front desk. He came by. He wasn't happy when I told him you weren't in. He thinks I was covering for you."

"What did it say? I know you read it." The kitten purred and she nuzzled it against her chest.

"Yeah, you know me too well. It was pretty sappy, by the way." She could hear the rustling of papers. "Here it is. It says, 'Love is the closest thing we have to magic. Yours always, Kev.'"

It was another line from a movie. It had to be. The man was aggravating. Even after their talk he still dismissed the idea of friendship and went straight for relationship. "Just throw it away," she said. "Are you still at the office?"

"Yep. But, I'm about ready to take off."

"Is Lance in?"

"I haven't seen him. Why?"

"One of us should search his office, see if he has the tape."

"One of us meaning me, right?" He chuckled at her silence. "It's already done. I didn't find anything. He's not stupid. He destroyed it the minute he discovered what was in his hands."

Why? Why would he destroy it? Why would he undermine the case? She spun at the ringing doorbell. "Gotta go. Someone's at the door."

Outside her window, a man who looked to be in his forties stood pointing his finger at her. *Me?* She mouthed the word. He understood and shook his head, pointing lower.

The kitten?

He nodded.

She brushed the top of its head with her lips. "So, you're not a stray after all."

She opened the door and the man was standing uncomfortably close to the threshold. His eyes were brown. Mud brown. His face was full and round and was much too close to hers. He adjusted the ball cap on his head. A size too small, it failed to cover an odd tan line that curved in a low arc across his wide forehead.

His arms shot out and she jerked back, stepping out of his reach. What was he doing?

He gave her a scolding look, his brows raised. "My cat?" he said, informing her in two words what his intentions were.

Heat crept into her face. She felt foolish.

"May I?" he asked, his tone snide, he gave her a lofty look as if she were stupid. She plunked the cat into his open palms, and he tucked it like a sack of potatoes under his left arm.

"I've been looking everywhere for this cat."

She looked down at his foot. It was resting inside the doorway now. Did he mean to keep her from closing the door? Jaida slid her hand lower and gripped the knob.

He didn't move. He had the kitten, why wasn't he leaving? Was Marilyn watching? She hoped so. Her eyes darted to the left, but from inside the door, she didn't have a clear view of her neighbor's window.

He removed the tattered ball cap from his head and swiped an arm over his brow then replaced it. "Could I trouble you for a glass of water?" he asked. "It's a bit hot out here."

163

She eyed him, uncertain if she should turn her back on him. Something about him gave her the creeps.

Jaida said nothing and then nodded, pushing the door partially closed before she went to the kitchen. Her gaze darted to the drawer that held her weapon. Could she use it if she had to? Pull the trigger and put a deadly bullet into another human being?

She didn't want to find out. She skipped the ice, filled a glass with tap water, and was back at the front door in less than a minute.

She handed him the glass. "How did you know I had your cat?"

"Actually I didn't. I've been walking up and down the boardwalk, knocking on doors. Lucky for me you happened to be holding it."

He could see in her window from the boardwalk? She gave him a skeptical look. Did he have binoculars? Was he a peeping Tom?

He drank the water down. With his head tipped back, she took a better look at the strange tan line, trying to recall what it looked like when he took his hat off. His balding scalp was pale compared to the rest of him. Did he wear a toupee?

"Looks like he wears a rug." That's how Marilyn described the man who was snooping around her house. Was this the same man? She studied his fingers pressed into the crystal tumbler. The prints would be a clear set. Her fingers twitched. She wanted to grab it from him, but she didn't have to. He was already handing it back.

"Thank you for the water, and again for taking care of this little fellow."

Jaida offered a parting smile and closed the door. She slid the deadbolt in place, relieved when she heard the solid click locking him out.

She stood at the window and made sure he left the premises then set the glass on the counter and set the alarm, Gale's warning still ringing in her ears. First thing in the morning she would run those prints.

22

Jaida screamed. Her eyes jerked back and forth in her head. Blackness descended, the weight of it bearing down on her chest until it sealed the air from her lungs.

She gasped. Writhing, she thrust the crushing pressure from her body. And then it was gone. The evil fled, the bees had chased it away.

She swatted a limp hand where they swarmed about her head. Livid little creatures, they ranted, the noise swelling in her ears. She pressed clenched fists to the sides of her head and shook it. "Go away."

But they were persistent, a nuisance that plagued her until their murmuring pulled her from this present torment and into another realm. Her eyelids, pinched tight, relaxed and then fluttered opened, the ceiling over her bed no longer dark with evening shadows, but awash in sunlight.

Another nightmare. Exhausted, Jaida turned her head on the pillow, damp from the hair that clung to her neck and the sides of her face. She reached for the alarm. With the push of a button, she silenced the throng of bees.

Her nightgown was twisted around her hips and thighs. She swept her fingers over her collarbone and inside the well of her neck where fear had collected in a shallow wet patch. She had to get up, had to go to work.

A few minutes later she stood hunched under the showerhead like a frightened child. It was only a nightmare, a trick of the mind, but it was so vivid, so real. Hot water streamed over the back of her head, running down her spine, yet still she shivered. She pinched her eyes tight, squeezing out the twisted and grotesque face that terrorized her in her sleep. She'd read about hell, and last night she swore she had paid it a visit.

Work and coffee was what she needed. Caffeine and getting her focus back on her objective would chase away the residual effects. Maybe.

She had considered talking to someone. A counselor or a friend, but the dreams had been less frequent since she'd started running. The trauma of last night's terror had made up for the lull.

Jaida slipped a lime green sundress from the hanger and pulled it over her head. Her eyes were puffy with purpled grooves carved underneath. She covered the evidence of her miserable night with a layer of concealer to the dark circles, and a dab of blush to her cheeks then examined her work. No one would be the wiser.

She sat on the edge of the unmade bed and slipped on a pair of low-heeled sandals, her hands trembling the whole time. She had to shake this off, but her coping skills were failing her.

What she couldn't resolve in her waking hours hounded her in her sleep and left her barely functional during the day. She needed peace. But there was no peace for the wicked. Isn't that what the Bible said? Is that what she was? Wicked?

Not willing to go there, she shook her head at her own question and stood, her legs as unsteady as the rest of her. She climbed in the car and headed out, picking up a large coffee at the McDonald's drive-through.

The familiar stretch of freeway she drove every day was behind her, her exit a distant blur in the rearview mirror. The detour was unplanned, and she would be late, but after last night, it was unavoidable.

The coffee was too hot when she took her first sip, and she scorched her tongue. She popped the plastic lid off and set the cup in the drink holder, the vented air blowing down on it. She didn't want to feel anything. Not fear, or shame, or remorse. Emotions scared her. They were dangerous. They left you weak and exposed. Just like love. But today she couldn't seem to override them.

The one-hour drive to Los Angeles had taken her two. She pulled into the dim light of the parking garage, the sound of her tires and the hum of her engine echoing in the concrete box. She took the ticket the machine spit out, waited for the red-and-white bar to raise, and found one lone spot near the front of the garage.

Her car was just one among rows and rows of vehicles. More SUVs and fewer hybrids filled the spaces. Was it only a couple of years ago that the Prius dominated the Los Angeles freeways?

Jaida unhooked her seatbelt and reached for the door, then drew her hand back, dropping it into her lap. When the reality of what she was doing sank in, she was no longer in a hurry to go inside.

She reached for her coffee and sat back, her gaze scanning the garage looking for one car in particular. She didn't see it, but there were two more levels above her.

Instead of sitting here worrying over seeing him again, she should be in Fullerton, working on her cases. At least working on *the* case. She set the cup down and shoved the key back in the ignition, hesitated, then pulled it out again, her shoulders slumping.

Why did she need him? She didn't understand it, but she couldn't deny it. She needed Spencer. She looked up at the sound of an electronic squawk. Three cars down to her left, headlights flashed and a tall brunette with waist-length hair climbed inside a silver Audi. Jaida slipped the keys inside her purse and got out.

The elevator ride was smooth, not jerky like some of the older buildings. It shot to the top floor in seconds. *Seraph* was painted in gilt script on the top half of the glass doors and displayed prominently in large carved lettering over the information desk. The woman behind the marble topped counter pointed her in the direction of Spencer's secretary.

It was incredible, what he'd done with this place. The house she lived in, the car she drove, and Spencer's monthly checks were a testimony to his financial accomplishments, but seeing all of this with her own eyes left her speechless. He had done quite well without her.

The nameplate situated on the edge of the desk read: Rebecca Childers. Ms. Childers wore her graying hair coiled and pinned into a knot at the nape of her neck. The navy basket-weave skirt and blazer she wore, Jaida guessed to be from St. John.

She looked the woman over for any flaw and found none. No young sensual secretary for Spencer. His hiring habits were another example of his virtuous character, the one that widened the rift between her less-than-stellar one.

She took a breath and stepped up to the desk. "Excuse me, Ms. Childers?"

Eyes the shade of cinnamon peered up from the open book she cradled in her hands. "Can I help you?"

"I'm here to see Mr. Gordon."

"Do you have an appointment?" She tucked a thin ribbon marker in the pages, closed the book, and set it aside.

Before Jaida could answer, the woman slid a date book in front of her and flipped the cover open.

"I'm afraid you won't find my name in there," she said. What would she do if she refused her?

Ms. Childers straightened, her spine not touching the back of the chair. "I'm sorry, dear, but Mr. Gordon doesn't see anyone without an appointment. I can make you one now if you'd like." She reached for a pen.

Jaida shook her head. "It really is a shame when a woman has to make an appointment to see her husband." It was the lack of sleep she told herself. She hadn't meant to say it, to strike a blow to Spencer, but there was no taking it back now.

Ms. Childers gave her a doubtful look. Her lightly penciled brows rose in silent question. It looked like she wasn't the only one who had kept their marriage a secret.

"Mr. Gordon is your husband?" It sounded more like an accusation than a question.

"Yes, he is."

"May I ask your name?"

"Jaida," she said, hesitating when it came to her surname. The name Gordon would be a given. She didn't need to explain her use of another name, or her reason for taking it on.

"Please." She gestured to the russet suede chairs in the far corner. "Have a seat. There's a pot of fresh coffee and blueberry muffins from the bakery right over there." She pointed, indicating a little nook on the other side of the waiting room.

"Thank you," Jaida said then sat in the chair nearest to the woman's desk, which was still a good stretch away. Her stomach churned. She'd had enough coffee on the drive over. A muffin

171

might quell the shakiness overcoming her, but she didn't think she could hold it down.

Ms. Childers picked up the phone and their eyes met. She turned away with her head dipped low and her hand cupped around the mouthpiece. The woman didn't believe her. Wasn't she in for a surprise? Did she think she was some lunatic with plans to bribe Spencer or sue him for alimony?

Her palms were clammy, like the skin under her arms. She wove her fingers together and clasped her hands in her lap. Why was she so nervous?

She blew out a breath and straightened. Ms. Childers couldn't have spoken more than a few words before she hung up the phone and looked at her from across the room. Jaida moved to the edge of the seat, preparing to rise. Would he see her? She couldn't imagine him turning her away.

A door across the hall opened, and Spencer stood in the doorway. She automatically came to her feet when he saw her.

"Jaida." He gave her a brusque nod. The light from the window behind him gilded the blond in his hair like a halo. She half smiled at the image.

He held the door for her, stepping back in silent invitation. She entered and her hand grazed his. She wanted to reach for it, wanted to absorb the comfort and strength she knew it held, but she held back, afraid he would refuse her, just as she had refused him.

She breathed in. "It smells like citrus," she said.

He shut the door, his hand sliding from the knob and into his pant's pocket. "Air freshener." He gave her a quizzical look, his penetrating gaze asking her what she was doing here.

She shrugged in response and tried to smile, but it felt false and he saw right through it. Her nerves tightening, she slid her fingers together then pulled them apart. She ran them over the desk's marble top. The wood base was a warm cherry, and it complemented the chocolate suede couch on the other side of the office.

"You outdid yourself, you know. Everything is so well done." She touched the aluminum shade on the desk lamp. It was a Pablo Pardo design. She lifted her eyes, daring a glance in his direction. He still hadn't moved away from the door.

His silvery-green gaze was fastened on her, but he didn't respond, didn't take part in her weak attempt at conversation. And the way he watched her only served to heighten the anxiety unraveling her on the inside.

She tried again. "I haven't been here since the real estate agent walked us through." The building was in poor condition back then, inferior next to the neighboring structures. But Spencer had a vision, and he had more than fulfilled it.

"I'm glad you appreciate it."

She heard the familiar clicking and looked down at his left hand. His fingers were wrapped around the pen, the end of it at the mercy of his nervous thumb.

She looked into his eyes. "Old habits die hard."

"Why are you here? Is this your way of getting even? Letting my staff know that I have a wife who wants nothing to do with me?"

It was the calm he had greeted her with, but the storm was just beginning to brew. He moved away from the door. "I apologize, Jaida. I'm sorry I told your friends about us. Are you able to call it even now?"

"That isn't why I came. I…I just needed to see you." She lowered her face and closed her eyes. She'd been caught up in the moment and didn't think before she spoke.

"Why?"

She looked up at that, a mixture of hurt and offense tightening around her heart. "What kind of question is that?"

"A reasonable one. Why did you suddenly need to see me? You made it known you didn't want me around. What changed?"

"I *am* your wife."

"Do you tell that to the men you're with? That you're my wife?"

She jerked her chin up. "Do you think that matters to them?"

"I would think that it should matter to you."

Her hands started to shake, and like an electrical current the trembling spread up her arms and through the rest of her body. She remembered the gnarled hands that reached for her, the hideous faces that mocked and tormented her.

Fear flashed in Spencer's eyes. She was scaring him. Did he think she had lost her mind? Maybe she had.

Their spat forgotten, he stretched out his hand, beckoning her. She stepped into his arms and pressed her face to his chest. He was her lifeline, and she clung to him, her fingers digging into his back. *Don't let me go.*

But Spencer didn't hear her silent plea. He stepped back and lifting her chin with his fingers, he angled her face toward him, his own need exposed and as raw as her own.

It was she who made the first move, touching her lips to his. He responded, his ardor unexpected. Instead of pushing her away, he welcomed her, his hands capturing her waist and drawing her closer.

Yes, this was it. This was what she needed. This was what she wanted. She missed him. Missed what they had. Missed what she had kicked, and scratched, and fought so hard to free herself from.

He dragged his fingers through her hair whispering her name over and over again. His lips moved to her jaw, her neck and then without warning, he gripped her shoulders and pushed her away.

"Stop," he rasped.

"I don't want to." She tried to shrug from his grip, to get beyond the barrier he'd erected with his arms, but he was too strong for her.

"It's no longer about what you want. I thought love would be enough to bring you back." He pressed his lips into a tight line and shook his head. "But I was wrong."

He watched her then slowly lowered his arms and moved away, placing himself behind the safety of his desk. Her mouth went slack. What was he doing? Why was he ruining this?

"Are you asking for a divorce?" The thought terrified her. But why should it? She'd been living without him. What difference did a piece of paper make?

His eyes glistened. Fear gripped her when he didn't answer. Was that it? A divorce? He said he never would, but everyone had their limits. Had she pushed him beyond his?

"No, Jaida. I'm not asking for a divorce. I'm asking you to love me." He waved a hand to where they stood clinging only seconds ago. "And that's not what this is about. Is it? Not for you anyway."

The truth was a rapier—razor sharp and precise—and it cut to the quick. She dropped her gaze to her bared toes peeking up from her sandals. Spencer was right. He was always right when it came to her.

She closed her eyes. "I wish it was Spencer." *I wish it was.*

23

Spencer was still reeling from the whirlwind that ripped through his office, nursing a fresh gash to an old wound. Jaida would never know the carnage she left in the wake of her hit-and-run, but he was feeling it all over.

She came here seeking comfort, or at the very least, a distraction from whatever it was that had her spooked. He'd never seen her so shaken. She was teetering on some unseen precipice, and she was afraid…afraid enough to come running to him.

He rounded the corner of his desk and softly closed the door she left open when she fled. He stood there a long moment, his palm pressed to the back of the door, remembering the apology she offered before taking flight. It was sincere. And that alone was a bitter pill to swallow since she was lamenting the fact that she didn't love him.

She doesn't love me. His hand fell to his side. The admission was long overdue. She may not love him, but true to form, she had no reservations about tempting him with the physical. They were still married, and he had every right. But once she mastered control of her fear she would bid him farewell and be on her merry way leaving him to pick up the pieces all over again. No thank you.

Spencer lowered himself to the couch, easing the burden of weight from his limp knees. She had noticed the orange-scented oil warming in the outlets enough to comment on it. Citrus, she'd called it. But the only fragrance stirring in his nostrils was the scent of her perfume. It was on his clothes and his hands, and he didn't welcome the reminder. He got up, went to the bathroom, and washed it from his skin, then cupped his hands and splashed his face. What was he going to do about her?

Pray for her.

Spencer's gaze darted to the ceiling and he laughed to himself. What good would that do? He'd made a career out of praying for her, and nothing had changed.

Pray for her.

He sighed, dried his face, and sat back down at the reprimand. Hunched on the edge of the couch, he dropped his head to his hands. *Help my unbelief.* What good was praying if he didn't believe?

He prayed for his wife and for himself, his head lifting at Rebecca Childers' voice amplified through the intercom.

"Landon has the car waiting at the front door."

Spencer rose, slipped his arms into his jacket, and picked up his briefcase. "Tell him I'll be right down."

Jaida hurried down the hall avoiding eye contact with anyone in her line of sight, but she wasn't fast enough to escape her coworker's notice. Aimee called her name from behind. She pretended not to hear the receptionist and kept moving toward her office where she could close herself inside.

Why had she thrown herself at Spencer like that? Her face flamed, and she ducked her head down, walking faster. She ran to him because he made her feel safe. It made sense at the time. But now that her head had cleared…now that he had refused her…

Aimee caught up to her and stepped in her path. "Didn't you hear me?" She was walking backward, the sound of her heels clicking hard against the tile. "You don't look so good. Are you okay?"

Jaida kept her eyes on the floor, blinking away any trace of moisture. "Everything is fine."

Aimee sounded skeptical. "Okay, whatever you say." She handed Jaida an envelope, her name inscribed in calligraphy across the front.

"It's an invitation to my bridal shower."

Bridal shower? Jaida stopped at the news and looked up at her. "I didn't know you were getting married. Eric?"

Shy, little Aimee blushed, her cheeks matching her strawberry blonde hair. "It was quick. The decision to marry, I mean, and you haven't been around much."

No, she hadn't. She'd been so wrapped up in her life that she hadn't seen anything else going on around her. "I'm really sorry, Aimee."

"Jaida, come in here," Auggie yelled from his office. She rolled her eyes. She just wanted a few minutes to herself. Was that too much to ask?

His light was off, and he was sitting in the dark, his olive complexion pale from the glow of the computer screen. Without looking away from the monitor he instructed her to close the door.

She did as he asked then sat down beside him, leaning in to get a better view of the open file. Was he going to fire her? She had expected it sooner.

She scanned the screen for her name, the names of their superiors, and the reason for her termination, but it wasn't her name that popped up on the page. It was Lance Palermo's.

Auggie clicked the mouse cupped under his palm. "I have some information that you're going to want to see."

She watched the list of names and addresses rolling down the screen. What was this about?

She gave him a sidelong look. "I'm not being released?"

He leaned back and looked up at her, the chair creaking from his weight. "You thought I called you in here to fire you?"

"You have good reason to." She violated policy and lost the evidence because of it. "I would have fired me."

"That's because you're not as charitable as I am."

She shoved his shoulder. "Not charitable. Desperate. Admit it. You need me."

He squinted at her. "Have you been crying?"

She shook her head and sniffed. "Allergies."

He opened his top desk drawer and handed her a box of allergy medicine. She shook her head, refusing it. "I'm good."

"You sure?"

She nodded. "Now, why am I here?"

"About that. I told you I was doing everything I could to get us out of this mess." He jutted his chin at the screen. "And this is part of what it's going to take. I don't have enough proof to try Lance Palermo in court." He shot her a calculating glance. "But this isn't court, is it?"

He rolled the mouse on the pad, clicked 'print' then rifled through the papers in front of him. Pulling one from the middle, he handed it to her. It was a duplicate of a digital photograph.

"That's our good friend, Lance doing a little business with William Gale," he said. She took the next two pages he waved in her face. With each line she read, her stomach sank a little lower.

Lance works for my father? She wanted to laugh at the irony and cry over the betrayal. Did he know she was his flesh and blood? His daughter?

It explained a lot. This was how Gale managed to stay one step ahead of her these past few weeks. Lance was tipping him off.

There were two pages worth of reported money transfers between Gale and Lance. She lifted her face and saw Auggie watching her. "The dates go back about thirteen weeks." Just about the time Gale kicked off his campaign.

"Must be hurting for funds."

"Maybe." Or was Lance here for more than the money? If he'd been hired to silence her he'd had plenty of opportunities.

She handed Auggie the papers and squeezed her temples with her thumb and forefinger, willing away the migraine that was forming. Was it time to quit? Time to give up the search for her mother and let someone else pursue Gale? He still wanted his money back. And maybe even her life. Giving up everything she wanted wasn't going to stop him.

"So, Lance was never a cop or special forces? How did we miss that?" She'd been completely fooled by some con artist for hire.

"No, no, no. I didn't say that. He is what he says and more, along with the credentials to back it up. But he's as dirty as they come."

She reached for his bottle of Tylenol, uncapped it, and popped two in her mouth. Auggie handed her his can of tea, and she washed them down.

She took another drink and shook her head. "I just can't believe it. Where did you get all this information?" For as good as Lance was supposed to be he wasn't covering his tracks very well.

"Computer forensics. Lance cleared out everything, but I hooked up with a pro—a former CIA agent, and he's the best there is at breaking encryption codes, hacking, you name it. This guy can resurrect the dead, including post-mortem emails."

He spun the computer so she had a better angle on the screen. He pointed at the fifth paragraph from the top. "Take a look. This has Lance linked with some real bad boys. Criminals that make Gale look like Mr. Rogers."

"You got all of this out of the computer in his office?" Lance couldn't be that sloppy.

"His home computer." He grinned. "And don't ask me how, because I would have to kill you."

She rested against the edge of the desk. "Have you confronted him?"

"No, and I'm not going to." He leaned back in his chair and spun it until they were face to face. "I don't want you saying anything either. Not yet."

"What about Mr. Baseel?" Had he shared this information with him?

Auggie shook his head. "I don't want Baseel to know anything either."

"What do you plan to do then? Nothing?" She thrust her arm up in the air and straightened, turning her frustration on him full force. "Why did you go digging around in his business if you were just going to roll over?"

"Calm down. You're getting all bent out of shape for nothing. I'm not rolling over. I've got someone watching him.

Baseel would fire him if he found out. And if you were thinking clearly you'd recognize the advantage of keeping him on."

"Sorry, but I don't see how this is a good thing."

He began to spell it out for her. "Palermo has a direct line to Gale. We can tap into his communications with him. If that doesn't get us what we need, it looks like he may or may not have a felony or two under his belt, and if we have to use a little police department muscle to convince him, we just might get him to cooperate."

He had it all neatly planned out, but he was the one who wasn't thinking clearly. "Those *felonies* as you call them are so vague no cop would touch it. And Lance would know that."

"They would if they want my Lakers' season tickets."

She snorted. "Who's dirty now?"

"Not dirty. Smart."

He could spin it any way he wanted to, but even she knew it was wrong. Besides, the way he went about getting the evidence against Lance was illegal. It couldn't be used. But then it wasn't Auggie's intention to have it sent to the prosecutor; he only planned to threaten him with it.

"And in the meantime?" she asked.

"Just go about your business like nothing has changed."

Jaida bobbed her head in a slow nod. She'd never done well at concealing her emotions. Not when it was personal. How could she come face to face with Lance and not let on that she knew?

She moved to leave then stopped and turned at the door. "I need the rest of the reports you have on the Hawn case."

He closed out the window, logged off, and shut the computer down. "I'll get them to you tomorrow. Don't forget this." He held out the invitation she'd left on his desk.

Safely closed inside her office, Jaida leaned back against the door. All the way down the hall she felt the ache she'd stifled making a slow ascent. The information Auggie unearthed on Lance stung her ego, but that would recover. It was Spencer's rejection that did her in. He held the power in his hands to crush her, and he didn't even know it. She blinked at the tears welling in her eyes. *I will not cry.*

She looked down at the envelope clutched in her fingers. Aimee was actually getting married. Jaida shook her head at the enormity of it all then tore through the seal and slid the postcard from the casing. It was a simple, but pretty card. A heart wreath of white daisies was centered on a pale yellow background. She held it to her nose. It was scented, and it smelled like a field of summer flowers. She'd never seen anything like it before.

The invitation instructed her to write down a piece of advice for the bride to be, the collective wisdom of the masses intended to insure a successful union. She was the last person who should be offering marital advice.

Fear and selfishness weren't quality traits in a spouse, and she possessed them both in excess. She supposed she could share what not to do in marriage. Don't be afraid of love, don't live your life with your guard up, and don't make the promise before God and the groom if you're going to break it. And don't have too much pride to admit when you're wrong.

"Sometimes we don't even know what it is that we want. Sometimes our strongest desires deceive even ourselves."

Lance the prophet. Of all people, he understood something about her that she didn't, and until ten seconds ago only God knew what it was that she really wanted.

Ask of Me.

She felt rather than heard the tender overture. Was it God? She closed her eyes, listening with her heart, hoping to hear the invitation just once more. Just to be sure. But with what she'd done, how could she ask Him for anything?

Ask of Me.

Jaida looked up at the skylight above her. Was it that simple? She wet her lips and swallowed. "I want to love my husband. If you're listening, God, please help me to love my husband."

She stood there a long moment looking up into the filtered sunlight, waiting for a transformation. But she was the same; nothing had changed. She chuckled to herself. What was she expecting, some dramatic conversion?

Her face flushed with heat, ashamed of her hope, and she quickly busied herself, marking the date and time of the bridal shower on her calendar. Aimee would make Eric a wonderful wife.

Jaida reached for a pen, and her hand brushed the budvase sitting on the edge of the desk, knocking it to the floor. She picked up the crystal tube and tossed the dried-up rose in the trashcan. She should have tied it with a ribbon and returned it to Lance. He'd used her to get at Gale's money, and the evidence. He was the one who took the tape. She was sure of it now.

She sat at her desk, sorted through the stack, and pulled the accident report on the Hawn case. It was an accident reconstruction. They'd been hired by the liable party to overturn the citation. It should be a quick job once she got the rest of the reports from Auggie.

She reviewed the witness statements. All five were consistent in the retelling with very minor discrepancies. That was rare. It was commonplace for differing perspectives to skew the facts.

Maybe that was why relationships faltered and fell like bloodied corpses by the wayside. Everyone approached the scene of their offenses with their own bias, their minds interpreting words and seeing things entirely different than the other person. Not false witnesses necessarily, but tainted witnesses. Tainted by a distorted worldview.

Hadn't she done the same? Insulated her heart and broken Spencer's, because in her mind her abandonment had defined her as unworthy; something meant to be discarded? She rubbed her forehead with her fingertips. There was no sense looking back. What was done was done.

Jaida looked up. The red light was blinking on her phone. She'd been so distracted she hadn't noticed. Maybe Ray had finally called. She pressed the 'play' button.

"It's me, Kev..." Not in the mood to deal with him, she deleted the message midsentence. Carina's silky, almost-bored tone followed the second beep. "Let's meet later. Call me." Jaida returned the call and scheduled a late dinner with her at a new mom-and-pop Italian restaurant not far from her house.

That was it. Kevin and Carina, nothing from Ray. She was beginning to wonder if she would ever hear from him again.

24

Jaida turned her left blinker on and pulled into the alley behind her house. The narrow street was lit well enough by the streetlights along the sides of the drive, but the windows on the backside of her house were dark.

She frowned at the blackened glass and touched the brake with her foot. Had the timer malfunctioned? It failed once before, when she first moved in, but that was before she'd become acquainted with Gale. Now it mattered.

She sat in the idling car in front of the garage, her hands wrapped tight around the wheel. Should she go inside? Marilyn warned her to be careful. But what more could she do? Her alarm was set, her lights were on a timer, and she had deadbolts installed on every door. If anyone got past that...

But what if that man had returned? The one Marilyn saw lurking around? Her heart pumped faster, the surge of adrenaline a keen blade that sharpened her senses, bringing her fully alert.

Jaida lowered the car window and scanned the grounds, watching and listening for anything out of the ordinary. The couple that lived in the gray single-story clapboard behind her was home. From the sounds and smells filtering through the screens, Dave was practicing scales and arpeggios on the drums, and Shelly was banging around the kitchen, cooking something tomato based for dinner, her silhouette visible from the window.

She could ask Dave to do a walk-through with her, make sure it was safe before he left her alone. He was tall and stocky, a former fullback for the UCLA Bruins; he could take care of himself…and her, if necessary, unless weapons were involved. She was unarmed, her Ruger stashed behind the phonebook in one of the kitchen drawers.

Her only experience handling a weapon was at the shooting range. She was precise, accurate. She didn't miss. But at the range, the targets were paper. They didn't bleed.

She was getting ahead of herself, assuming the worst. The timer probably failed, and in a few minutes she would walk inside and find out she was overreacting to some fluke, a simple mechanical glitch.

Jaida opened the garage and pulled inside then lowered the automatic door as soon as she hit the brakes. She fished the flashlight out of the glove box and tucked it under her arm.

She slung the strap of her purse over her shoulder and looked up at the house. It stood about fifteen feet from the garage. She sucked in a breath and hurried up the concrete walk, her cell phone and house keys clutched in her fist.

Inside, Jaida dropped her purse on the floor and kicked off her shoes. If she had to run, barefoot was easier than heels. She moved her hand blindly over the nubby plaster, feeling for the light switch. She flicked it up, and her stomach sank. *Nothing.* No light, not even the flicker and pop of a dying bulb.

She felt like the unsuspecting victim in a horror film. A ripple of fear licked up her spine, and she cast a longing glance at the door behind her. Now might be a good time to turn back.

Remembering the flashlight, she slid the switch on the shaft. It didn't light up. She shook it, the batteries rattling inside the case. "Great. All this technology, and here I stand in the dark."

She tightened her grip on the flashlight and took another step down the hall, the weight of the heavy-duty steel tugging against her wrist. It was durable, solid, and would do some damage to an intruder if there was one.

The electric bill! A nervous laugh bubbled from her throat. That was it. That was why the lights were out. She never paid it. The tension that drew her shoulders into a rigid line drained away. It made perfect sense. She remembered Carina sitting at the counter waving the notice around like a flag. Edison had never been that quick to turn it off in the past, but apparently they changed their policy.

There were utility candles and a box of matches in the pantry. Her steps more confident, she moved down the hallway toward the kitchen. She would pack a few things and crash at Carina's after dinner. Tomorrow morning she would take care of the bill and get the lights turned back on. It was inconvenient, but a simple fix.

The side of her foot brushed against something soft and unfamiliar as she swept down the hall. She paused and jerked it back, her toes curling on contact. *What was that?* She skirted the object then looked down at her feet, but it was too dark to make out the shape. Dirty laundry, maybe? She'd carried the basket down this morning. Had some fallen out?

The clouds shifted and the moon's white light split through the pitch turning it a hazy slate. She could see the outline of the dining table below the front window and the arc of the chair backs surrounding it.

Visibility was still restricted, but it was sufficient to orient herself and easily find her way into the kitchen. She set the cell phone, moist with sweat from her palm, on the counter then moved toward the pantry. Her knee slammed into something solid. The flashlight sailed from her hand and her body buckled. She tumbled to the floor, landing in a pile of pots and pans, the clanging steel splintering the eerie silence.

Someone *had* been here. Were they still? Whoever it was had emptied her cupboards, dumping the contents onto the floor. She rolled onto her knees, wincing at the fresh stab of pain then dragged the flat of her palm over the front of the drawers, counting. One, two, three… She pulled it open and slid her hand inside an empty drawer. Her gun was gone.

Was it among the debris? Jaida slid her hands over the tile, shoving pan lids and ladles out of her path as she went. Her fingertips grazed something light, the contact sending it skittering across the marble floor. She reached out and slapped blindly at it, pinning it down, recognizing the familiar feel and shape under her palm.

She sat back on her heels and ran her fingers over the weapon. She checked the clip. It was intact and loaded. She pushed up from the floor, released the safety, and turned enough to observe the stairs and hallway. She shifted her position again to view the living room, crying out when she glimpsed the destruction.

The gun trembled in her hands. She stepped out into the open, her eyes darting back and forth over the lower floor. She saw no movement, heard no sound.

Tables and lamps were overturned. She edged her way around them. Lumps of fiber from the couch cushions covered the area rug like a layer of fresh snow. That must have been what she'd brushed against in the hall.

She reached down, and gripping the rim, righted the lightweight table that was tipped on its side. As if it made a difference. Everything was ruined. Her collection of sculptures was smashed, and the shards of porcelain scattered across the tile. Something in the pit of her stomach sank. Priceless, irreplaceable art destroyed. Remembering that her feet were bare she backed away from the glass.

Jaida spun at the noise on the landing, turning her weapon on the open staircase. Her grip on the gun no steadier than before, she waited and watched, but darkness obscured the top steps where they rose and blended in with the shadowed landing. How could she shoot if she couldn't see?

She tightened her hold on the grip, her ears alert to any movement. She cocked her head. There it was again, the same rustling noise. Her stance eased, her fingers relaxing. It was only the palm branches brushing against the window in the spare room.

Strange how fear made the familiar alien, how the creaks of a settling house or the rustling of windblown branches were the sounds of an unseen enemy.

She stepped back behind the walls of the kitchen, away from the illuminating moonlight and picked up the phone, making a quick call to 911. After filling in the emergency dispatcher, she was told a squad car was already on its way.

Jaida disconnected and dialed Auggie. He answered on the first ring.

"Hey, what's up?"

"Someone trashed my house." She pressed a palm to her forehead, her voice taking on an unexpected quaver. "They destroyed it, even slit the cushions. They were looking for something."

"Did you call the police?"

She nodded though he couldn't see. "Yeah. They should be here soon."

He didn't ask what they were looking for. They both knew. All it would take to end this was a call to Spencer. She would request a loan; he would make it a gift. But it was the principle that kept her from asking. She didn't take Gale's money. She owed him nothing.

She heard a car door slam on Auggie's end. "I'm on my way," he said. "Stay on the line until I get there."

Her legs suddenly weak, Jaida rounded the kitchen wall and sank down on the single barstool left standing. She was so tired. Tired of fighting what she couldn't conquer, tired of trying to control what she had no power over. Her shoulders slumped and she wept softly, silently.

"Jaida? Are you there?"

"I'm here," she said. She hadn't meant to go quiet on him.

"Any sign of the police?"

In the distance, sirens wailed. "I can hear them." If it was for her they blared. "Thank you for coming out, Auggie."

"Did you think I wouldn't?"

"No, I knew you would. I just wanted you to know I appreciate it." She could always count on him.

"Have you been through the house? Made sure no one is still hanging around?"

"No, the lights don't work." Jaida slid off the barstool and flipped the switch in the dining room. The lights lit up instantly, making a liar out of her.

She looked up at the recessed lights in the kitchen. They were ripped from the sockets, gouged out eyes staring lifelessly at the floor. The hall light was probably in the same condition. Was it

Lance? Would he do this to her? Of course, he would. He was owned by Gale.

"A passbook," she muttered to herself.

"What?" Auggie's voice in her ear startled her.

"The lights in the ceiling are gutted. I think they were looking for a passbook. You know, for the money?"

She moved toward the hall to have a look at the damage then stopped cold at the lump on the floor. The light from the dining room spread only so far, but it must be what she'd grazed with her foot. It wasn't filler from the couch like she'd thought.

"No!" she cried, backing away.

"What's wrong? Is someone there?" Auggie's stricken voice shouted at her over the airwaves, but she couldn't answer.

"Jaida!"

"He killed it. I can't believe he killed it."

"Okay, now you're freaking me out, chica. Who killed what? What are you talking about?"

"A kitten. A stray I took in. He killed it and left it in my house." Its white fur was streaked with pink and red and matted to its body.

"Hang on. I'm almost there."

She turned away from it and moved back toward the dining room, toward the light. "I know who did this." And it wasn't Lance.

"Who?"

"I don't know his name, or why, but I know who did this," she repeated.

"Mind sharing it with me?" he asked, frustration seeping into his tone.

There was a knock at the front door. Flickering red and blue lights from a squad car on the side street flashed in the windows and streaked across the walls. "The police are here."

"I'm five minutes away," he said.

She hung up, set the phone on the dining table and rushed to open the door. Two male uniformed officers greeted her. One looked to be in his forties, his temples flecked with gray, and the other one was a good decade younger, his close-cropped black hair stark against his fair complexion.

"I'm Officer Reynolds," the older one said. "We got a call from this address, a break-in." He jabbed a thumb at the man beside him. "This is Officer Wilson."

Wilson gave an abrupt nod. Reynolds leaned to the right, tipping his head to peer inside. He scratched the side of his jaw, the sound of stubble scraping against his trimmed nails. "Somebody sure did a number on the place." His gaze swung from the house to her face. "Can we come in?"

"Oh, yes, of course," Jaida stepped back to let them in. "Sorry, I'm a little shook up."

"That's perfectly understandable, ma'am."

They cleared the threshold in two strides and the younger man let out a low whistle, meandering deeper into the living room. "Have any idea who might have done this?" He turned, eyeing her in a way that made her flush with guilt. Why? She hadn't done anything wrong.

Yes. No. What did she say? She had every physical trait, every minute detail etched in her mind. She could describe him to a sketch artist, but she had no name to give them. And how did she explain everything without sounding like some crazy woman?

"No," she said, deciding it was the best answer. Reynolds' face suddenly turned hard. What? Didn't he believe her?

Before she knew what was happening his hand clamped around her wrist and he jerked it up her back. She gasped, crying out for help. He yelled at her to be quiet then shoved her against the wall, her cheek smashing into the plaster.

What the...? "What are you doing?" Were these cops dirty? Were they even cops at all?

"What's this?" He yanked the gun from her hand and shoved it in her face where she could see it, her head still pressed to the wall.

Stupid, stupid; how could she be so stupid? She pressed her eyes closed, wincing when he jerked her arm further up her back, pain searing her shoulder. "It's mine," she said, her voice muffled against the wall.

"Is it now?" He pressed his weight against her, leaning his face close to hers. "What's your name?"

"Jaida Martin." *And you're cutting off my oxygen.* "I have a permit."

The other cop joined in. "Do you live here?"

"Yes." What did they think, that she staged this? Or worse, that she vandalized the house and did away with the real owner?

"I'm going to need some proof," he said.

And how was she supposed to provide proof with her face shoved into the wall? "Is this force necessary? You have the gun. This is all an honest mistake. If you'll just let me explain..."

"Where's your ID?"

"In my purse at the end of the hall."

"Wilson, go check it out."

"I know this looks bad, and I understand your alarm," she said. "But someone was in my house. I didn't even realize I was still holding the gun."

"Why were you hiding it behind your back?"

"Not hiding, holding. It wasn't a conscious choice, I just was that's all." Her argument sounded lame, even to her. But it was the truth.

The patio gate clanked shut. Auggie! He was here! Thank God! He would set these two straight.

Dressed in jeans and a tee shirt, he appeared in the foyer and took in the scene. "What's going on here?" he demanded. "What are you doing to her?"

Officer Reynolds barked at him to stay where he was, spittle spattering the side of her face. She had this guy good and scared, which didn't bode well for her.

Warm tears spilled down her cheeks and she laughed. She was hysterical and her untimely outburst earned her another painful body slam against the wall. Auggie was right. She was too much trouble, and without even trying. No wonder he wanted to marry her off.

"That's what we'd like to know. Your friend here planned to pull a gun on us."

"That's a lie!" she said.

"There's obviously been a mistake. If you let her go, I'm sure we can clear everything up in a satisfactory manner." Calm and professional, Auggie was handling this well, but then he wasn't the one being roughed up.

She heard Wilson's approach, his radio squawking. "This is her house all right, and she has a permit."

Reynolds was reluctant, she could sense his hesitation, but he eased away from her, his hand still tight around her wrist.

Wilson eyed Auggie. "Who are you, and what's your business with this woman?" Her wallet was still flung open in his hand. She wanted to reach for it, take what was hers, but she thought better of it.

"Name's Auggie Garcia." He flashed his identification and Wilson snatched it from him. "I'm head detective at Baseel Detective Agency, and Miss Martin here works for me."

Wilson looked it over and nodded at Reynolds, confirming his identity then handed it back. Reynolds released her then, his hand sliding from her wrist. "I don't take it lightly when I encounter a *victim* and they're concealing a loaded weapon."

"I didn't…"

He raised his hands silencing her. "I could take you in, press charges, but I'm going to let it go this time. I hope you learned something from this?"

She rubbed the raw skin at her wrist then nodded, holding her tongue, refraining from offering her side of it. If his scolding tone was the worst she endured for her gaffe, she was getting off easy.

"That your cat?" Wilson asked glancing in the direction of the slain animal.

Auggie left her side and reappeared with a chair from the dining room. He set it in the foyer where they stood. "Sit down," he said, nudging her arm.

She did as he asked, then shook her head in answer to Wilson's question. "It's a stray I took in. The owner came for it yesterday."

"If the owner already claimed it, why is it in your house?" Reynolds asked.

Jaida dropped her head to her hands. She wanted to scream that she didn't know why it was in her house. Wasn't it their job to find out?

Auggie touched her head lightly, his voice soft. "It's okay, Jaida. Just take a deep breath and tell them what happened."

It took every ounce of her strength to compose herself, but she managed to do it. She lifted her face and looked Reynolds in the eye. "I think the man who came for the kitten was the one who did this. I don't think that it really belonged to him." She started to tremble but her voice held steady. "He used it to get to me…to my house."

"And why would he want to do this, ma'am?"

She blinked, confused. "I don't know."

Wilson asked, "Any broken windows or busted locks?"

"I haven't checked," she said. There were no lights. At least she'd thought that at the time.

"Did he come to the front door?" Auggie asked, joining in the questioning.

She nodded.

He stepped around her and knelt in front of the open door, sliding his hands over the doorjamb. "No sign of forced entry," he said.

He squinted inside the latch opening. Then reached into his pants pocket, produced a small knife and flicked it open, using it to pry something out of the hole.

"This would be the point of entry," he announced, holding up a smooth piece of steel. It was small enough to hide in the socket but large enough to keep the door from sealing tight.

That was why the man had requested a glass of water. It gave him the opportunity to jam her lock. But her alarm should have notified her that the door wasn't latched.

Auggie dropped the first piece of evidence inside a small plastic bag. "It's probably too small to pick up a full print."

It was then that Jaida remembered the water glass she set aside. "That glass on the counter should have a clean set of his prints."

She stood and hurried to the kitchen, found the box of gallon-size Ziploc bags and handed him one. "He asked for a drink," she said. "He said he was thirsty."

He picked up the glass with a dishtowel and held it up to the dining room light. "Perfect." He slipped it inside the bag then sealed the top.

Wilson came down the stairs. "Whoever did this is long gone." He wrote something down on a pad glancing up at Jaida. "They were definitely looking for something. Any idea what?"

Auggie caught her eye, silencing anything she might have said with a slight shake of his head. She frowned.

"No. I have no idea what they were after." She looked back at Auggie who handed over the bagged glass to Reynolds. Why didn't he want them to know?

Auggie came up beside her. "Why don't you pack a bag and I'll book you a room? We'll sort through this mess in the morning."

She nodded and did as he asked. It was probably for the best.

25

It was a small hotel, privately owned, and tucked away at the end of a residential street. It was safe. That's the way Auggie described it. He turned from the counter handing her the key card then took the overnight bag she clutched in her hands.

"You're in room 125," he said then started down the hall, his swift stride leaving her in the dust.

She quickened her steps to keep up. "Where's the fire?" She looked up at him for an answer, but he only grunted.

Was he angry with her? He'd hardly said a word on the drive over. She supposed he had a right to be. She had interrupted his evening to bail her out of yet another mess.

The hall they tramped down was narrow, but the light-colored walls made it feel broader than it was. They edged closer to the wall, single file, allowing another couple to pass. She agreed to this too quickly she decided. She didn't need to hide out in a hotel.

"Take me home," she said.

"No." He shot her a quick glance then turned a staunch face forward.

"We both overreacted. Whoever it was that broke in isn't coming back."

"It's one night, Jaida. It won't kill you." Her bag banged against his shin. He lifted it up and stuffed it under his arm, muttering a curse. "Besides, I already dropped eighty bucks on the room."

"I'll pay you back," she argued. "I need a friend not a parent."

"What you need is some common sense."

What was with the insults? "What's bothering you?"

He snorted. "Are you serious? A butchered cat in your house, your furniture shredded by some maniac, and you ask what's bothering me?"

"It's more than that." She gripped his arm, but he shrugged her off. "Talk to me. Why are you so upset?"

"This is my fault." His throat worked. "If something happened to you…"

His fault? "You're not making sense. How is this your fault?"

His jaw hardened, but he didn't answer.

Whatever he was warring against was winning. If it would ease his mind, she would do as he asked. Like he said, one night wouldn't hurt her.

Tired, Jaida slowed down and followed a half step behind, past the ice machine, the vending machines. He stopped abruptly and dropped her bag in front of her door.

"Do *not* leave here. I'll be by in the morning and we'll go back to your place together."

She nodded. "Alright."

His face softened. "You gonna be okay?"

"I always am." She tipped her chin up. He chucked it, and she jerked it away.

Jaida watched him walk back the way they came, the usual swagger in his stride and his cocky demeanor were doused by something unseen. But whatever was troubling him, he wasn't sharing.

She turned and slid the card in the slot surprised he hadn't done that for her too. The light blinked green, and she pushed the door open.

"Home sweet home." She turned on the light, looked at the outdated furnishings and frowned. If a room could be called frumpy, it was.

Two double beds draped in brown bedspreads were along the wall to her right. She dropped her overnight bag and purse on the bed closest to the door. There was a clock and a lamp with an orange shade on the nightstand.

She turned on the television with the remote then tossed it on the bed and went into the bathroom. It was compact, but clean and smelled of disinfectant. She unwrapped a bar of complimentary soap and washed her face, then fetching her toothbrush and toothpaste from her bag, she brushed her teeth and swallowed two aspirins with a cup of tap water.

Jaida left the bathroom and turned on another light, her mind churning with haunting images of the dead kitten. Just how far would Gale take this?

She paced the worn carpet and then went to the window. Lifting the curtains, she looked out. The parking lot was only partially full. Auggie was gone. She told him that she was safe in her own home, but was she?

Maybe it was time to call Spencer and request his help. By tomorrow morning, she would have a cashier's check in her hand, and this would all end. She released the drapes, letting them fall back into place. The remedy was simple enough, but she still couldn't bring herself to do it.

She sank down on the edge of the bed and aimed the remote at the television, raising the volume. A man's face filled the screen, his scripted words urging her to call their toll-free number for a free credit report.

Numb, she slid her shoes off with her toes and scooted to the top of the mattress then leaned back against the pillows. The shock was just too much to process.

The window unit shuddered, the ancient appliance giving its all to keep the room cool. Fatigue pressed down on her eyelids, and they slid closed. The newscaster on TV reported on the storm damage over hurricane-force winds rising up out of the south.

She should say a prayer for the residents, for their safety. Her mother, Eva would have. They would have joined hands and lifted up their voices together. It seemed a lifetime ago that her heart was soft and her faith sincere. When she still believed that God was a God who answered.

When she packed her bag tonight, she came across the Bible Eva left for her. She'd brought it along, tucked it inside the bag, under her change of clothing.

She had kept it hidden away at the back of the closet shelf. Tonight was the first time she'd picked it up since her mom had passed, the first time she even came close to keeping the promise she had made to read it.

Jaida opened her eyes. Flecks of glitter sparkled in the popcorn ceiling. Her own pursuits had lost their sparkle and left her wanting. She rolled from the bed, dug the Bible out of her bag then lay back down with it, the pillows swallowing her up.

She flipped the book open. A frayed purple ribbon was caught in the crease. Had the page been marked for a purpose? She propped her knees up and balanced the book across them then began by reading the verses that were highlighted in yellow. She would read a few of them and be done with it, promise fulfilled.

"In You O Lord, I put my trust; Let me never be put to shame. Deliver me in Your righteousness, and cause me to escape."

Could she ever trust God as the psalmist did? Did she want to? She reread the verse a few times, memorizing the words and absorbing the meaning, then flipped the pages until she found more highlighted verses.

"Your close friends have set upon you and prevailed against you; Your feet have sunk in the mire. And they have turned away again."

What had her mom found in these lines that moved her to permanently mark them? Were they a glimpse of her struggles? Did they encourage her? Bring her hope when she had no hope?

Flimsy pages rustled beneath anxious fingertips. Verse after verse, line after line, Jaida read on, her motive shifting from keeping a promise to feeding a newfound hunger that gnawed at her soul.

The book of Ezekiel was riddled with highlighted verses, and notes were penned in blue ink along the margins. It must have held some significance.

"An Allegory of Unfaithful Jerusalem." Jaida skimmed the heading of the sixteenth chapter then read the sentences overlaid in yellow.

"But you trusted in your beauty and used your fame to become a prostitute. You lavished your favors on anyone who passed by and your beauty became his."

Tiny pricks stung her eyes and the words blurred. It was for Jerusalem, it was for her. It was for the unfaithful. It was for her.

She wanted to be wanted. But the men, the relationships, they were never enough. Want was shallow; love was deep, and she had settled for the lesser.

Truth rubbed like coarse salt at the raw spot alternately aching and soothing, cleansing the blackness and rousing small sparks of life to a soul that had been dead for too long. She wept. *God, please help me. Please forgive me.*

Jaida slid the Bible from her lap and pushed it away. This was too much, too fast. She needed to get out of here, needed some air to clear her head. She slipped her shoes on and reached for the key card, stopping abruptly when she saw the yellowed Scotch tape curling up at the edges inside the back cover of the Bible.

What was this? She wiped her eyes and dropped the key card on the table then picked up the Bible, curious at the envelope that was taped inside. She scraped a thumbnail over the edges of the peeling tape and pried it away from the lining. Inside was a handwritten letter. It was four pages long and addressed to her.

Before she'd read through the first page she was crying again. When her mother said the Bible held the truth, she wasn't just referring to the Scriptures.

26

Carina was sniffing around as though she was on the scent of something big, and it was making Auggie nervous. What did she know?

Close on his heels, she followed him down the concrete steps of his second-story studio to where his Expedition was parked at the curb. He twisted the crick from his neck and opened the car door. He had to get to Jaida before she did.

"Have you heard anything, anything at all?" she asked. "I'm worried. Jaida stood me up last night, and she's not answering her phone."

He gave her a sharp look. "I heard you five minutes ago when you asked me the first time."

"But you never answered me."

He offered just enough to quiet her. "She's fine," he said. "Rough night, that's all. She needed some time away."

She pressed her palms against the fender and leaned in. "You know where she is then."

"I didn't say that."

"But you do know don't you?"

For the first time since she came to his door asking about Jaida, he really looked at her. She was dressed down. The typical dark, tailored power suit she grilled her victims in was replaced with designer jeans and an orange knit shirt, the sleeves cut out at the shoulders.

"Not working today?" he asked.

Her laugh was low. "I'm not thrown off that easy. Now, where is she?"

It wouldn't serve either of them to engage her. Neither one would be satisfied with the results. He slid behind the wheel, closed the door, and started the engine. He half smiled at the look on Carina's face; the shock, dismay, and then the fury, her eyes lit up like two fiery coals.

She pounded her fist on the hood, yelling curses at him, the sound filtered by the sealed windows, but he read her lips loud and clear. "Tell me where she is!"

She ran to her car parked two vehicles down from his. He pulled out onto the street and hit the accelerator hard.

Jaida stood under the shade of the palm tree, her gaze fixed on the bronze marker at her feet. She finally got what she'd been fighting for, but with it came no triumph.

"I know her name. You left me her name." Tears swelled in Jaida's throat. *Sofia Carlisle was my mother.* She pressed her eyes closed long enough to stay the welling tears then opened them to look upon the name of Eva Victoria Payne, embossed in the burnished nameplate.

She had given her more than a name. The letter Eva left behind told the story of Jaida's premature birth and her hasty desertion. It was recorded in detail along with the particulars of Sofia's death.

She explained the need for secrecy; that it was necessary for Jaida's protection and that Sofia requested it. But in the end Eva wanted Jaida to know that her abandonment wasn't an act of rejection. It was an act of mercy.

How had Eva kept silent all those years?

Jaida knelt in the grass. The ground was cool and damp through the knees of her jeans. It was green, well watered by the groundskeeper over the dry days of summer. She was through digging into the sordid past of strangers. That's what they were. What they would always be.

The air was warm. The light breeze that ruffled through her hair filled her nostrils with the scent of earth and the fragrance of lilacs. She closed her eyes and thought of God, of Spencer, and of Eva. What she wouldn't give to have back all that she'd taken for granted, all that she'd rejected. But some mistakes couldn't be undone.

After offering a silent prayer, she rose and brushed the grass from her knees then struck out on the cobbled path toward the parking lot. Her phone rang, and she frowned at the number on the screen. His timing was epic.

"Hello," she said, her feet carrying her swiftly toward the car parked at the front of the lot.

"Hello to you. You look lovely today. So much like your mother. Except for the hair. Hers was dark and curly."

She was offended by his familiarity and angered by his flippancy. And how did he know what she looked like today? Jaida spun around, her eyes scanning the layout of the cemetery. Was he watching her? Her body shivered in the heat.

"What do you want?" She picked up the pace, fairly running to her car and then remembering how Sofia died, she stopped, slowly backing away, her heart pounding.

She looked around her and visually searched the vicinity. Where was he? Had he rigged her car too? Would she be trapped inside a molten furnace and burned beyond recognition with the turn of a key? There was no proof he was behind Sofia's untimely death, but sometimes you didn't need proof. You just knew.

"Have you considered my offer?" he asked.

"I know her name. Sofia Carlisle. She gave birth to me and then hid me from you." That's why she'd been hidden in the bushes. Not discarded as she once believed, but protected. Her own father would have ended her life before she drew her first breath, but Sofia fled, Gale's men hunting her down like an animal.

"Looks like I've lost my leverage."

"You never had any."

"Be that as it may, I'm still out a substantial amount of money because of you, and I will collect."

"Good luck on that." She backed further away from the car until she was at a safe distance then pressed the starter on the remote. She ducked her head and shoulders, cringing, waiting for the worst. But there was no explosion. She lifted her face. Still skeptical, she watched the car idle, listened to the soft hum coming from under the hood.

She thought again of Sofia and spoke without thinking. "You killed her, didn't you? You used a young girl, got her in trouble, and then disposed of the problem before the public could discover what kind of a man you really were."

His anger pulsed through the airwaves. "You think you have it all figured out, don't you?" His question was rhetorical, his sarcasm belying his innocence.

"Yes, I think I do," she said. Mother and child, her mother a minor, they were a threat to his budding political career. If he couldn't destroy the child, the mother would do. Take her out before she could talk, and no one would be the wiser.

The puzzle pieces were finally coming together, and she could see the picture more clearly. This was why he refused to reveal her name. It linked him to her, and ultimately to her death.

"I told you to leave the past alone." The malice in his tone made her skin prickle. She got in her car and locked the doors.

"I'm still coming after you," she said.

The smile in his voice was spine chilling. "I wouldn't expect anything less."

Auggie let the phone ring a few more times then hung up. Jaida must be in the shower. Better be in the shower.

The lab called this morning with the results. The fingerprints on the glass belonged to Terrence Black. He also picked up a couple of the man's prints from the light fixtures in her kitchen. The man was a two-bit thug who was likely on Gale's payroll.

At the next red light, he dug the wallet from his back pocket and fished out the card Spencer Gordon gave him. He held it up to the sunlight, memorized the number, and dialed.

Jaida would probably go off on him for involving the man, but she wasn't around to consult. Besides, he was her husband, and he had a right to know what was going on. He shook his head at that, still stunned by the new revelation. She hid her secrets well. Just like he did.

211

"Good morning, this is Seraph. You've reached the office of Mr. Spencer Gordon." The woman's words were concise and perfectly enunciated.

Auggie leaned forward in his seat. "Uh, yeah, yes, can I speak with Spencer Gordon?"

"Mr. Gordon stepped out for a moment. May I take your name and number?"

He reached for the business card he set on the console. No cell or alternate number was listed. "Yes, ma'am. Please have him call Auggie Garcia. Let him know I have some urgent information about a mutual friend."

Auggie shook his head at how hokey that sounded. It came off as clandestine, like some cheesy line out of a dime-store detective novel. He left his contact information, hoping the man remembered him then headed for the hotel. Jaida still wasn't answering, and he needed to know that she was right where he'd left her.

After leaving the cemetery, Jaida went back to the hotel and waited for Auggie. A half an hour later Ray called. He was ready to talk.

The address he gave her was on State Route 142, the house located somewhere in the canyon. She wrote the directions down and headed out, deciding against returning Auggie's messages until after she had what she wanted from Ray. She couldn't risk him trying to stop her.

Ray's terms were non-negotiable, and this time she would follow them to the letter. No wire, no police, just her and a promise for his protection.

She accelerated up the snaking incline, her tires hugging the centerline. A car shot past her on the other side of the two-lane highway. She slowed, searching for a tan house with the numbers 1902.

Gale believed himself to be invincible, but his days were numbered. She could forget about Ray, walk away and call a truce with Gale, but for Marcus Dennison and Sofia, she had to follow through. It wasn't just for their sakes. If she didn't do this, didn't stop Gale, she would be watching over her shoulder for the rest of her life.

Jaida slowed the car again, skimming the numbers on the houses. The fear that washed over her was unexpected. She tightened her grip on the wheel and shot a quick glance at her cell phone lying on the passenger seat. She could leave Auggie a message; give him the address where she could be found as a precaution. He didn't need to know she was meeting with Ray.

She picked up the phone. No signal. She lifted her foot from the gas pedal. She should have let someone know where she would be, but she couldn't turn back. Not now.

Thirty yards ahead the incline topped off. She started a slight descent and hit the brakes when she saw the house. She'd almost missed it. Two weeping willows blocked most of the tan stucco house. The black resin digits she memorized from the sheet of paper were barely visible, an overgrown hedge concealing the numbers.

She pulled into the gravel drive and shifted the car into park. The apprehension she felt only moments ago returned in full force. She picked up the phone again, but her hope that there might be even a weak signal here in the driveway was immediately doused when she looked at the screen.

From inside the safety of her car she contemplated the yard, the house. The property appeared to be abandoned. She reread the address and looked up at the numbers mounted on the pillar.

It was the right place. Ray said he would be waiting for her out front, but there was no sign of life. Had he backed out again?

Jaida turned the key off and waited a few minutes before she opened the door and climbed out. She tucked the keys in her palm. It cost her a small fortune in cab fare to pick her car up. But it was worth it. It was her only way out if this meeting went badly.

She made a quick study of her surroundings. The nearest house was about forty feet away from where she stood. She could see it well enough through the dense landscape. But would the occupants be able to see her or hear her if she found herself in trouble?

Here goes nothing. Jaida moved toward the porch, toward the front door obscured by shadow, and waded through the knee-deep grass. If he wouldn't come to her, she would go to him.

She knocked. Behind her, a car whizzed through the canyon. She raised her arm to knock again. With her fisted hand still cocked in the air, she froze. It was odd, the sensation that coursed through her, the limp limbs, the swaying of her body. She stumbled backward. She felt...so...strange.

A delayed pain registered in the back of her skull, and she winced. She jerked back. Darkness fell.

27

Jaida!" Auggie pounded his fist on the hotel room door until the side of his hand throbbed. Where was she?

He should have known better than to leave her alone, to trust her with the simple task of staying put. Why hadn't he brought her back to his place? He could have forfeited his bed and slept in the recliner.

He jogged down the hallway toward the front desk then reached over the counter and gripped the arm of the clerk before he could pick up the ringing phone. "The woman in room 125, did she check out?"

The man looked down at his arm where Auggie had latched onto it. He released him, and the clerk straightened. "I'm not allowed to give out that information, sir."

"I checked her in last night, I paid for the room. I think I'm entitled to know if she's still here."

He shook his head. "I'm sorry, but I can't give out that information."

Auggie reached in his back pocket, pulled out his wallet and flipped it open, flashing his identification. Not a cop, but close enough. He worked with the police department enough to be looked upon as an authority.

"She might be in trouble," he said.

His face blanched. "What kind of trouble?"

"I'm not at liberty to say."

"What do you want me to do?" he asked.

"For starters you can tell me if she checked out."

He tapped his fingers on the computer keys. "What was the room number?"

"125."

A couple more clicks and he said, "It shows the room is still occupied."

"I need to get inside. She isn't answering the door."

The clerk shook his head. "She might be sleeping or in the shower. I can't just walk in on a guest like that."

"You won't be walking in, I will." He stuffed the wallet back in his pocket.

The clerk stammered then slid the card across the counter. "If anyone asks, I had nothing to do with this."

Auggie went to the room and let himself inside. Jaida's bag sat unzipped on the bed she'd slept in, a white tee shirt and pink pajama pants were left in a pile on the pillow. She planned to come back.

He flicked on the bathroom light, looked inside then walked to the window. There was no sign of a struggle. He pushed the curtain back and noticed the diner across the parking lot. Had she gone for breakfast?

Her purse was gone, and she hadn't left her cell phone behind, why wasn't she answering? She knew he was coming for her. He moved to the laminate desk and picked up the notepad. No message, nothing.

The light caught the surface of the paper when he tossed the pad back down. He picked it up again and took a closer look, angling it under the desk lamp until he could make out the faint impressions left from the previous page. It appeared to be an address. It could be nothing, but then again it could be everything.

Using the pencil on the desk, he swept the lead over the center of the sheet in light strokes. It was an old grade school trick, but one that worked.

A street address took shape and Auggie examined the writing. He wasn't certain, but it could be Jaida's. He copied the data on the bottom of the sheet and tore it off. Rule number one: Leave no stone unturned.

28

Spencer hung up his suit jacket, sank into the leather desk chair, and sifted through the stack of messages in the bin.

Joan Garrett called requesting a meeting for new Seraph accounts. He tucked the slip of paper behind the rest, grinning at the next message. They would have to remove the panic button they installed at the Nixon's Beverly Hills estate. The owner, June Nixon, was a feisty ninety-year-old. She was setting off the alarm then timing how long it took EMS to arrive.

Spencer made a notation at the bottom of the form then set it in the box of outgoing documents. He hoped to have that kind of spunk when he got old.

He read the next name, tried to remember where he'd heard it before, and then sat up straight. "Auggie Garcia," he mumbled. The name, the face—they came back in a rush. What was this about a mutual friend? The only mutual friend they had was Jaida.

His heart slid to his stomach. He dialed the number and stood, slipping his arms into the sleeves of his suit jacket. Something was wrong.

Jaida lay curled up on her side, drifting in and out of consciousness. Pain pounded at the base of her skull, the internal violence sending the world spinning behind her eyelids.

She stirred, and her nerve endings screamed in agony. She let out a cry, but it was little more than a feeble whimper. A cold sweat broke out over her body. She was going to be sick. *Lie still. Don't move. Don't open your eyes.*

She drew in a long, slow breath. The air in the room was tainted with the musty scent of animals and stale urine. Where was she? She sensed movement. An animal? A person?

"Help." The plea croaked from her dry throat, and someone laughed. A man. Jaida cracked her eyes open. Pain crashed through her head, and she turned her face away from the light.

She was on the floor, but whose floor? And then she remembered. She was at the house in Carbon Canyon. She was supposed to meet Ray here.

He hovered over her. She could sense movement, feel the heat from his body. The scent of his woodsy cologne was familiar, triggering memories she couldn't quite grasp.

She opened her eyes again and tried to make out the face, but her vision was still too hazy.

She threw out a name. "Auggie?" Is that who it was? No, it couldn't be.

"Not as tough as I thought you were." She knew the voice. Knew it well. She squinted then blinked, willing her eyes to clear. Why couldn't she figure it out?

The man circled her. He lifted his foot and ground his heel into her raised shoulder, pressing it to the floor. She cried out for him to stop.

His foot slid from her shoulder and he stepped back. "You've been out for over an hour."

"Where is Ray?" she asked. What had they done with him?

He laughed and the sound hurt her head. "Your blonde is showing. Haven't you figured it out yet? I am Ray."

Her forehead bunched, her eyes strained, but her mind could not make the connection. This was not Ray. This was someone she knew, someone she had done more than converse with on the phone, but she just couldn't put the voice to a face.

She stared hard until the shadowy details of his features took on a shape she recognized as human, but the similarities ended there. The voice, the laugh, and now the face all came together, but the cruelty was incongruous with the eyes staring down at her. Was she delirious?

He squatted down beside her and spoke gently this time. "I need that money, Jaida." His fingers trailed the side of her face as if he held some affection for her, then he stood.

She closed her eyes again, listening to his footsteps, the creak of the floor as he moved away from her. When she opened them he was peering through the slats in the blinds. He straightened and pulled the cord, sealing up the gaps. What was he watching for? Was he expecting someone else?

He turned and gazed down at her. "I've tried to be nice, to handle this in a gentlemanly way, but I'm running out of time."

As if he were exercising the ordinary task of checking the tires on a car, he bent down and tested the duct tape banded in snug loops around her wrists then moved to her ankles.

He leaned over her with his palms pressed to his thighs, his green button-down shirt open at the collar. "For what it's worth, I did love you."

Tears streamed down her cheeks, and he brushed them away with his thumb. This wasn't love. Did he think she was crying over him?

"I have an errand to run," he said, "but don't you worry. I'll be back."

She raised her head and watched him walk out the door. Was he just going to leave her here? She closed her eyes and rolled to her back, wincing at the pain. It was lessening and her vision had improved, but what did it matter?

She'd seen his face. She could identify him; testify against him. And just like he said, he would be back. And when he got what he wanted, he would kill her.

"God is my refuge, a very present help in times of trouble." She meditated on the verse she'd learned as a child, preparing herself for the worst.

Auggie hit 'redial' on his phone and let it ring. Sweat curled a trail down his spine. He rolled down the car windows and let the hot air hit his face. The air conditioner picked a fine time to quit on him.

He hung up, hit 'redial' again, and two rings into the call the ringing stopped. He made a connection.

"Jaida, where the…" He bit back the oath. "Where are you?"

Harsh laughter, and then the phone went dead.

He had her.

Southbound traffic on the 101 was deadlocked, and Spencer was caught in the middle of it, his vehicle packed in like a sardine.

"Nothing is moving," he said into the receiver of his cell. If it didn't break soon, he would abandon the car and walk to the nearest exit.

The news of the vandalized house and Jaida's disappearance shook him to the core. If anything happened to her, he didn't know what he would do.

Auggie said, "I'm calling in some favors on my end.

By the time you get here, we should be ready to roll."

"Tell me why this man would take her?" What did he have to gain? Didn't the nature of his career demand that, at the very least, he be perceived as upright and law-abiding? Why would he risk that?

"Under my supervision, Jaida has been investigating Gale. It's her job, and this is one of the hazards," Auggie said.

"Well, since you explained it that way, I don't need to worry, do I?" he asked, unleashing the sarcasm. Why was this man so defensive? Was he normally this callous, this uncaring toward his subordinates?

"Look, I'm sorry. I know that sounded bad. I just meant..." He sighed. "I don't know what I meant. I'm afraid for her."

"That makes two of us."

The traffic still wasn't moving. Spencer pounded the steering wheel with the heel of his hand. *Get out of the way!*

His imagination ran wild, fear for her safety coloring his sanity. He dragged a hand over his eyes. *Lord, keep her safe, and show me where she is.*

"I blame myself," Auggie said. "I should have pulled her off of the case. I almost did, but it wouldn't have stopped him."

"You're sure he's the one who has her?"

"Probably not Gale himself, but one of his underlings."

Spencer leaned out the window, craning his neck. It was too early in the day for this kind of gridlock. Why weren't they

223

moving? As if in answer, red lights flashed in the distance. There was an accident, which meant he could be sitting here for hours. He needed to get off this freeway.

"George Rowan," Spencer said, more to himself than to Auggie.

"What's that?"

"I have to make a call." Spencer hung up. George owned and operated a private helicopter. If George had a clear schedule, he would contract his services to fly him to Fullerton Municipal Airport.

Vehicles closest to the off-ramps were exiting the freeway. The compacted traffic loosened enough for Spencer to edge into the lane to his right. He would be crowded out, or someone would show a little mercy and let him in.

He eased the car all the way into the next lane and took advantage of the narrow opening in the lane to the right of that. He punched the gas and squealed onto the exit.

If he had to drive the rest of the way in this madness, he would need to be strapped into a straitjacket by the time he got there.

29

Lance Palermo's cherry red Mustang was parked in the driveway of his rental, a two-bedroom, brick ranch home on a cul-de-sac. Auggie pulled in behind the car and parked him in.

He got out and looked inside the Mustang's windows then opened the front door, driver's side, and searched the interior. The car was empty. Not so much as a soda can or gas receipt. Freshly vacuumed too. Had he cleaned it out for a reason? He popped the trunk. It held a spare and jumper cables.

He closed the trunk then cleared the two concrete steps to the front porch in one leap. The windows were dark, the living room curtains drawn.

He tapped the brass knocker and the door swung open. Lance stood there clutching a briefcase in his left hand.

"Going somewhere?" Auggie asked.

"Very observant."

"You meeting up with William Gale?" Auggie flicked the collar of Lance's olive green shirt, his fingers grazing his chin. Lance jerked back, his mouth a hard line.

"I'm in a hurry," Lance said.

He moved toward the edge of the porch, and Auggie stepped in front of him. Chin to chin, nose to nose. "Where's Jaida?"

"What am I, her keeper?" Lance snapped his gum, slipped past Auggie, and descended the steps.

Auggie chased him down and grabbed his shoulder. Lance flung off the restraining arm and spun on him. "Back off."

"Not until you tell me where she is." It was déjà vu. Hadn't he just played this scene out with Carina? But in the reprise the roles were reversed. "Gale will get his money," Auggie said.

"With this bunch it's dangerous to make promises you can't keep. Besides, what's with all this white knight, hero stuff? She's a big girl, she can handle whatever she's in for."

Auggie's anger burned. He wanted to grab hold of Lance and give him a preview of what *he* was in for, but the neighbor on the other side of the street was watching their exchange. He couldn't afford to get hauled in right now.

Lance looked past him to the driveway where he'd parked him in. He smiled. "Nice try, by the way."

A black four-door sedan rolled up to the curb and Lance quickly climbed in the back. The driver turned his head on a thick neck, his eyes narrowed in silent warning.

Auggie watched him pull away with his key suspect. He would have followed, but Lance would be watching for it. He memorized then texted the plate number to Caleb Daniels. He would put a tail on them. One they wouldn't recognize.

She'd passed out again, or maybe she'd just fallen asleep. Jaida looked up at the ceiling. It sagged in the center, the paint a dull and dirty yellow from where the roof leaked.

"I'll be back." His promise rang in her ears. How long had it been since he left? In her current state, could she get herself out of this house and somewhere safe? Her senses had cleared enough to focus and think rationally, but physically...

Jaida worked her wrists, twisting and pulling against the thick gray tape. It would take something sharp to sever it, and the room she was in had no furnishings, no personal belongings, nothing she could use to free her hands.

She closed her eyes and pictured the layout of the front yard, the frontage along the road, and the house just west of this one. Making it to the road with her feet bound was a long shot, and being out in the open put her at risk if he should return before she hailed a passing car that was willing to stop.

But the neighboring residence might be doable. It was close enough, and once she passed a certain point it was concealed by foliage.

She braced her feet and right elbow on the floor and pushed herself upright. Her head throbbed from the shift in position, her eyes stung with tears, a reaction to the pain. What had he hit her with, a lead pipe?

She sat unmoving, waiting for the nausea to pass, then rolled to her knees and pushed up with her knuckles. She was on her feet. Blackness passed behind her eyes and her body swayed. There was nothing to grab onto to steady herself, but just when she thought she would topple over, the reeling subsided.

Thank You, God. The words were foreign of late, but strangely enough they came naturally. How long had it been since she'd given thanks for anything, or even recognized the provision, the help?

Blood channeled its way through her limbs, her veins on fire, the circulation reviving the deadened nerve endings. Mustering her strength, she hopped toward the wall, but the jarring movement set off another bout of pain. She dropped back down to the floor and crawled, inching along like a worm.

She'd made it as far as the hallway then went still. *A car.* She closed her eyes and listened, thanking God again when the rumbling engine faded away.

Jaida crawled to the edge of the kitchen tile, pulled herself up with the doorframe then sagged against it. There had to be a knife, a razorblade, something with a sharp edge that she could use.

She took stock of the galley kitchen. It had painted white cupboards and a pearl gray floor. There was a door on the far wall. It was adjacent to the side yard where a straight, unencumbered path led to the house next door. That would be her way out. Even if she had to crawl.

She hobbled to the gas stove built into the center of the counter. Maybe she could heat the tape, soften it enough to loosen it and pull free. She turned on the front burner. No gas, no flame. The utilities must be shut off.

The surfaces of the counters were bare save for an open ravioli can with the lid pried up. She leaned her elbows on the counter and dragged her body down the row of cabinets and drawers, searching through all of them. She slammed the last one shut. They were empty.

Time was running out. She could feel it. She cast a glance at the front door then looked back at the can. Why not?

Jaida dragged herself back to the front of the kitchen, pinched the steel rim between two fingers and slid down to the floor with it. The circle was jagged and sharp. Hopefully sharp enough to work through the tape.

She pinned the cylinder between her knees so that it wouldn't shift, centered the tape that met between her wrists over the makeshift blade and worked her hands back and forth.

The fibers thinned, weakening with each stroke until the layers began to snap and pull apart. She was almost through the thickness. Her movements quickened, and she bore down harder on the blade when the lid collapsed inside the can.

"No, no, no!" She tucked her fingernail between the can and the lid and pried it out.

A few more sweeping movements over the mock blade and her hands were free. She tore the tape from her wrists then went to work on her ankles. Startling at the crunch of gravel in the drive, the can lid slipped, slicing across her palm. She bit back a cry as blood ran down her arm.

The engine cut and a car door slammed. Her heart was pounding in her ears. *Focus. Concentrate. Just get the tape off your ankles, Jaida.* She worked frantically until the adhesive band split in two then she ripped the loose ends from her jeans.

God, please get me out of here!

She stood up prepared to flee, pausing at the sudden wave of dizziness. The lock on the front door rattled, and she turned. It was too late.

30

The chopper that carried Spencer had bypassed the accident and landed safely at Fullerton Airport.

Spencer gripped George's hand. "I can't begin to tell you how much I appreciate this"

"Oh, yes you can. I think you did that all the way here." He paused and the quirk of his lip slid into a serious line. "Spence, just go take care of business."

Spencer reached for his bag behind the seat and disembarked. In his mind, he was already sprinting across the blacktop, and his feet soon caught up. With his bag tucked under his arm, he darted toward the building.

He still had questions, a lot of them. And he wanted an answer on how many hours Jaida had been missing. From the particulars Auggie Garcia relayed, the window of time in which she could have been taken spanned from one to twelve hours. That was a broad range.

The more time that elapsed the harder she would be to find. He pushed away the peace God offered and clung to his fear like a drowning man. Where was his faith? His hope?

Spencer stood waiting outside the double glass doors in the no-parking zone. A black Expedition is what he was told to look for. Auggie would be picking him up. Beyond that, he came prepared to follow whatever plan the man had laid out. He hoped it was a good one.

A few minutes later the SUV pulled up beside him. The lock clicked and Spencer got in, dropping the bag at his feet. "Have you heard anything?" he asked then tugged the visor down.

"No, but I do have a lead I want to follow up on." Auggie circled the parking lot then pulled out onto Commonwealth Avenue.

"What kind of lead?" Spencer asked.

"I have an address. It might not be anything, but we should check it out." He scratched at his chin where day-old stubble was taking shape into a goatee then flipped on the turn signal. He was turning right.

"Address for what? A business, a house?" The location they were holding Jaida? The thought chilled him. Would they find her? When Spencer looked down at his watch, his hand was shaking.

"A vacant house in Carbon Canyon. I think Jaida may have written the directions down, possibly gone there."

Why a vacant property? That should raise some red flags. This couldn't be good. "You know a lot about this man, William Gale. What he's capable of, possibly his intentions." He didn't want to hear the answer, but he had to ask. "Is Jaida's life in danger?"

He watched Auggie's reaction. He was controlled, his expression neutral, but he observed the sudden tension that ran along his forearms to his hands knotted around the wheel.

"Possibly."

Spencer closed his eyes at the reply and said another silent prayer for her safety.

"Don't worry," Auggie said. "We'll find her."

But would they find her in time?

"You said you had some favors to call in?" Spencer questioned him, expecting him to elaborate. What favors, and what did that mean for Jaida?

"I've got the key suspect under surveillance, connections on the police force on alert, and a couple more irons in the fire."

Was this really happening? He should have kept her safe somehow, monitored her life from a distance. Wasn't that his area of expertise?

Auggie's phone played the theme song to Star Wars. He took the call and Spencer listened to his half of the conversation, memorizing what he'd heard. He said something about fingerprints, a parking lot, and an abandoned car.

Auggie hung up. "Jaida's car was found in the parking lot of the Brea Mall. No prints. It was wiped clean."

"What about her phone? Have you zeroed in on its location?"

He shook his head. "GPS isn't picking up the signal."

"This vacant house, is it the only thing we have to go on?"

He didn't answer.

Spencer loosened the knot on his tie then yanked it through the tunnel of his buttoned collar. "I'll take that as a 'yes'." He folded it in half and tucked it into his jacket pocket then reached for and unzipped the bag at his feet.

"We do have a tail on Palermo, but he's probably wise to us."

"*Lance* Palermo?" Spencer felt the familiar burn of jealousy. What did he have to do with this?

Auggie looked at him with more than a little surprise. "You know him?"

"You might say that," Spencer said, and then asked the obvious question. "Palermo works for Gale?"

"He does."

Jaida sure knew how to pick them. Spencer stared straight ahead. How could he love her and want to throttle her at the same time? He remembered the bag on his lap. He reached inside and pulled out a digital recorder, a cell phone, and the rest of his gear.

Auggie glanced over. "What's all that?"

"Just some tools of the spy trade." He managed a half smile and unplugged one of the cords.

"You're eavesdropping?" he asked. "How did you hack into her phone?"

"Simple code," Spencer said. "Not as James Bond as most people might think." He hit 'rewind' on the recorder then 'play.' "I've been recording any activity since I left Los Angeles."

Spencer glanced over at him. "Given your occupation, you should be familiar with this."

"I am, but if GPS can't trace it, what makes you think that'll pick anything up?"

Spencer held up a silencing hand. "Just listen."

After five minutes of dead air, Auggie gave him a sympathetic look. He held the speaker up to his ear and frowned. He wasn't skilled in this area. It was a curiosity, something he tinkered with. What made him think he could actually...

Spencer sat up straight and brought the recorder back to his ear. "Did you hear that?" There was a faint shuffling sound followed by white noise.

"I did."

Someone on the recording spoke. "Did you get it?" *Get what?* The sound was muffled. There was enough clarity to discern the words, but not the gender. Could be a man or a woman.

"Patience. I had an errand to run. I'm heading back in a few minutes." It was another voice, distinctly different in pitch, but still garbled too much to define.

Back where? That house?

"Do I need to hold your hand to make sure this is done right?" It was the first voice.

"I can handle her."

The conversation ended. Had the other one left, gone back to finish the job? There was no current activity. Spencer didn't like what he heard.

"We need to call the police now and get them to that house."

"Not yet." Auggie whipped the car around in a sharp U-turn. "You said this was taped?"

"Yeah. What we heard probably took place between now and just before you picked me up." Prior to that, he'd been listening in.

Spencer leaned forward, and Auggie looked over at him. "That's not gonna get us there any faster."

"I want the address to that house." If he had to, he would make the call to the police himself, but he needed to know where to send them.

"Just sit tight. We're going to that house ourselves. I need to make a quick stop at the office. I know someone who can help find her."

He didn't like the delay, but Spencer agreed. He would give him five minutes, and then he was taking matters into his own hands.

The stoplight turned red and Auggie sped through the intersection. "Can I ask you a personal question?"

"Sure," Spencer said, instantly regretting his heedless assent. Not wise when the question had yet to be posed. But then again, he hadn't committed to answering either.

Auggie shook his head. "I love Jaida," he said. Spencer gave him a dark look, and Auggie held up a hand. "Like a sister. I love her like a sister. She's one of my closest friends, but I know how she lives." Spencer knew where this was going, expected it sooner. "Why haven't you divorced her?"

He'd asked himself that same question a hundred times over, even made appointments with attorneys, only to cancel. He loved her. But it was God's love for her that kept him bound to her in spite of her infidelity.

His eyes turned to water. "Love suffers long, Garcia. Love suffers long."

31

From somewhere in the house, her captor raged, shouting obscenities loud enough to leave her quivering like a frail leaf in a violent wind.

The closet shelf was narrow and scarcely wide enough to accommodate her. The pine board she lay on was thin and weak, the center of it bowing under her weight. Jaida made herself small. Curled up on her side, knees bent, she tucked her chin tightly against her chest, praying the board wouldn't snap in two and drop her to the floor like a heap of bricks.

"I know you're in here, Jaida. And I *will* find you." He slammed what sounded like a fist into something hard, and against her will, her body jumped at the impact. She clutched at the edge of the drapes piled on top of her and fought the tremors that threatened to give her away.

Cupboard doors banged and another door slammed shut. She hunkered down deeper, pressing her back into the wall. If he did find her she had one advantage over him and that was her hiding place. The moment she sensed him near, she would lunge at his head and fell him to the floor.

"You know, they say that clothing makes the man, but what about the woman?" he yelled. Something else slammed then rattled. Was it the oven? "But you...you're the exception. I think you made the clothing that night you sat in the bar. It showed the world exactly what you are."

A prostitute. That's what he meant. It all made sense now, the reason he insisted she dress that way. Something inside of her withered with renewed shame.

"As far as the east is from the west." That was how far God had removed her sins from her last night. But it was another day, and the accusations he was making rang all too true.

Jaida swallowed, tasting the musty odor from the aged fabric that cloaked her. Was she kidding herself to consider her acts forgiven? No penance? No price? She knew the truth, had learned it as a child, but she also knew well the things she had done. The arrows of doubt hit their mark.

His threatening rants were a violent squall. He swore again, and the close proximity of his voice altered the rhythm of her heart. *God help me.*

He wanted the money. He wanted it badly. Bad enough to kill for it, and whether she had it or not, she was as good as dead.

She'd left blood behind on the kitchen floor. She had stanched it with the hem of her shirt. There shouldn't be a trail. But this house was small with few places to hide. If he really believed she hadn't escaped, he would find her, and it would be over.

She was suffocating in here. She gulped in the hot stale air, anxiety tingling her hands and feet. Beads of sweat trickled from her hairline and into her eyes. She blinked and then held perfectly still. The floorboard creaked. He was only a few feet away. Her muscles tensed, prepared to attack, prepared to flee.

Please don't let him find me.

As though mocking her request, the closet doors rattled, and Jaida imagined the horror of him jerking the curtain and peeling away her covering. She pressed her eyes closed, her trembling mouth moving in silent recitation. *"I will trust in the shelter of Your wings."*

She saw the image in her mind, God's protective wing forming a shadow over her. He was her shelter; not this closet, not these drapes, not anything else.

"Come on out, Jaida. Time to pay up." She could hear him breathing, see his shadowy visage through the loose weave of the fabric. He was close enough to reach up and yank her down.

Adrenaline surged, and she knew what she had to do. She would aim for his head and lunge, dropping him to the floor. Then she would gouge his eyes, and make her escape through the front door...if she didn't pass out first.

A phone trilled, and her heart jerked in her chest. His shadow thinned and disappeared. Jaida closed her eyes and breathed. He had left the room.

Spencer followed Auggie down the hall to a door on the right. It looked like every other door inside Baseel Detective Agency—hollow steel coated in blue paint. Auggie withdrew a small tool from his pocket, bent down and worked it inside the lock.

He looked up from where his head was level with the knob. "Jaida's office," he said, then pushed the door open. He stood.

"You're pretty good at that," Spencer said.

"I've learned a few skills in this business."

Auggie fetched the sweater draped over the back of her chair and tossed it to him. "Hold onto this." The white cashmere, soft and scented with Jaida's perfume, whipped against his chest and dropped to his hands.

"What's this for?"

"Just hang with me. I need to make a quick phone call. I have a connection that will tell us if she is or ever was at that house."

Spencer tossed the sweater over his shoulder. "Two minutes, Garcia." He held up two fingers to reiterate his point. "That's all I'm giving you."

"Yeah, I know." With that said, he disappeared into another office, one he had the key to.

Cell tracker in his hand, Spencer paced the hallway, listening for any new developments. He didn't like this waiting around.

"Can I help you with something?"

Spencer turned. A woman of about twenty-five, with reddish-blonde shoulder-length hair, sat at one of the desks.

He shook his head. "No, thank you. I'm just waiting on Mr. Garcia."

She laughed. "I know that's his name, but it sounds too serious for him. He's never been Mr. Garcia to me. It just doesn't suit him."

She stuck out her hand. Spencer looked down at the offering. Not up for the pretense, he hesitated, but manners won out and he took it.

"I'm Aimee," she said.

"Spencer Gordon." He engaged in the social game then slipped his hand away, burying it in his pocket.

He leaned to his right and peered inside the office Auggie was in. He was planted on the edge of a desk with the phone to his ear. Spencer urged him with a look to wrap it up. Couldn't he handle this while they drove?

A hand on his elbow, he turned. "Can I get you anything to drink? Coffee? Bottled water?" she asked.

He shook his head. "I'm fine, but thank you."

"There's a comfortable chair." She pointed to a waiting area just off the main lobby. "You can have a seat if you'd like."

Auggie strode up beside her and handed her a sheet of paper. She looked it over and nodded then smiled up at him. "Nice meeting you, Mr. Gordon."

"Same here."

They headed back out to the street where they'd parked. "I just talked to a friend. He owns trained search-and-rescue dogs." Spencer's hand tightened around the sweater, understanding now why he was holding it. "If she's in that house in the canyon or has been there, we'll know."

Auggie started the engine when someone tapped on his window. He rolled it down. A man, blond and in his early thirties stood there.

"Don't you answer your phone anymore?" he asked.

"What?" Auggie unclipped his cell from his belt, looked over the unit and swore. "It isn't working. When did you call?"

"About an hour ago."

"What do you have?"

"Nothing, but why did you have me following Palermo? He's one of us."

"Why aren't you following him now? You have someone else on him?"

The man shook his head. "No. Palermo spotted me, got out, and we had a few words. Figured you'd made a mistake. I tried to call you to see who I was supposed to be tailing, but I wasn't getting an answer."

Auggie spewed out a sentence in Spanish. The man shrugged. "Sorry, man. I didn't know. A little information goes a long way. You should have told me who it was. Have you heard from Jaida?"

"No. Phone's not working, remember?"

"So you think Palermo has something to do with her going missing?"

"Yeah, I do."

"Shows what I know. I thought this was over Gale's money."

"What money?" Spencer asked.

"I'll catch you later, Caleb." He shifted into drive and took off.

"I don't know what kind of game you're playing, Garcia, but this is my wife we're talking about, and I expect you to be forthcoming."

"All right. Long story short, eight and a half million dollars belonging to Gale, vanished from his accounts. Jaida was in possession of the account numbers at the time, and Gale accused her of taking it. That's why her house was ransacked. He was looking for it, looking for a bank book."

"Why did you lie to me?"

"I didn't lie. She was investigating him, and he took her. And that's what I told you. What difference does the money make?"

"I could have paid it. Put an end to all this." Why hadn't she come to him? Asked him for it? She knew he would take care of it...take care of her.

They drove a few miles east then pulled into a residential driveway where a two-story house sat on top of the rise. A man emerged from the side gate, a harnessed German shepherd at his side. Auggie threw the vehicle into park, hopped out, and opened the back door, ushering them inside.

"Spencer, this is Carl Brooks. Carl, Spencer Gordon." Auggie ran the introductions while he backed out of the drive.

"Good to know you, Spencer."

"Same here."

Carl stroked the thick fur around the shepherd's pointed ears. "This is my girl, Tobi."

Auggie took over and filled the man in on the details: where they were going, the potential danger involved, and the layout of the grounds.

"Carl has a hundred percent rescue rate." Auggie said it with a confidence Spencer hoped the man was worthy of. He looked over the team—man and dog—and wondered how many of those rescues were live ones and not just recoveries.

Carl said, "Actually, Tobi is the one with the skills. I just follow her lead."

Spencer didn't care which one of them was the lead or who took the credit. He just wanted Jaida found. Alive.

Spencer shifted to get a better look at Carl. "So, Carl, how exactly does this work?" He didn't want to dawdle over details and directions; he wanted to be prepared before they arrived, wanted to hit the ground running.

Carl slid to the center of the backseat and leaned forward. "Tobi is an air-scenting dog. She works off-lead, which means I direct her in a search pattern, and she sniffs the air to catch the scent we're looking for."

His hands moved rapidly, explaining as much as his words. "You see dogs can discern one particular odor in a sea of odors." His eyes dropped to Spencer's lap. "Is that the sweater Auggie mentioned?"

"It belongs to my wife, if that's what you're asking."

Carl's brows rose as he shot a surprised look at Auggie. Guess he must know Jaida too. The wife part managed to leave everyone who knew her dumbstruck.

"Can I see it?" Carl recovered admirably, bypassing the uncomfortable questions.

Spencer handed it back, and Carl held it out to the dog. "I can smell perfume on the sweater, but a trained dog will home in on the odor of skin cells that flake off the body, the scent enmeshed in the fibers. Skin cells float in the air and then fall to the ground, and once the dog knows the scent, she can track it."

"What about bloodhounds? I thought they were better for hunting down missing people," Auggie asked.

"That's a prime breed for picking up older scents, but since it's only been a matter of hours, Tobi can handle it."

Carl's passion for his work was evident, and he ran with the opportunity to share what he did in depth, but after his initial questions were answered, Spencer retreated into his own little world, Carl's raspy voice fading into a distant drone.

The day he told Jaida that he wanted her to love him, he was asking the impossible, and he knew it. Events of the past week had opened his eyes to the truth. And he was through waiting, done humiliating himself.

Love suffers long. Isn't that what he'd just told Auggie? The reason he'd given him for not divorcing Jaida? He might be labeled a hypocrite, but he knew when he'd been beaten. It was time to let her go.

He wouldn't stop searching until he found her, and when he did, he would set them both free.

32

He was a monster, not a man. In the aftermath of his tirade, a calm fell over the house. Jaida lowered the curtains from her face and breathed in the quiet.

The natural light in the room had dimmed, the sun reaching its peak some time ago. She pushed the covering to her waist then sat up. From prone to upright, a wave of dizziness assaulted her. Afraid to move another inch, the board under her bottom slouched even more at her centralized weight.

Everything around her was still. Was he in the house? She dumped the twisted pile of fabric to the floor, a cloud of dust rising on impact. She needed the bathroom. Needed it now. Slowly, softly, she slid from her perch and dropped to the floor without a sound.

At the end of the hall to her right, sunlight cut a wide swathe across the living room carpet where the front door had been left open. He didn't close it this time. Why? Was it a trap?

To the left was the bathroom. She darted inside, closed the door and locked it.

She turned a circle in the cramped space. A thin, yellowish flow of water trickled from the spigot on the sink. Her hand was bleeding again. She used the facilities then searched the mirrored cabinet for bandages. An empty prescription bottle and an uncapped tube of lip balm was all she found.

⤛⤜

The front tires of the Expedition rolled over the cracked lip of the entrance and bounced over the chunked cement. A thin layer of gravel covered the rest of the driveway.

The property was private. Cloistered by sweeping willow branches, dense boxwoods, and junipers left to grow wild, it was an ideal environment for detaining the unwilling.

The dollhouse-sized dwelling at the end of the drive stood alone, an outcast; its humble structure banished from the notable houses on the property's outer perimeter. Spencer had made a call to a realtor, confirming the house was vacant. It was a foreclosure on a single-acre parcel, but the name on the loan wasn't familiar to any of them.

Car doors opened. The posse exited the vehicle. Tobi strained against the leash, and Spencer fell in behind her, curbing his instinct to rush ahead. It was all on the animal now.

⤛⤜

Jaida stilled. He was back, and from the sound of it, he wasn't alone this time. Had he called in reinforcements?

The window was her only way out. There was no screen. She rolled open the privacy glass in the track, boosted herself up on the toilet and climbed out.

The front door was open. Auggie entered first. Weapon drawn, he announced his presence. But Tobi fought for first position with an urgency Spencer understood.

When there was no response from within, Auggie let the canine lead. The animal circled the living room, homing in on the center then followed the invisible trail of skin cells down a narrow hallway. His adrenaline spiked. She was here. Or had been.

Spencer started to follow then broke from the pack, checking out a coat closet at the front of the house then heading into the kitchen. His shoe hit the side of an empty can, the hollow tin ringing out as it tumbled over the tile. He looked down at his feet. *Duct tape.* Two half circles of layered duct tape were discarded on the kitchen floor.

He picked them up, looked over the side with the adhesive then walked to the window and held them up to the light. A thin layer of blue lint coated one of the bands; fine blonde hair on the other, with a crimson stain. *Blood?*

"Hey, Auggie," he yelled, fear doing a number on his heart. He was no detective, but even to the layman, it was clear that the tape was used to lash hands and feet. Jaida's? But where was she now?

He spotted two stains on the floor similar in color to the one on the tape. Spencer bent and pressed his finger into the center of the larger one. It came away wet.

"You find something?"

Spencer stood and held out his stained finger. "Blood."

Auggie grabbed his wrist and looked for himself. "Where did it come from?"

"The floor, this." Spencer held up the duct tape.

Auggie swiped a hand over his mouth. "We're closing in," he said. "Tobi is picking up a strong scent at the back of the house."

They may be closing in, but what were they going to find?

Carl joined them in the kitchen, Tobi at his side. "Looks like our girl slipped out the bathroom window."

———

Jaida stood at the front door of the adjacent house and jiggled the button on the doorbell. It was stuck, jammed in the socket. She knocked on the door and then the window. *Please, please, let me in!*

Inside, the television blared. She cupped her hands on the window and looked through the layer of sheers. A table lamp lit up the far corner of the room, and beside the table was a man slumped down in the recliner, asleep. She tapped on the glass again. *Wake up! Please!*

He didn't rise, didn't so much as flinch. She could smash in the front window with a rock. That would wake him. He would call the police, report her vandalism, and she would be safe. But the commotion would alert more than the sleeping man, and she knew it wouldn't be the police that got to her first.

Jaida kept out of sight, her body pressed close to the house. She looked to the tree line that separated the two properties and pressed her eyes closed against the sudden sting of tears. What was she doing out here playing hide-and-seek with a lunatic? She pounded on the door this time then shook the knob. "Let me in!"

It was useless. He wasn't going to hear her.

She tripped and nearly fell as she scurried around the far side of the house to the back deck. It was two steps up, a rectangle constructed from redwood planks. Jaida tried the sliding glass door and the two windows that ran along the back wall, but they were locked…all of them.

She turned at the unsettling sounds of rustling and the whispers of movement all around her. Fear played tricks on her eyes—his face was hidden in the collage of leaves, and then it was gone. He was out there watching, waiting for her.

She scanned the grove of trees at the back of the lot. She was trapped. Where could she go for help? She looked out toward the canyon then back at the house she'd fled. There was no safe place.

"Under the shadow of your wing…" No safe place but there.

Voices carried from the house next door. They grew louder, closer. Jaida ran. Hurtling the steps of the deck, she stumbled in the dirt, caught herself with an outstretched hand and sprinted into the canyon.

"Into the canyon and out to the road," she said, repeating her plans like a mantra. Her legs flew in long, unsteady strides over uneven ground, carrying her deeper into the canyon.

A fresh spate of blood rolled from her palm and dripped from her fingertips. Her head throbbed. Somewhere behind her a dog barked, but she didn't stop, didn't look back.

33

Spencer stood in the center of the yard feeling utterly lost. He intended to go after Jaida, but which way should he go? How long had it been since she left? Was her exit made by force, or had she slipped from captivity unseen?

Carl exited the front door, the leash wrapped around his wrist. The dog leading, the two of them took a turn around the house, Jaida's sweater still bunched up in Carl's hand.

Auggie came to stand beside Spencer. "I know this is hard on you, but we'll find her. If she did go out the window, it's likely that she got away. She might be on her way home right now or headed to the police department."

Spencer shook his head and walked away. He didn't need a pep talk he needed results. He unclipped his cell phone and looked at the screen. The signal was weak. He dialed Jaida's home number and then her cell. There was no answer.

He snapped the phone back in the holder and headed into the backyard of the house next door where Tobi was going wild.

Jaida scampered up the jagged incline, sucking the hot, dusty air into her lungs then skidded down the other side. She ran her tongue over her lips, tasting the gritty film and swallowing against a parched throat. Two miles deeper and she would be at the end of the canyon. Her limbs were like Jell-O, and her lungs were on fire, but she pushed harder.

Somewhere behind her, the dog still barked. She cast a quick glance over her shoulder. Did her attacker see her run? Had he followed? The stitch in her side slowed her down. She needed to stop. Just for a little while. Up ahead was a hollow. Not a cave, but there was enough of a depression in the hillside that it would conceal her.

She ducked inside the cleft and sank to the ground, her eyes instantly closing. *Please show me the best way out, God.* She reached up and felt the back of her head, wincing at the tender lump. It was the size of a golf ball.

Her time of rest expired, Jaida sat up and leaned forward, looking over the topography of the canyon. She could continue on as she planned or head for the road now. But that might put her out in the open too soon.

If she chose the road, then it made sense to wait until traffic was the thickest. Judging by the light of the sky, in a couple of hours it would be rush hour, and vehicles would clog the two-lane highway from end to end.

She pushed up from the ground, teetered then regained her balance. Two hours was too long to wait. She would go now.

Spencer stood at the top of the rise and looked over the canyon. Below him to the left, a stream of blonde hair whipping in the breeze caught his eye.

She's alive. "Jaida!" he yelled then scrabbled down the hill. The soles of his shoes offered no traction, and he slid, struggling to keep his footing.

Behind, Tobi was closing in. Spencer didn't stop for Carl and Auggie. He wasn't about to let Jaida out of his sight.

※

Her name carried over the open air, breaking up as it tumbled down the hilltop. He was right behind her. Jaida ran. No longer into the canyon, but out to the road.

※

"Jaida!" Spencer called after her again, but she didn't stop. His shoes an impediment, he took them off and leapt across the rifts of packed dirt, running at a speed beyond his ability.

He punched the air with his fists, propelling himself over the next hilltop and down into the gully. She was staggering, her pace slowing, and he was closing in from behind.

He ran faster, the gap between them forty feet, then thirty, twenty, ten. "Jaida!" He reached out and grabbed her shoulder. She stumbled back into his arms, and he wrapped them around her.

She writhed and kicked. "Let go of me! Let go of me!" she screamed. One hand slipped free, and she slapped at his face, her nail catching his jaw.

Spencer caught her free arm at the wrist. "Stop. Jaida, it's me. Stop it."

She looked up at him. Her face was splotched red from the heat and smudged with dirt. Confusion clouded her eyes. He drew his arms tighter around her as she crumpled against his chest. Her keening cry rippled through the air and tore at his heart. What had this man done to her?

"You're safe now," he said. He held her close and pressed his lips to the side of her brow, easing her trembling.

It was a slow, irrational tumble he took, falling prey to his longing. He closed his eyes. *I can't do this. Not again.* He held fast to her, kept her braced upright, but in his heart, he'd opened his hands, stepped back, and let her go.

A scuffling sound came from the hill. Spencer looked up. Auggie jogged a crooked path down the incline then leapt over a short row of scrubby growth. Carl and Tobi were beside him, the shepherd barking, recognizing the find.

"She all right?" Auggie asked. Carl gave Jaida's arm a light squeeze for reassurance.

"I think so." But who was he to say? She needed to be checked out by a doctor or an EMT, someone who could evaluate her physically and emotionally.

Her fingers dug deep into his back when Auggie laid a gentle hand on her head. "I'll take care of this, chica, don't you worry. Gale and his boys are going down."

She raised her head the slightest bit. "But it..."

He shushed her. "Let's get you out of here then we'll talk."

"Can you bring your car around to the edge of the canyon?" Spencer asked. It was a shorter distance and the terrain less challenging to cross.

"I'm on it," Auggie said then took to the hills, back the way he came.

"I'll stick with you," Carl said. "Probably not a good idea to leave you two alone out here." He sat down on the flat of a large rock and massaged the shepherd's head, fishing a treat out of his pocket for the hero.

"Thank you," Spencer said. "Not just for staying, but for finding her." He'd had his doubts.

A half smile lifted the corner of Carl's mouth. "I'm just glad it turned out well."

Jaida loosened her hold on him and drew back. Her flushed skin had paled, but her eyes shone with gratitude. She looked meek, fragile, almost breakable.

"How did you know?" she asked. A bruised reed, she swayed. He reached out and gripped her hand, steadying her.

"Auggie called me and told me what was happening. Said he found an address in your hotel room."

"And you came," she said, her tone matter of fact rather than surprise.

"Of course."

She shook her head and lowered her gaze until she was staring at the ground. "Thank you," she said. She was different, almost shy with him.

"What happened to your shoes?" she asked.

Spencer looked down at his dusty socks then smiled up at her. "They weren't made for running."

Neither was she, only she realized it too late. Would he give her another chance if she asked?

"I know who my mother is," she said.

He stiffened, withdrawing from her as if her quest to learn of her parentage was what had destroyed them and ruined her. Ultimately she bore the blame. It was her failing, her transgression, and no one else's.

"Was it worth it?" he asked. "Did it fill that void?" His tone was sharp, honed by years of hurt and anger she had caused.

"No. But I know who I am now. And it isn't Sofia Carlisle's and William Gale's daughter." She belonged to God. And if Spencer still wanted her...

She could feel Carl's eyes on her, sense his shock at her announcement as clearly as she saw Spencer's jaw go slack. She half smiled at their reaction, but there was no pleasure behind it.

"Yes, William Gale is my father," she said. It was a confession of sorts, and a truth she'd just as soon forget.

Jaida wanted to say more, but movement near the road captured her attention. *What in the world?*

"Carina?" Carina was entering the canyon, descending the slope at an angle, her ankles wobbling in shoes too high to be trekking through the brush. What was she doing out here? How had she found them?

Carl asked, "Where did you come from?"

"I'm parked up on the road," Carina said. "Auggie told me where you were." Carina rushed at her then and threw her arms around her. Jaida staggered backward at the impact. "I was so worried about you. You didn't show up at the restaurant, you didn't call."

"I don't understand. Is Auggie coming back?" Spencer asked.

"He had a call," Carina said. "He'll be by to pick you and Carl up. He should be just a few minutes behind me."

Carina turned to her. "He asked me to take you to the emergency room." She pressed a hand to Jaida's back urging her forward. "He had me in a panic until he explained you were fine and just needed a once-over by a doctor."

Jaida dug in her heels. "I am fine. I don't need to see a doctor."

"You heard the lady. Do as she said." The familiar voice silenced her and sent her heart slamming against her ribs.

He was about five feet behind her to the right. Jaida turned. The hammer of his pistol was raised; his finger on the trigger, and it was aimed at the center of her head.

"Who is this?" Spencer stepped in front of Jaida, shielding her. The moment was surreal, a scene from a movie, a clip from the news, but it didn't translate as cogently to real life.

He brushed his hand across the surface of his cell phone clipped to his belt, and prayed he still had a signal.

"His name is Kevin," Jaida said. He could hear her swallow, feel her fear.

Sensing danger, Tobi hunched down and growled, ready to spring. Kevin swung his foot at the dog. "Shut that thing up, or I'll do it for you."

Spencer watched as Carl knelt down beside the animal, soothing her with a soft command, then suddenly and without warning Carl swung around and went for the gun. But Kevin was ready for him. He brought the handle down on the back of Carl's head, knocking him unconscious.

Jaida cried out, and Tobi let loose a throaty bark, unleashing her distress over the form of her prone master. Spencer took advantage of the split second of chaos, did a half-turn to his right and lunged at Kevin.

He didn't hear the sonic crack until it was too late. The bullets came in succession: *bam, bam*. His body jerked, and he felt the blows like a ball bat to the chest, the impact hurling him to the ground. A crimson stain spread across the left breast of his white shirt.

"No!" Jaida screamed. Kevin laughed. Both sounds faded in and out like bad reception. His left lung squeezed. Was this what it felt like to die?

A shadow hovered above him lording over the kill. "There is a time for daring and a time for caution, and a wise man knows which is called for."

34

Blood pumped from Spencer's torso. "What have you done?" Jaida cried.

She dropped to her knees and squeezed his fingers. They were clammy, his breathing shallow. His skin was losing its color, his lips pulled tight with pain. Were the physical changes shock or a prelude to his death?

"Don't die Spencer. Please, hold on." She had so much to say, beginning with 'I'm sorry.'

Carina slowly backed away. "You shouldn't have shot him, Kevin. We need to get out of here now."

"Just shut up! I need to think!"

Was Carina involved? "You're a part of this, Carina?" Jaida's head whipped back. She heard the crack of Kevin's knuckles against the side of her face, felt each raised angular knob of bone digging into her muscle and jaw.

He leaned down and got in her face. "This is your fault. You shouldn't have run." Marble hard, his eyes burned with hatred for her. This wasn't the Kevin she knew. This was an animal. His timidity, his concern for her had all been an act.

Jaida stared back with equal loathing then reached for Spencer, pressing the heel of her hand into the worst of the two wounds. With every beat of his heart, a warm gush seeped through her fingers, his drenched shirt clinging to his chest. How long before there was nothing left in his veins to sustain him?

His lungs rattled when he inhaled and the last trace of color in his cheeks drained away. She was losing him. "Carina, please get help," she begged.

"Get away from him." Kevin grabbed her by the arm and jerked her to her feet.

Only a few feet away, Carl was coming to. He groaned and pushed to his knees. Kevin spun and shoving her aside, he aimed the gun at Carl.

Carl raised his hands. "Put the gun down, son. You don't want to kill anyone."

Carina shouted, "You can't do this! You can't just shoot everyone!" She paced like a caged animal. "This wasn't supposed to happen."

Jaida rushed back to Spencer's side. Again she applied pressure to the wound. He was fading fast. What if he didn't make it? *But he had to.* "Carina, please, you can make this right. Just go get help."

A legion of screaming sirens drowned out the rest of her plea. Lights flashed, car doors slammed, and orders were barked. The ground pulsed with pounding feet. Weapons drawn, law enforcement barreled down the hillside. Auggie stumbled behind.

An ambulance was parked at the top of the bank. "Help is coming, Spencer. Stay with me. Please." She pressed a kiss to his forehead. "I love you." Tears came so hard now she couldn't see the face that was only inches from her own.

"What's going on? What happened?" Auggie's questions were muffled by the commotion. He stood there in the hub of the fray looking bewildered. But what answer could she give him when she was confused herself?

Kevin ran, and Carl chased after him.

Jaida sensed someone beside her and glanced up. *Carina.* Carina knelt down in the dirt. There was humility in the penitent pose, but it went no deeper than her hunched form.

"I swear, this was all Kevin's doing, you have to believe me," she said.

Jaida kept her eyes fixed on Spencer. She couldn't look at the woman, couldn't bear the sight of her. They had set her up. She could see it clearly now, understood what was behind the push for a relationship with Kevin and his offer to assist her with her finances. It was always about the money.

"I came for you. I could have left you, but I came to take you to the hospital." She grabbed Jaida's arm and clung. "You'll tell them that won't you? You have to tell them."

Mercy, absolution, a get-out-of-jail-free card, Carina wanted it all, including Gale's eight and a half million dollars.

"You came after me because you thought I had the money. Just leave." Spencer was her concern, not Carina's guilt or innocence.

A policeman approached, his uniform thick with dust. He asked about Spencer then yelled for a paramedic. From a distance she saw Carl point at Carina, and within seconds handcuffs clicked shut around her wrists.

Carina shrieked. "I am a prosecutor!"

"Then you should already know your rights, ma'am, but I'll give them to you anyway." Carina dug her feet in, but the policeman dragged her. Soon she would be sitting in the back of a police car. "You have the right to remain silent…"

"Tell him, Jaida. Tell him I tried to help you," Carina yelled over her shoulder.

"Anything you say can and will be used against you in a court of law."

Paramedics swooped in and surrounded Spencer. Skilled hands worked quickly to plug the holes in his chest. Though barely responsive, they asked him a question, checked his pulse, and slid an oxygen mask over his head. Everything around her instantly fell away. All that mattered was right here in front of her. She couldn't lose it. Not now.

Someone tugged at her arm. "Leave me alone."

"Let the paramedics do their job, chica. It'll be okay. You'll see."

She stood, dodging Auggie's awaiting arms. She didn't want to hear his promises or be comforted until she relaxed into a false sense of wellbeing. He wasn't God. He couldn't guarantee her anything.

She touched the arm of a policeman, and he turned. "Who called you? How did you know what was happening?" There were no houses near enough to witness the violence and call for help.

He held up a cell phone. "This has a panic button that accesses emergency assistance. Someone pressed it, and it alerted the authorities to the situation. It was also kept live, so everything that was happening was heard. We found it on the injured man."

Spencer's actions had saved everyone, but him. If only they had arrived before he was shot. She watched as they strapped him to the stretcher and lifted him up. Their steps swift and sure, they carried him toward the waiting ambulance.

"Wait!" Jaida ran after them. When she caught up, she kept pace alongside the stretcher. *I won't leave you, Spencer. Not this time.*

She followed them up the embankment where they secured him in the ambulance. The doors slammed shut. "Can't I ride with him?" she asked.

"Too serious. Follow in another vehicle." The driver rattled off the hospital as he climbed in, the sirens already blaring.

Spencer shouldn't have come. This should not have happened. Not to him. She felt Auggie come up beside her. "How did he get in the middle of this?" she asked.

"I'm not sure myself," he said. "But no matter what happens, you need to know that this is what he wanted."

"He wanted to die?" She wrapped herself in her arms, holding in the pain.

He looked at her as if she were slow on the uptake. "For you? Yes."

She closed her eyes, the earlier pain that pummeled her skull had returned. Or maybe she'd slowed down enough to feel it. He shouldn't want to die for her. Shouldn't have to.

The officer she spoke with earlier approached, peppering her with questions for his report. The area had thinned out with only a few stragglers working around the crime scene. Carl was with them.

"I can't do this now," she said. "I need to go. I have to be with my husband." *Husband.* It had been too long since she'd referred to Spencer as her husband. She turned to Auggie. "Will you take me to the hospital?"

En route to his vehicle parked thirty yards ahead, Auggie said, "Now is not the best time to tell you this, but under the circumstances it's wrong to keep it from you."

Jaida shook her head. Whatever he had to say, she didn't want to hear it. No more grim news. No more Jerry Springer-like surprises. "Not now," she said. "Just take me to Spencer."

35

The hospital waiting room was full, the cloying air tinged with the smell of sweat and fear. The room reached legal capacity an hour ago, but family and friends waiting to learn the fate of their loved ones continued to trickle in. Must have been an accident.

Jaida sat slumped in a vinyl chair, her eyes fixed on the clock above the door. The hands had channeled around twice since she arrived and still no word on Spencer's condition.

He'd been rushed to the operating room on arrival, but the nurse she spoke with offered little more than vague replies to her concerns.

"Has he lost too much blood?"

"Probably."

"Is he strong enough to be operated on?"

"We'll find out."

"Will he live?"

"No one can say."

What *did* they know? And what was taking so long? Auggie remained beside her, a sentry standing watch, his back pressed to the wall.

She pushed herself upright in the chair, stretching the stiffness from her spine. "You don't have to stay. I'll be all right."

He stuffed his hands in his pockets. "Yeah, I've heard that one before."

Jaida slumped back down. She shouldn't have left that hotel room. She studied the clasped hands resting in her lap. Dried the shade of Indian clay, Spencer's blood lined the tips of her fingernails. She'd scrubbed them at the bathroom sink until they were nearly raw, but her guilt still marked her.

If she hadn't ventured out on her own, none of them would be here right now. She turned her hands over and gently pressed a finger against the gash from the can. Raw and bruised, it ran the length of her palm, but the blood had congealed.

"You should have that looked at," Auggie said.

She shook her head. "Not now." When she told him about the blow she'd taken to the head he insisted she be examined. She'd already had her head probed, tests done, and a CT scan. She wasn't up for anymore examinations.

Jaida closed her fingers over her palm, hiding the laceration in the center of her fist. Besides, what did it matter if her hand rotted to the bone and fell off? There were holes in Spencer's chest, and he was dying.

Fear seized her at the thought of losing him. She squeezed her eyes shut. *Please, God, don't let him die.*

Auggie touched her shoulder. "Go ahead and cry. You'll feel better if you let it out."

She shook her head. "He's been in there a long time." How much longer could it take?

Across from her a young woman's eyes welled with tears before she broke down and wept. The man with her wrapped his arm around her and led her out into the hall.

The only reprieve from the somber atmosphere was the random bursts of childish laughter from the two toddlers playing in the corner. The sullen mood was broken long enough to breathe in hope, but that hope evaporated before she exhaled.

She dropped her head back against the wall, and rested her eyes. She should pray, but she was at a loss. How many more times and ways could she beg God to let Spencer survive?

"You're dirty."

Jaida opened her eyes. Standing in front of her was a child, her round face scrunched up, her green eyes narrowed.

"I guess I am," she said then sat up and smoothed her rumpled shirt.

A rail-thin woman with fine pale curls swept the little girl away, apology in her face. "I'm so sorry."

If it didn't hurt so much right now she would laugh. "Whatever smart remark you have lurking around in your brain, I don't want to hear it."

When Auggie didn't respond, she rolled her head to the side and looked up at him. No humor curled the corners of his lips as she anticipated.

"Why don't you go wash up?" he said. "There's a bathroom down that hall." He jerked his thumb toward the door and to the right.

What if the doctor came while she was gone? She couldn't leave. Not yet.

"I'll come and get you if I hear anything before you're back." He must have sensed her concern. He nudged her shoulder, and she pushed herself to her feet.

The bathroom was a single occupancy. Jaida shut the door and locked herself inside then leaned her palms on the cool porcelain sink. When would this nightmare end? And how would it end?

She lifted her face to the mirror. Pale and drawn, dirt smudged her left cheekbone, her forehead, and her chin. She twisted her hair into a loose knot at the back of her head then ran the water until it went from cold to warm. She tested it then plunged her hands in the stream. She splashed it on her face and watched the dirt swirl down the drain. The little girl was right.

Drops of water clung to her eyelashes and dripped from her chin. She tore off the paper from the bottom of the towel holder and pressed it to her face. She was as clean as she was going to get with liquid soap and paper towels.

She dropped the wet paper in the trashcan then shook her hair free, running her fingers through the tangles. It was a modest improvement, but an improvement nonetheless.

Jaida turned out the light, and when she stepped from the bathroom, she saw Auggie speaking with a doctor across the hall. The man was in his scrubs. Her throat suddenly felt too thick to swallow. Good news or bad? She tried to gauge his expression, but it was unreadable.

She hesitated before joining them. Auggie saw her and reached for her arm. "Jaida, this is Dr. Bowman, the surgeon who operated on Spencer." He turned back to the doctor. "This is Spencer's wife."

She dipped her head to acknowledge the man then asked, "How is he?"

His mouth worked as if he didn't know what to say, or perhaps how to say it; how to deliver the awful news. Didn't they usually do this in a private room?

I can't do this. I can't bear to hear him tell me what I already know. Sensing her need to flee, Auggie set a staying hand on her arm.

Dr. Bowman shook his head. "I'm at a loss here."

Jaida pressed her eyes closed. *Just hurry up and say what you have to say.*

"His survival is nothing short of a miracle. I've been a surgeon for over twenty-eight years, and I've never seen anything like it."

Her eyes flew open. *"What?"*

"By no means is your husband entirely out of the woods, Mrs. Gordon, but he is doing very well."

"He's alive?" She didn't mean to sound so skeptical, or shocked, but he'd sounded so dire and she'd been so sure.

He nodded his head as if he still couldn't quite believe it himself. "Yes, he is. And he's been asking for you."

"Where is he?" She had to see him, had to touch him to believe it was true.

Dr. Bowman walked her to a room at the end of the hall in the critical care unit and pulled the curtain back, the metal rings scraping across the rod.

"Oh my..." Jaida gasped, unprepared for what she saw. So still, he lay there like a corpse groomed for the casket, prepared for the grave.

She hesitated then touched his face, felt his breath on the back of her hand. He was sleeping now. His skin was colorless, nearly translucent, his face and bared arms blending into the bleach-white linens he dozed on.

The doctor said he was doing well. He didn't look well. She turned to question him, to reassure herself, but he was gone. *Don't leave me here alone.* She stood staring into the empty hall. She couldn't do this by herself.

She gripped her hands at her waist and turned back, her throat thickening at the sight of him. "I wasn't worth this, Spencer."

Oxygen was piped in through the tubes in his nostrils, his breathing light and raspy. The doctor said he would be in and out of consciousness, but the potent painkillers transported through his veins kept him so deathly still it frightened her.

Jaida slid a chair next to the bed and sat down. The pinging of the monitor stole her attention. She watched the numbers flicker and change—Spencer's pulse, his oxygen, the weak, but steady rhythm of his heart. It was beating, and that was good.

She turned her eyes on Spencer. *God's will.* It was in her desperation that she had prayed for God's will, not considering what that might mean. What if it was His will to take Spencer from the earth? What would she do then?

She didn't want to think about that. She reached for his hand and cupped it in her own, dreading the confession she was about to make. There were no reparations, nothing to right her wrongs, only repentance and a hope for grace. She'd received forgiveness from God, but would Spencer be equally merciful?

She pressed the back of his hand to her cheek. "You promised me something the day you brought me home. Do you remember? You told me that you would always take care of me." Jaida paused and watched his chest rise and fall, rise and fall, making sure…

"I was fifteen when you shared that secret with me." She didn't understand the weight of his promise, the burden he carried. Not at the time. "You're a man of your word, Spencer. You always have been. But you were only a child when you made that promise. You didn't have to follow through on it." *You didn't have to marry me.*

"I knew you would never leave me. Not physically, anyway, but it was only a matter of time before you realized your mistake." Just like her father and her mother. "So I left you first."

"The truth is, I've always loved you." Until last night, she thought she'd eluded that love, outwitted it. But it lived. It was a force, a being that possessed a will of its own. She couldn't run from it any more than she could run from God.

Hot tears slid down her cheeks. "I've done so many unforgivable things, and I am so sorry. I want…I need you to forgive me." *Please forgive me.*

She glanced up at the monitor, at the digits that blinked erratically. The numbers stumbled, falling, falling like a spiraling stock market crash, the steady ping of the monitor replaced with one long uninterrupted tone.

Jaida leapt to her feet. "Somebody, help!" she cried. But they were already there, a trained faction preassembled before they tore into the room and pushed her out into the hall, the medical team crowding around Spencer.

No, God, no!

36

Jaida folded at the ache in her middle and sank to her knees on the tile floor as though it was quicksand. She startled at the high-pitched cry then sobbed when she realized it came from her.

Inside the room directives were shouted, and questions asked. The amalgamation of commands and inquiries bounced back and forth like a tennis ball alive in a match, one colliding with the other. And from the sound of it, they were losing him. *She* was losing him.

It didn't happen the way she thought, but her fears had not been unfounded. Predictive or just an unlucky guess, she'd been right all along. Spencer would leave her.

Hard rubber soles slapped against the tile. A pair of white lace-up shoes stopped in front of her, coffee stains speckling the finish. Or was it blood?

"Excuse me, but you can't stay here." It was a woman's voice. A thick hand with nails clipped short swung down in front of her face. "Let me help you up."

Jaida slapped it away. "Leave me alone."

"Honey, we have the best in the field in there doing everything they can."

Jaida processed the woman's words then lifted her gaze from the stained shoes to the round face. It was a nurse. "Are you saying he'll live?" she asked.

Her lips flattened. "I'm saying he's getting the best of care."

God's will. Just like she'd prayed, Spencer's healing—his destiny—was in God's hands. Not the surgeon's.

The hand swung down again in a second attempt to remove her from the hallway. This time she could sense the demand. Jaida gripped it then rose to her feet.

The woman's hand went instantly to the small of her back. "We need to keep this hallway clear." She ushered her past the nurse's station and out to the main hall.

"We have staff available, specially trained to help you through the grieving process."

"Grief counseling?"

"I know this is a difficult time." Her cold, efficient manner turned motherly, the woman patted her arm. "If you'll just wait right here, I'll call someone for you."

"No thanks, I'll pass," she said.

The nurse appeared agitated, unsure what to do with her. "The cafeteria should still be open. Why don't you go downstairs and get a cup of coffee?"

Coffee? Her husband was dying, and she was sending her for coffee? Was she that desperate to be rid of her, to make her someone else's problem? Jaida turned and walked away. She found the elevator at the end of the hall and rode it down to the first floor.

The double doors of the chapel were arched, fashioned in maple, and propped open at the far side of the lobby. She hurried inside, desperate for an infusion of hope.

Pillar candles on either side of the altar sat centered on tapered silver holders, silent white flames licking up the wicks. The light drew her in, and the cross that hung above the altar—it was a beacon for the lost and hurting.

"Come to me all you who labor and are heavy laden, and I will give you rest." The invitation was almost audible, and Jaida responded, moving toward the rough-hewn beams joined by crudely twined rope. She knelt, surrendering to the grief.

God would answer her, she knew He would, but would it be an answer she could live with? She plucked a tissue from the box tucked under the pew and blew her nose. It was time she went back upstairs and faced whatever awaited her, but she didn't want to do it.

"Jaida."

She turned. Auggie was standing in the doorway still as a stone, his features flat and unsmiling. He was the messenger, the bearer of bad news. It was written all over his face. She stood and discarded the wadded tissue in the trashcan stowed in the corner then looked up at him, steeling herself.

He took a step inside and pulled both doors closed behind him. Was he afraid she would make a scene?

"Is he...?" Unable to finish, she swallowed, warding off a fresh wave of tears.

His eyes darted around the room, looking at everything but her. "Next to a confessional, I guess this is about the best place to do this," he said.

He wasn't making any sense. She reached for the back of the pew, her fingers digging into the wood. Waiting.

"I don't know how to tell you this. I knew it wasn't going to be easy, but..."

She was a coward, she kept her eyes on the floor, her fists clutching tighter around the pew back.

"You need to hear this from me. Not from Baseel, or the news if it comes down to that. And I know this is the worst possible time to drop this on you, but I have no choice."

She looked up at him then. "What are you talking about?"

He slid his hands into his pockets and raised his chin. "I took Gale's money," he said. "I was the one who emptied the accounts."

What was he saying? Was Spencer dying? She didn't understand. Wasn't Spencer the reason he was here?

His eyes never left hers. "I'm sorry," he said.

Sorry for what? Did Spencer die? Her mind couldn't make the leap, but slowly his words sank in. *The money. He was talking about the money.*

"It was you?" she asked. How could he have done this? She trusted him.

"Please, don't look at me like that."

"You betrayed me."

He rubbed a hand over his head and then looked away again. "I'm taking care of it, making it right the best I can. I've already talked to the head of the agency. He knows."

"All this time…you had the money all this time, and you said nothing?"

He nodded. "Yes."

She railed, unleashing her rage. "Spencer is dying because of you." She closed the gap between them and shoved at his chest. "How could you do this?"

"I know. I didn't think anyone would get hurt or that Gale would go after you. I'm sorry."

A humorless laugh jerked from her chest. "I thought you came here to tell me that Spencer didn't make it. That he was dead."

"Why would you think that? The doctor said he was fine. I was right there with you."

Her gaze fell to the floor. "Not anymore. His heart stopped."

"Chica, I had no idea." He reached out to comfort her, but she held up a hand to warn him off.

Together they headed back to CCU in silence. Dr. Bowman stood in the hall. He had his head bent over an open chart spread out on the counter at the nurse's station. One of the nurses saw her approach, whispered something to the doctor and pointed her out.

He looked up from his paperwork, his eyes meeting hers. "Mrs. Gordon, we've been looking all over for you." He clicked the pen in his hand closed and tucked it into his shirt pocket.

"How is he?" she asked. Was he alive, dead, or still teetering somewhere in between? The uncertainty was tearing her apart one piece at a time.

"Your husband had been doing so well that we couldn't understand what went wrong. But there was just too much blood loss, and with the trauma to his chest..."

He never answered. Not in words, but she filled in the blanks. He started down the hall. So this was it? This was how it ended? He turned suddenly and waved at her to follow. Was he taking her to the body?

When she caught up to him he said, "As I was saying, we're baffled as to why his heart stopped, and equally so as to how he pulled out of it. It's a miracle, really. Not that I put much stock in them, but there's no other explanation."

She grabbed his arm. "You mean he's alive?"

"Isn't that what I just said?" He waved a hand in the direction of the room she'd been pushed out of. Spencer still occupied the bed, his head propped up and a sheet covering him to the waist.

She went inside and drew the curtain closed, acutely aware of how closely Spencer watched her. Heavy lidded, his eyes followed every move she made. Did he not want her here after all?

Her heart pounded so hard she could feel it in her throat. She didn't deserve to be here, to be taking her place at his side as his wife. She'd burned that bridge a long time ago.

His intense gaze made her uncomfortable. She busied her hands. Reaching for his box of apple juice, she tore off the straw and plunged it through the top.

"Did you mean it?" he asked. His words were soft, a mere whisper.

She stilled. Mean what? And then she remembered what she had said to him in the canyon when she thought he was going to die. *I love you.* The declaration came back to haunt her.

Jaida wrestled with the denial that was on her lips, the fear that crept in, but this time she won. She pushed the tray away from the bed, slipped off her sandals, and carefully stretched out beside him, molding her body to his. It was only a matter of time before they tossed her out, but for now...

She lightly brushed her lips against his cheek, the soft skin bristly with a day's growth of whiskers, then laid her head against his shoulder and closed her eyes, reveling in the moment. "Yes, Spencer. I meant it."

37

S hell pink and antique white. It was the color scheme chosen for Laurel's party. The Victorian touch was elegant but slightly out of sync with the modern dayroom decorated in shades of blue and brown.

"I'm here," Jaida said. "It took awhile to get this wrapped." She held up the pint-sized square box dressed in yellow and white paper and topped with a frilly white bow.

She dropped her purse on a chair then set the gift next to the bouquet of English roses. The blooms were freshly cut and arranged in a blown Bohemian glass vase, the cranberry shade complementing the pink and white roses perfectly.

"Everything looks perfect." She tipped her head back and looked up at the crepe streamers, twisted and draped in a delicate arc overhead.

"Yes it does," Spencer said, sliding his arms around her waist. Jaida sank back against his chest, absorbing every wonderful beat of his heart.

"I'm glad you're here," he said. His soft breath tickled her ear, and she found herself tearing up.

She turned in his arms then and kissed him lightly on the mouth, too choked up to say what was in her heart. He brushed his thumbs under her eyes and gave the sides of her chin a quick squeeze until she smiled back.

He knew her too well. Knew that she was fretting. She'd missed out on so much and failed those she loved most. He kept telling her not to look back, but forward since that was the direction she was going, but some days were harder than others, and days like today were when the regrets came out to haunt her.

He held her away from him and clasped her hands. "You look nice," he said. "*Really* nice." Grinning, he took in the azure dress she wore. The way he looked at her warmed her insides and brought a blush to her cheeks.

It wasn't the sensual leer she'd become accustomed to, but an adoring gaze that reflected the high value he placed on her. Her heart swelled with love for this man. A love she didn't believe was possible.

Seated in a wing-backed chair, Laurel looked regal in her knee-length ginger-colored dress. Jaida set a hand on her shoulder. "Happy Birthday," she said then planted a kiss on her cheek.

Laurel reached up and squeezed her hand. Though her words were still shapeless and unformed, she responded to her presence, more alert and aware than she could recall.

The progress they were seeing was something the doctors kept telling them was impossible, but they couldn't dispute the proof sitting in front of her now. With all of their combined years of training and experience, something greater had taken place and proved them wrong.

Spencer seated her first then took the chair beside her. She reached up and smoothed the lapels of his charcoal hounds tooth jacket. Austin Reed—it had to be. He always looked impeccable. Even in a hospital gown.

She bit her lip and gave him a mischievous smile, wondering what he would say if she told him that.

"What?" He grinned back at her.

"I'll tell you later."

"Am I late?" Mrs. Childers, Rebecca, joined them. She carried a small wrapped parcel. Mary followed behind bearing a bouquet of pink, yellow, and orange balloons and a smile that lit up the room.

Spencer jumped up and turned on the video camera mounted on a tripod in the corner. "Actually, you're just in time," he said then started the first few bars of the traditional birthday song.

Rank amateurs, they all joined in, their rendition off-key, but Laurel seemed to enjoy the attention. Inside she was probably having a good laugh at their expense. The final note was dragged out and slaughtered at the finish. Laughter filled the room.

Spencer offered up a prayer of thanks then slid the knife into the center of the cake. The blade sliced through the yellow fondant and chocolate devil's food, but spared the edible butterflies and rosebuds.

Working as a team, Jaida picked up the paper plates stacked at the end of the table and laid them out while Spencer came behind and filled each one with a hefty slice of cake.

She took the one with the largest butterfly and set it in front of Laurel. "For the birthday girl," she said. Then she offered a plate to each of their two guests.

"This is so moist. What bakery did you get it from?" Rebecca reached for a napkin and dabbed at her mouth.

Jaida ladled some punch into a cup. "No bakery. My friend Aimee does this on the side." She handed it to Spencer.

"I want her number," Mary said. "My daughter is getting married, and this is the best I've tasted."

"Write down your email address and I'll send it to you." With such rave reviews, maybe Aimee should quit Baseel and do this full time.

Laurel lifted a bite to her mouth. Jaida set her plate down and filled Laurel's cup, topping the plastic with a lid and straw. She set it in front of her.

"You're messy." Jaida grabbed Spencer's hand and licked the smear of cream filling from his knuckle. "Mmm, that's good."

"You think so?" He smeared a slab of frosting across his lips and puckered. "Have at it."

Jaida laughed. "Behave or they're going to kick us out of here."

He looked down at her, his gaze warming her clear through. "It would be worth it."

Rebecca clucked her tongue. "You two are incorrigible."

Spencer grinned at her and wiped the frosting from his mouth with a napkin.

Mary said, "I am amazed at how well Laurel is doing. Even the doctors marvel at her improvement. It's unprecedented." She looked from Jaida to Spencer. "And I think it has everything to do with the change in your relationship."

The room fell silent, and Jaida pressed her fingers to her lips. Mary's observation had been a theory of her own, but to hear it expressed by someone else only served to confirm it.

A small part of the afternoon was spent eating cake and sharing stories. Laurel's eyes drooped. It was time for a nap. Rebecca left, and Mary went back to work leaving the three of them alone.

Jaida sat back in the chair, and Spencer stood. He stacked the soiled plates and dropped them into the lined trashcan then collected the gift-wrap strewn across the table and tossed the wadded paper in the can.

Jaida picked up a ribbon that had slid to the floor and handed it to him. He gripped her fingers and kissed the back of her hand.

"You're hopeless," she said as though she disapproved, but she was learning to let her guard down, to let him love her. And in truth, she wouldn't have him any other way.

Jaida rubbed at the tickle above her elbow then turned when she felt it again. It was Laurel. She set her hand on Jaida's arm. "I m-m-missed you," she said, the *m* held out in one long hum. It was a complete sentence and nearly perfect.

Stunned, Spencer laughed, it was soul deep, exultant. He kissed Laurel's forehead then squeezed Jaida's hand. "Stick with me, and we'll have her back to normal in no time."

But then she realized what Laurel had said, and her joy quickly faded. She looked up at Spencer. "But, what about…I've been coming to see her all this time, and she doesn't remember." Her speech was returning, but what was becoming of her mind, her memory?

Spencer set a warm, reassuring hand on her back and she relaxed into it. It would be all right, she told herself. It was improvement. Maybe it would come a little at a time.

"Mom, Jaida's been here every week," Spencer said. "Don't you remember?" Would her response be as coherent as her statement a few seconds ago, or was that shining moment a flash in the pan, a singular event?

Laurel's fingers tightened around her arm. "N-n-not the same. Different," she said, her voice trembling.

Jaida's worry fell away, and a smile pulled at her mouth. *Different*. She said she was different. Laurel saw the new…well maybe it was the old Jaida—the youthful, idealistic one, but all grown up and shaped by a fresh worldview.

"Knock, knock."

Jaida turned. Auggie stood in the doorway. Their eyes connected. His were soft and hopeful, hers...well she could only imagine what he saw considering what she felt. She glanced at Spencer and then down at the table, at the crumbs that had fallen from her plate. Why was he here?

Her cool reception didn't deter Spencer from playing the gracious host. He shook Auggie's hand warmly and introduced him to Laurel.

Her eyes brightened when she saw the bouquet he carried. They were her favorites, lavender delphinium and yellow daffodils, the stems tied together with a limp white ribbon. Spencer must have told him. Must have invited him too.

"These are for the birthday girl." Auggie set the flowers in her arms, and from the look on Laurel's face he'd scored some major brownie points.

She'd hardly spoken with him since that night at the hospital, the rift between them carved wide by her struggle to get past his offense. She believed in him, put her trust in him, and he'd betrayed her.

Just like you betrayed Spencer. The truth that set her free now snared her. Sharp and piercing, shame at her lack of mercy sunk its teeth into her soul. She was a hypocrite.

Forgive him.

I've tried.

Forgive him.

She closed her eyes, swallowing the knot in her throat. Auggie turned and landed a peck on her cheek. Why was this so hard for her?

"It's good to see you, Jaida. Real good." He was tentative, almost meek. Two characteristics she never would have used to describe him. But he'd been in the fire, and its heat had a way of burning away the dross. She knew that firsthand.

"You too," she said, almost meaning it. He lingered at her side as though he might say more but then moved away from her.

She *was* different, just as Laurel said, but the change in her was incomplete. She had so far to go, and her reaction to Auggie proved it.

Spencer offered Auggie a chair and handed him a piece of cake, a fork stabbed into the top. The two men talked and laughed like old friends catching up. This was a good thing. Wasn't it?

She watched Auggie from across the table. Gone from his eyes was the pride that once rivaled her own. He'd been broken by his circumstances and looked as fragile as she felt. Sympathy swelled in her breast.

She rolled her lip in and bit down on it. *Move forward, Jaida, and let Auggie do the same.* She reached across the table and clasped his hand. "I'm sorry," she said.

He glanced down at their joined hands looking surprised and pleased. "I'm the one who owes you an apology. More than an apology."

Spencer slid his arm around her shoulders and leaned close. "Now that that's out of the way. How is everything coming along on the legal front?"

"I have a good attorney," Auggie said. "We'll see where things go. But I do have some news." His attention shifted to Jaida. "Palermo was hired by Gale *and* by Baseel. You were right, he was with internal affairs."

He'd been telling the truth, half of it anyway.

"He was working both ends and using his position at Baseel to locate Gale's cash and the tape."

"He admitted to taking it?" To stealing it right out of her house?

Auggie's head wavered back and forth. "Not directly. But according to my sources, he said enough."

"He goes down, but once again Gale comes out unscathed," she said. It wasn't right.

Auggie cracked a smile. "Don't be so sure. Charges are being brought against Gale as we speak. Palermo is working with us in exchange for leniency. Oh, and the police picked up prints from your house. They matched the ones on the glass. It was one of Gale's punks who trashed it."

"What do they have on Lance?" she asked. No one could prove he was the one who took the evidence, and using her to get it was hardly a criminal offense.

A bit of the former cockiness returned. "I told you I'd been checking him out. I don't care how good someone is at what they do, sooner or later they slip up, and he left a decent trail of chargeable offenses."

"There's also talk of reopening an investigation over the death of a young woman Gale was involved with years ago."

Her mother? "Sofia Carlisle?" she asked.

"Yeah, that was the name. How did you know?" Carl didn't tell him? But then she hadn't told him that William Gale was her father. Not yet.

She shook her head, her stomach sinking. Her instincts had been right about Sofia's death. "That is a story for another day," she said.

"I wasn't going to give you this, but..." Auggie pulled an envelope from his shirt pocket. Tossing a guilty glance at Spencer as he handed it to her.

"It's from Palermo. He asked me to see that you got it."

Spencer's eyes darkened, and he looked away. She handed it back. "I don't want it," she said then reached for Spencer's hand and squeezed. "I have everything I need right here."

Auggie crumpled the paper in his fist as though he enjoyed it then went on with the update without missing a beat.

"The dates for Kevin and Carina's trials have been set. Are you up for testifying? It's going to get ugly."

Spencer had protected her, kept her out of the limelight and the fray, but soon she wouldn't have a choice in the matter, and she would have to face these people standing on her own two feet.

Instinctively Spencer's arm went around her. Provided by God, it was a wing, a shield, a buffer from everything evil, and Jaida welcomed it.

"I'll be ready."

EPILOGUE

The roar of shattering whitewater, the squawk of circling gulls, and the distant tinkling of windblown chimes, the medley was God's opus. And the woman curled up snugly beside him, her head cradled in his lap, was His gift.

Spencer stroked gentle fingers over the curve of her brow, sweeping wispy strands of hair from her face. In this finite moment, everything was right in the world. Jaida shifted and burrowed in, snuggling closer. *Keep needing me, keep loving me.*

His gaze traveled from one delicate feature, perfectly shaped and formed, to another, and wondered at how beautifully made she was; more beautiful than he remembered. But then he was partial.

A breeze rolled over the water ruffling the short sleeves of her white blouse. He loved watching her sleep. She was so peaceful and content.

He didn't want to wake her, but the day had gone on without them, absconding with the sun it was sneaking into another part of the world, leaving theirs dusky and damp.

"Jaida," he said. When she didn't stir, he brushed his fingers under her chin and called her name a second time.

Velvety blue and fierce with love, her eyes opened, and the way she was looking at him did crazy things to his insides. "We have to go."

"Kiss me awake," she said then closed her eyes.

God had already awakened her. He had been the one to open her eyes and bring her back to him. "I thought you were already awake. Or are you talking in your sleep?"

In feigned repose, she didn't answer. He stroked his finger around the perimeter of her face, marveling again at how lovely she was.

He nudged her shoulder and without opening her eyes, she sighed. "Are you going to argue with me, or are you going to kiss me?"

His mouth tilted. "What do you think?"

THANKS!

I want to thank those who graciously assisted me in the completion of this novel.

To editor, Renee Gray-Wilburn, thank you so much for your labor, your advice, and your encouraging words.

To my 'readers', Deb Weyandt and Deb Momyer, I greatly appreciate you giving up your free time to read through and critique my work.

To Leah Nawrocki for passing on her Photoshop skills even when it hurt.

And a special thank you to my husband and children for always being there. You are the best part of my life.

And an extra special thank you to Jesus Christ, lover of my fickle soul. Thank you for the promise, and for giving purpose to this crazy life.